NAMING THE HANGMAN

ERIC PLUME

2ND Edition

This book is a work of fiction. The people, places and organizations within it are either fictitious or used fictitiously. No commentary on the behavior of extant corporate or government entities is intended.

For Michael

Acknowledgments

Once again I have to thank my wonderful staff of volunteers Barbara, Jose and Jennifer, for all the assistance and advice you've given me as I wrote this book - including the harsh parts. Some of it stung but I couldn't have done without any of it. You people rock.

Likewise to my lady Faye for her cover design and research, not to mention taking the internet away from me so I would work. I may have grumbled, but it was necessary. Specific mention must go to her tolerance and forbearance during the frantic scramble to get this book out on time.

I must also raise a glass to the Iowa Association of Private Investigators for throwing open the doors of their yearly conference to me, just because I asked nicely. All the shared stories and insider tips are valuable beyond words to my career. I cannot thank you enough. See you all next year!

As always I thank my family, literal and adopted, for all your encouragement. It's nice to be believed in.

Love isn't put there to make us happy. I believe it exists to show us how much we can endure.

\- Hermann Hesse, *Peter Camenzind*

Chapter 1

The phone always rings at the wrong time.

Mine rang while I stood on the sparring mat against an opponent bound and determined to beat the crap out of me. I ignored the chiming tones and focused on my adversary. Scott Hardy was convinced women shouldn't learn fighting and aimed to show me his point of view. I aimed to end the match without acquiring too many bruises.

Hardy opened with looping rights much stiffer than the rules allowed for, but I'd expected it. I blocked with upraised forearms and gave ground, waiting for the right moment. He gave it to me, lowering his shoulders and spreading his arms in a bullish attempt at a shoot tackle. I dodged left, grabbed his arm and twisted his tackle into a counter he hadn't planned on. Physics played to my favor and my overconfident opponent found himself kissing canvas with my knee planted in his back.

"Hold," Alvarez called out in a firm teacher's tone.

I obeyed. Hardy wriggled under my knee, tried to improve his position. I leaned into my hold to prevent that.

He grunted and glared at me from beneath my knee. "Goddamn it Amber, you trying to break my arm?"

I leaned harder. "Only when you try to break my jaw."

"Enough," Alvarez said. He was a wiry Latino, fashioned from leather and braided cable; at five-five he looked me right in the eye, but a doctor could have taught anatomy using the muscles in his chest. The gold cross around his neck matched the three gold teeth in his grin. "Let him up, Amber."

I released Hardy and stood. He glared at me and I ignored it, moving across the mat towards the pile of stuff which held my phone. My arms throbbed where I'd blocked Hardy's punches.

"You can bench-press her," Alvarez said to Hardy, "but that don't mean you can beat her up."

Scott Hardy's ears turned red, face trying for impassive but ending up at sullen. He was twenty and looked it despite two hundred pounds of water-weight and show muscle laced with testosterone.

"She got lucky," he muttered.

No, she didn't," Alvarez said as I dug out my iPhone. "You went in with your dick in your hand and she took advantage of it. Just like last time." Alvarez shook his head. "Hardy, what part of 'never underestimate your opponent' isn't making sense to you?"

"My foot slipped while I was setting up for the shoot," Hardy said as I queued up the call. "Could've happened to anybody."

Alvarez's grin didn't fade. "It happened to you. Which is why you lost."

He blinked. "I don't get it."

"That's why I'm teaching you."

My phone's screen glowed with the number that had just called me; Julian Wu, the office assistant I'd recently promoted to journeyman investigator. I redialed him, pressing the phone to my ear. It rang several times, followed by a clumsy pickup.

"Hey boss." On most days Julian's voice was pleasantly vibrant; what I heard in my ear was flat, clogged and dead. My internal alarm went off.

"Talk to me," I said.

"I'm at the clinic," he said. "That Copeland guy tried to punch my teeth in."

"Jesus, are you okay?"

"I'll live." A slight pause. "My face hurts like hell though."

"Julian, I thought I told you to keep your distance." Ray Copeland was the subject of a workman's compensation case, a thoroughly unpleasant character who had several priors for assault and battery. The fact that he was supposed to be out with a broken collarbone had made me feel only slightly better about putting Julian on his trail.

"I did, boss. He made me anyway...just walked up and socked me right in the face. Told me to mind my own business. I'm okay, just...ow."

"I'll be there shortly. We can talk more when I get there."

"Cool." His voice got some life back. "When you do, I've got a surprise."

"I think you've given me enough of those for one day. For now, just stay put and do what the nurse tells you to."

"No problem. She's cute. I think she likes me."

"Why am I not surprised," I said with a chuckle. Julian Wu could pick up a date in a nunnery just by walking in the door. "See you soon," I said before hanging up.

Alvarez wandered over. "I take it you gotta go."

I nodded. "Sorry. One of my employees got himself decked on the job. I'll take my critique later."

He grinned. Juan Alvarez had fifty-seven years on the meter but every time he smiled I had trouble believing it. "It'll be a short one."

I threw him a wave and headed off in the direction of the changing room. Alvarez's gym had a woman's shower and locker area but there was almost no one who used it, a fact I didn't object to. I washed away the sweat of my workout and swapped my exercise clothes for jeans and a blouse, noting that both fit differently than they had six months ago. The jeans were loose around my waist, the shirt tight through the shoulders. Both made me smile.

I'd never been smaller than a size eleven since growing into my adult shape; I would have been right at home pulling taps in a medieval tavern, a look helped along by straight country-brown hair and a dusting of freckles. I knew I'd never end up a waif no matter how much gym work I put myself through, but that didn't mean my belly had to overlap my belt. Getting fit had been a lot of work and it was pleasant to see some progress.

I worked at my grooming with the speed of practiced ritual, wondering what twist of circumstance had caused Julian to end up in the hospital. Investigative work came with a wide selection of hazards but physical violence was seldom on the menu. I also wondered about what he meant by a 'surprise'.

Creak.

The locker room had a double set of doors for privacy, and the inner ones squeaked like a stepped-on mouse. I was the only woman on the premises, which was why I pulled my unbuttoned blouse closed with my right hand and reached into my gym bag with my left before I turned around.

Scott Hardy stood in the doorway with a smirk, arms folded across his bulging chest. The smirk told me he wanted a real fight and thought he could take me down; I didn't want to find out what that meant to him. An atavistic portion of my psyche climbed into the driver's seat.

"One of us doesn't belong in here," I said. I kept my voice calm with effort.

"Yeah. You." He took a step forward.

"Hardy, I don't have time for this just now," I said.

He moved closer to me, arms and legs sliding into a fighting stance. "Looks like you'll have to make the time."

"If you insist." I pulled my H&K P7 automatic out of my bag and squeezed its grip. The striker cocked with a satisfying *click.* Hardy's eyes bulged.

"Holy shit," he muttered.

"Go away." I didn't point my gun at him. I didn't have to.

He stumbled away from me, hands splayed out in front of him. "You're fucking crazy."

"Which is why you'll want to be going away," I said.

Hardy backed out of the room, eyes never leaving the ordnance in my hand. I watched the doorway until the door stopped swinging, fingers flexing around the checkered grip of my pistol as I did my best to will the adrenaline away. It didn't go easy, but it went. I shook my head and stuck my gun back in my bag.

"Boys will be boys," I said to the empty room.

Chapter 2

I couldn't afford to send my employees to Harborview Medical on the rare occasions when they got hurt but that was all right with me; the traffic between where I was and there would have gotten me injured before I even set foot in the parking lot. Instead I used a dingy Occupational Health clinic on the shady side of Kent, and that was where I found Julian. He was sitting on the edge of a gurney when I walked through the door, ice pack pressed to his left cheek, texting one-handed. He looked up as I approached.

"Hi boss." Most days Julian's face held the sort of angelic appeal which caused fathers to hide their teenaged daughters; chiseled cheekbones, smooth skin, long black hair framing brilliant green eyes.

Today those chiseled cheekbones were swollen, purple with bruises. There was blood on the ice pack's wrapper and more crusted under his nose.

"Jesus," I said. "What'd Copeland work you over with, a tire iron?"

"He only hit me once," he said. "The rest is when I fell against my bike." He moved the ice pack and winced.

"Your nose broken?"

"No, thank God." Julian's grin was crooked. "He didn't break any teeth either."

"Small favors, I guess." I relaxed. "What'd you tell the cops?"

"I didn't," He said. "I also got what we were after."

I blinked. "How do you mean?"

He flicked his fingers across his phone's screen. "So there was a busker right near where I was staked out, doing a juggling show. People were taking videos and pictures with their phones. When Copeland came out and started yelling a couple of them moved their cameras onto him. After he hit me I convinced this one girl to email me her clip...you know, for pressing charges." He held up his phone. "Check it out."

I hit the play button and watched. The clip was typical cell-phone video fare, shaky and blurred. I recognized a section of Aurora Avenue at noon, people bustling up and down the sidewalk. A skinny hippie in a purple-and-gold unitard was working a juggling routine involving plastic spheres rolling up and down his arms; gravity juggling, made famous by David Bowie in *Labrynth.* The hippie was better at the juggling but didn't look nearly as good in tight spandex.

The camera blurred to the left and settled on a squat

bullish man in Carhartts and a denim jacket with his right arm in a sling, waving the other around and yelling something I couldn't catch. I recognized Raymond Copeland. He walked up to Julian and took his arm out of the sling to clock him in the face, hard. Julian went down like an unstrung puppet, crashing against his bike. I paused the clip. "Ouch," I said.

"Riddle me this, boss...is that the action of a man with a broken collarbone?" I looked up into Julian's beaming gaze. "I can vouch for his arm working pretty freaking well."

I raised one eyebrow. "Wait. You got him to hit you...on *purpose?"*

"I didn't know he'd go that far, boss." He shrugged, wincing. "I took the list of co-workers Izzy compiled and started asking them about the guy's injury, whether they'd seen him do anything he shouldn't be able to. They all told me to fuck off, of course."

"...And then you started tailing Copeland, figuring one of his co-workers would tell him there was a skinny Asian guy scoping him out, and when he saw you following him he came up to hassle you." I shook my head. "Jesus, Julian."

"Hey it worked, didn't it?"

"Except for the part where he could've killed you," I

said.

Julian's smile turned impish. "He could have, but he didn't, so I'm not going to fret about it."

"Dammit, this isn't a game."

"Boss, they raised the office rent on us again. We need to make progress on a case by the end of the month...you said so yourself last week."

I turned away and ran my hands over my face. Then I paced back and forth for a few moments, mostly because I didn't have a response.

"So I did," I finally said. "So I did."

What Julian had said was true; the property firm my business rented space from had gotten in the habit of raising rent every time one of our neighbors pulled up stakes and left, which had been happening at least once every couple of months. It was an ugly cycle I kept finding myself on the receiving end of but all my looking hadn't turned up a better option. Our location was a good one and all the competing firms charged more, not to mention the costs intrinsic in pulling up stakes - costs I lacked the capital to consider. Fiscal survival in the modern world was no longer an art form, but rather a game of chance.

I looked at my battered employee and didn't like

what I saw, mostly because I knew he'd done what needed doing. Some part of me wished it was my face with bruises all over it. Another wanted to go find Ray Copeland and put a set of bruises on *his* face. The rest was angry, unhappy with current events.

"I'm sorry about the hospital bill," Julian said. "I didn't know he'd actually go and hit me. I'll pay it myself."

"No," I said. "You got hurt on company time, the company pays the bill. That's the way it's going to be."

Julian leaned forward. "Look, boss -"

"Consider this a learning experience," I said. "Okay sure...what you did worked, and I have to give you points for cleverness. Ellison Shipwrights will be glad to have positive proof about Copeland's injury being faked, and we'll get a check by the end of the month. That's all great news."

I reached up and grabbed his shirt between my fingers. "But you pull one more whack-ass cowboy move like this and so help me I'll break your damn nose myself." I wasn't mad at him, not really, but sometimes emotions need an outlet. "We clear?"

He nodded. "Yes boss. Sorry." His voice was soft.

I let him go and patted him on the chest. "Don't be all that sorry," I said. "Like you said it worked, and we do need the damn money."

"Besides, now I'm a badass detective," he said. "I've been punched and everything."

"Last question," I said. "Why didn't Copeland beat the tar out of you? He certainly looked like he was ready to."

"When he bent down to grab me, I gave him a face full of this." He held up a small black canister; the pepper spray I had loaned him. "He sort of lost interest in me after I did that."

It was several seconds before I could form words.

"Julian," I said, "are you *trying* to drive me to gray hairs and booze?"

"I just did like I thought you would have."

I laughed. "From now on you do as I say, not as I do."

A red-headed girl in surgical scrubs walked up with a smile on her face and a clipboard in her hand. I stepped aside to make room for her. She prodded at Julian's injuries with careful fingers; I knew enough about medicine to know she wasn't doing anything necessary and enough about people to read the dewy look in her eyes.

I cleared my throat. "Is he going to live?"

The nurse turned around. "I don't see any permanent damage," she replied, "but head wounds are tricky. There might be something we can't see." She couldn't have been much over twenty-five, a slender waif with flawless ivory skin and a fetching set of blue eyes. "I'd like to keep him overnight for observation."

"I bet." I put my arm around her shoulders and led her away from Julian. "Look," I said, "I've had first aid training too, and my valiant employee here has about as much of a concussion as I do."

The nurse - her name tag read AMANDA - blinked and reached for her jargon. "Well, there is always the possibility of a subdural hematoma. I can't just - "

"I'll give you his phone number," I said.

She glanced back towards Julian with a look that bordered on hungry. "He single?"

"At the moment."

"Is he *really* a private detective?"

"Licensed and bonded," I said, "and bravely injured in the line of duty." I passed her one of my business cards. "Can I have him back now?"

She slipped the card inside her shirt, tucking it into her bra. "I'll go get him released."

I patted her on the shoulder. "Much appreciated."

I walked back over to Julian, whose eyebrows quirked in curiosity. "What was that about?"

I picked up the plastic bag which held all his possessions. "Me getting you out of here before Little Miss Nightingale chains you to a bed and throws away the key."

Julian tossed a puppy-dog glance at Amanda's retreating backside. "I wouldn't mind a bit of *that* peril."

"I gave her a card," I said. "If its true love she'll be calling. You can find your outpatient therapy on your own time."

A laugh bubbled out of his chest. "Boss, you're the awesomest."

"I bet you say that to all the ladies," I said.

"No, just you."

I chuckled as I handed him his coat. Though I'd never once entertained the notion of taking him to bed, Julian's charm had one undeniable effect; I never could stay annoyed with him for long.

A stack of paperwork a half-inch thick awaited us at

the front desk; I signed what forms I had to and handed others to Julian, wincing at the cost of his misadventure but certain that letting insurance take care of it would be worse in the long run. At least he'd had driven himself to the clinic, sparing me the thousand-dollar fee for an ambulance ride. Amanda did busywork at the copy machine and fed Julian sultry glances from her baby blues. He handed her his trademark high-wattage smile in return. I watched with detached humor.

We stepped out of the clinic into a wall of rain; early March in Washington at its finest. Julian scowled at the sky and zipped up his riding jacket. "Definitely a Monday," he muttered.

"But there was a redhead," I said.

He glanced over his shoulder at the clinic. "She really wanted my number?"

"Girls will be girls," I said.

Chapter 3

Once upon a time, the cheap office space I rented in the light-industrial part of Kent had been inexpensive. Thanks to economic reality and corporate greed it wasn't so any longer. Half my neighbors had either packed up or packed it in; the low white buildings sported more scars from absent billboards than active companies and more empty spaces than parked cars. At least it made Eckart Investigations easy for clients to find, as we were the only occupied office in our building.

As I pulled into my parking space I noticed another crack in one of the front windows. I frowned; the glass had not been properly installed by whatever third rate contractor Stillwell Property Management had hired, and last winter's frost had already damaged two of them. This made number three.

"Clearly the raised rent isn't going to the maintenance department," I said as Julian came up behind me.

"Yeah. I called them about the glass...they said they'd look into repairing it."

"When was that?"

Julian shook his head. "About a month ago."

I sighed and shook my head, glancing at the cracked glass, the weed-choked walkway, and the mold stains on the paneling. "Goddamn slum-lords," I muttered. At least our front door opened without trouble; I'd fixed that myself two weeks ago. It's amazing what a screwdriver and a can of WD-40 can accomplish.

"We should move," said Julian.

"No can do," I said. "Deposits, first and last month's rent...we can't afford them. Then there's getting everything from Spot A to Spot B, during which time we can't work. Don't think our landlords aren't aware of all that." I made a beeline for the coffee machine and found a fresh pot waiting.

Julian sat at his desk with a wince. "So what do I do now?"

"You write up your report," I said. "Document the entire process you used to discover Copeland's malingering. Be sure to make it look pretty for the courts and the client. I'll want it on my desk before you leave."

His face fell. "Boss, that'll take at least a couple hours."

"Better get started then," I said. "You're a badass detective, remember?"

"I think I preferred the hospital." He pulled out his keyboard tray and opened up a fresh document.

"Next time you're tempted to act the cowboy, stay calm and think of paperwork," I said over my shoulder as I headed for my office.

My employees keep the public areas of our firm's space neat and tidy, but anywhere real work gets done often resembles an explosion in an office supply store and today was no exception. I opened the door to a wall of noise; the musical styling of Ronnie James Dio belted out of my assistant's mp3 dock at considerable volume.

"Izzy," I called, "turn it down."

Izzy Alphabet looked up from her screen with a grin. "If it's too loud, you're too old," she called back. But she reached for the volume knob and put Ronnie's voice on equal footing with mine.

At five foot two Izzy would have been called 'petite' if she didn't carry eighty extra pounds on a frame wider than mine. Her clothes weren't even artfully unfashionable, her hair a frizzy rainbow of cheap dye. Under that hair sat the fastest chunk of gray matter this side of MIT. I ran a loose ship and she was most of the reason.

"I thought you liked metal," she said as I sat down.

"I do, but I like being able to hear even better. Besides, Dio's got the pipes, but he needed to fire his lyricist."

Izzy snickered. "And Queensryche didn't?"

I played at bristling in indignation. "Hey now, there will be no dissing of the 'ryche in my office."

"Dio's better," she said. "I'd know."

"Says the girl who was in pigtails when I was rocking out to both bands live."

Izzy made a disbelieving face. "You did not."

I grinned. "Iron Maiden, Queensryche, Scorpions...and yes, the great Ronnie himself."

"Dang, now I'm jealous," she said. "How's Julian?"

"He'll live," I replied. "After he finishes writing up his report he might even want to. Any calls?"

Not really. But, I've got a surprise for you." A file folder hit the desk in front of me.

"The Darrington case," she said, "finally moving forward."

"Oh?" Ronald Darrington was a possible cheating husband who'd proven to be quite the slippery little weasel; his wife was convinced of extramarital activities on his part but no evidence had surfaced.

She had hired us to track his habits, due to a prenuptial contract that would be null and void in the face of infidelity. I'd met with Elissa Darrington three times and I'd figured out his cheating hadn't provoked any hurt or moral outrage; she'd married money and wanted to make off with large amounts of it the easy way. Ronald had married pretty and was looking to eat his cake and have it. In some ways they were perfect for each other.

"What do you have?" I flipped through the file.

Izzy's pale eyes gleamed with mischief behind her glasses. "You know how we couldn't find any evidence of him screwing around other than a few suspicious absences?"

"No phone records, no emails, I remember," I said. "He claimed he was out playing golf with his business partners, had the receipts to prove it."

"Yeah. So I dug into his golf habit." She passed me a stack of printouts. "Found these...they're a set of private messages from the forum Darrington's golf course runs."

"What's in them?"

"Talk about hooking," she said. "The kind that has nothing to do with a five-iron."

I gave them a scan, not reading for comprehension.

I'd read plenty of illicit steamy missives in my time and didn't need another unfortunate use of the word 'hard' cluttering up my memory banks. "Times, dates, amounts...looks like the coat check girl is working two jobs."

"Yep. They use the forum to set up their meets and talk dirty and stuff. No record on Darrington's computer, and since he *does* use the golf course for business meetings he had a good excuse."

"So he got careless," I said.

"No, I'm just that good."

I grinned. "That you are. Okay, next question...how do we prove Mister Darrington wrote these?"

"I tracked the IPs from the metadata in the messages," Izzy said. "All of them originate from either his home computer or his work machine according to Comcast. The screen name he uses is the same as his instant messenger account, and I got that off his Facebook."

"How'd you dig up his password?"

"It took me three guesses," she said. "It was his Social Security number."

I laughed. "No kidding?"

"Another one bites the dust," she said with a

devilish grin.

"You called it," I said. "Divorce would have been cheaper…this way, Elissa Darrington will rip her husband's wallet out through his nut sack and we'll take home five percent of her gross." I squeezed her shoulder. "Well-played, Izzy."

She blushed. "Thanks boss."

The phone rang. As Julian was busy I snagged the receiver. "Eckart Investigations, this is Amber," I said in my shiniest voice, glancing at the phone.

A boyish tenor rang in my ears. "Amber! Just the lady I wanted to talk to."

"Kevin Andersen," I said.

"How'd you know?"

"I'm a detective," I said. "In this case I detected the caller ID displaying your number."

He laughed. If the voice in my ear dripped any more charm I would need a Q-Tip.

"I've got a piece of work for you, if you're interested."

"I like work," I said. "What's the situation?"

"Suicide up on Whidbey Island," he said.

I grabbed a pencil and scribbled *Andersen - Suicide*

Investigation on a nearby pad. "Insurance company?"

"Grieving wife," he said.

"Is there a financial settlement involved?"

Not a dime as of yet," he said. "The widow just doesn't believe the police report and wants it checked out more thoroughly."

Scribble, scribble. "She wants a second opinion," I said.

"Basically."

I made a thoughtful noise. I knew Kevin Andersen, having worked with him before on several occasions. He was a competent attorney who sent a fair amount of work my way, but collecting a bill from him was often a struggle and he had a habit of leaning on PIs to bend the rules. I wondered why he would take a case without a substantial sum to chase after. "How recently did this happen?"

"Very," he said. "The poor girl isn't even in the ground yet. Look, why don't you come down to my office. I'll introduce you to the client, make sure everyone's a good fit. You still do free consultations, right?"

I glanced at my 'incoming' box, already knowing what I would see; not a hell of a lot. Copeland's insurance fraud and Darrington's philandering were the only cases I had running, and both of them were all but closed. Other than a handful of penny-ante background checks Izzy could do from the office in a couple hours I was out of work. Much as I disliked Kevin Andersen and his smarmy ways I disliked the idea of sending business down the street even more.

"I'll give you a half-hour," I said. "After that it's on your nickel."

"See you soon," he said.

We exchanged polite good-byes. After hanging up I gave the phone a baleful stare.

Izzy glanced over. "Andersen Law again?"

I nodded. "Somebody doesn't believe the police, wants a second opinion."

"If he's coming to the office I'll count the pencils," said Izzy.

"I'm going to see him," I said.

"Steal some of his," Izzy said.

"He's not that bad."

"He's a jive-talking douchewidget," Izzy muttered.

I managed not to choke on a laugh. "That's...colorful," I said, "and more or less accurate, but we need more work. I'll at least go find out what the score is. If I smell too much dead fish I'll back out. While I'm heading over there, give Andersen one of your patented check-arounds." I'd worked with him before, but harsh experience had taught me to check out clients every time they called.

"With pleasure," she said, sitting down at her machine.

"I probably won't be back, so make sure everything's locked up before you leave," I said.

"Okay." She paused. "Boss?"

"Yeah?"

"You didn't *really* see all those bands live, did you?"

"*Brave New World* tour, Tacoma Dome, 2000," I said. "*Magica* tour, White River Amphitheater, 2002." I raised my hand in a popular two-fingered gesture I remembered well from my youth.

She grinned. "Ever flash your boobies at the band?"

"Anything's possible," I said.

"Oh come on boss, spill," said Izzy.

"Dear," I said with a wink, "that would be telling."

Chapter 4

Kevin Andersen was still in consultation with his client when I got to his office so I sat in the waiting room with a Starbucks mocha and my Kindle, ignoring the magazines on the table. I avoided magazines the way some people avoided fried foods or alcohol and for much the same reasons. Richard Stark's *Parker* novels filled idle time as easily as *People* and the sexism in the narrative was always a good deal more honest.

Around me the office was glossy and new, a five-year-old building trying earnestly to appear aged and stately; lots of reclaimed wood and faux-aged plaster, paintings on the walls, a pretty little secretary parked behind a big oak desk. The net effect resembled a teenage boy dressed in Dad's hand-me-down suit and I gave it the same level of amused respect.

I'd taken the time to change into the good clothes I kept at the office for business meetings; dove-gray suit, pencil skirt, hose, black pumps and a Macy's briefcase. A bit of makeup and a French braid rounded it all out. Except for the 9-millimeter tucked under my arm I could have been here to take the secretary's position. Of course, when one considered the realities of the current job market the pistol wasn't an unthinkable accessory.

My cell buzzed twice, dragging me out of Parker's latest one-sided revenge game. I set the Kindle aside and dug in my purse; a text from Izzy glowed on my iPhone's screen.

Boss, I did the digging you asked for. Weird news...Kevin Andersen is getting into politics. According to what I'm seeing he plans to run for city council next election.

I raised an eyebrow. **That IS weird,** I typed. **He have a party affiliation? A platform?**

Democrat, and kinda left-leaning from the sound of things. I tracked down some blog posts of his that are all social justice-y.

I filed that away because it was unusual. Kevin Andersen was about as idealistic as the average used-car salesman. **Not sure what to make of that but thanks for the heads-up.**

No problem boss don't get your pocket picked xD

I put the phone and Kindle away and sipped at my coffee. It was edging out of optimum temperature range for drinkable and needed to be finished. I'd just drained the last of it out of the bottom of the cup when I heard a door open. A figure approached in a gray suit almost the same shade as mine, but his had pants. Let's hear it for standards.

Kevin Andersen had one of those pleasant honest faces most people trusted and I didn't, accentuated by an ingenuous smile and the liquid brown eyes of a yearling deer. I stood and gave him a professional greeting while he lobbed a golden handshake and a friendly you're-looking-well at me; my brain flicked its BS detector from standby to active.

"I just want to warn you," he said as we headed for his conference room, "my client is pretty shook up. You'll need to be gentle with her."

"I'll keep my claws sheathed and my horns tucked away," I said.

He didn't laugh. "I'm serious, Amber. You can be quite a hardass."

"When necessary," I said.

"Well, it's not necessary now."

"We'll see," I said. He opened the conference room door and I stepped inside.

A dark-skinned girl in her mid-twenties sat upright in one of the chairs, hands folded in her lap. High cheekbones and arched brows lent her face a stern dignity reminiscent of a young Angela Bassett. Her hair was done in immaculate cornrows, gathered in a tail that fell just past her shoulders. As I walked up she stood, smoothing her slacks with her hands and offering me her right to shake.

"Rachelle Hooper," she said as I clasped it. She had a firm grip, work-roughened palms and the erect bearing instilled by military discipline.

"Amber Eckart," I said. "My condolences for your loss."

"Thank you." Her voice was a husky contralto, bruised by weeping.

"I know that doesn't mean much coming from a stranger," I said.

"It means enough." Up close her eyes were fresh grief and banked fire, the force in them as palpable as gravity. I was relieved when I could look away.

I busied myself with digging out a notebook, keeping a weather eye on my prospective client and wondering what Andersen had meant by needing to be gentle. On first inspection Rachelle Hooper didn't appear delicate in the slightest.

Andersen spoke first. "I've already explained to my client the realities of hiring you," he said. "That you aren't a police officer and any investigation you perform will be a finding of facts, nothing more. And also that it will be up to the police if they wish to reopen their investigation based on what you find."

“Excellent.” I glanced at Rachelle. “And you are still interested in hiring me?”

She nodded. “I’m interested in the truth.”

"I trust Andersen’s also explained to you that this will get expensive in a hurry," I said.

Andersen made a sound like 'ah' in the back of his throat. Rachelle's eyebrow twitched as she glanced at him. "What is she talking about?"

"I charge eighty-five dollars per hour," I said, "not including expenses...travel, lodging, administrative costs, that sort of thing. My standard contract includes a three-day retainer -" I stopped when Rachelle held up her hand.

"Now wait a minute," she said to Andersen. "You told me I had a case."

Andersen held up his hands. "You do, Rachelle. There's nothing to worry about here."

"That's a lot of money she’s talking about," said Rachelle. "I worry."

Silence descended over the table. I used the time to put facts together. It didn’t take me long. "I was under the impression this was a criminal investigation," I said, speaking to Rachelle but looking hard at Andersen. "Is there something I should know?"

The silence around the table stretched out further; Kevin Andersen's face grew pale as he found himself on the receiving end of a double dose of scrutiny. His warm friendly smile took on a brittle cast.

"Amber," he said, "can I speak to you for a moment?"

"Go ahead," I said, glancing at Rachelle. She watched Andersen's face with the intent calm of a security camera.

"I mean…my office," he said. *Please,* his eyes screamed.

I mulled it over. Already the scent of dead fish wafted off the situation; I'd had lawyers downplay just how much bringing me into a case would cost a client until the bill got drafted up and then inflate it on the final invoice. Though Andersen had never pulled that charade with me I certainly thought him capable of it. Also, while technically I worked for him I did need the client to trust me. A closed-doors conference with her present but in another room wouldn't help the process of building that trust.

"I'll wait," Rachelle said into the silence.

Andersen and I slipped into his office, a windowless space crowded with books. Like mine, it had the cluttered look of a place where real work was done. "Okay, spill," I said. "Who do you plan on suing?"

He sighed. "It's always about money with you."

"Of course it is," I said. "I'm in what's called 'business'. Now…who's the unlucky group and what did they do?"

"Amber, Rachelle really does want to know what happened to her wife."

"I'm sure she does," I said. "But on your end there's more to it than that. Spill."

Andersen ran his hands through his hair. "The Island County Sheriff's Department. My client believes she was mistreated during the course of their investigation into her wife's death."

"Racial insensitivity?" Despite the pervasive belief that the Pacific Northwest was a liberal paradise, Washington's law enforcement had a spotty history when it came to race relations.

"Maybe. Mostly it's a general lack of them giving much of a damn." He straightened his tie. "First they put my client in an interrogation room and grilled her for four hours…this was less than an hour after she had found out her wife was dead.

Then they termed the death a suicide after discovering the girl had been in counselling. According to poor Rachelle they never even looked at another option."

"You're thinking that if I can find evidence of foul play, you can sue the department for negligence and discriminatory policy and land a fat settlement." I tapped my finger against my chin. "Slick."

"Come on – an interracial lesbian couple, openly married and living in Oak Harbor…one dies under circumstances anyone would find suspicious and the police term it suicide after four hours of investigation? A case where their only real suspect had a rock-solid alibi, yet was still put under the hot lights and grilled while she's still grieving?" He shook his head. If I didn't know him I would have believed his disgust genuine. "Oh, and she just happens to be black."

"Money and credibility?" I grinned. "You're learning, Andersen."

"Amber, justice isn't being served here. Look at her."

"I'm looking," I said, "and what I see is a public-relations bonanza for an aspiring politician on the Democratic ticket...a would-be city councilman, say."

His jaw fell open. "I...you...Jesus Amber, I haven't even put my name in yet."

"I'm a detective," I said. "I've gotten in the habit of checking my clients."

Andersen shook his head once, a long slow sweep. "Whatever devil you cut your deals with, I'd like his number."

Her name is Izzy, I thought, making a mental note to give that girl a raise and soon. "Let me see if I have this correct," I said. "You're taking this girl's case because you figure to make some money on a negligence/discrimination lawsuit – and failing that, championing her cause will play well with the downtown liberals when you put in a bid for city council."

"Guess I'm caught," he said with a hangdog grin. "So what do you say?"

"I say I'll work for you," I said.

"Great!" He reached for his pen. "I've got the contract right –"

"Not so fast," I said. "Since it's clear I'll be working for you, my contract will be with you. As in, you'll be responsible for my bill instead of Rachelle Hooper. And I'll work by-the-hour, not on a commission deal."

Andersen winced. “And if I don’t agree?”

“I take my leave,” I said, “and tell your client all about this conversation over coffee.”

"Jesus, Amber."

"You should have remembered the claws," I said.

The look of strained pleading on his face might’ve won him an award if it showed up in a movie, but I wasn't a member of the Academy. At length he sighed, running his hands through his hair.

"All right, you win." He extended a hand. "I'll re-write the contract."

"Pleasure doing business with you," I said as we traded grips.

"I hope so," he said. "On your end this case is easy money. I'm the one risking my shirt."

"We'll see," I said.

Chapter 5

After trading a signature for a retainer check, I sat back down at the table with Rachelle Hooper to discuss her case. Right away I knew it wouldn't be a pleasant matter. I'd worked wrongful-death cases before several times; they weren't a part of my profession I enjoyed. I understood the need for loved ones to have closure, but as the person who did the digging I had always felt like a vulture, picking the bones of the dead for profit. There was something pointless and gluttonous about it that had never sat right with my public-service heritage.

Wordlessly Rachelle produced a photograph of the deceased. It had been taken on their wedding day; from the background I guessed the ceremony had taken place in a courthouse. Elaine Laurel Hooper had been a fragile girl with a young face and old eyes, pale skin in striking contrast with a wavy mass of hip-length sable hair. Rachelle had worn a Coast Guard dress uniform for the wedding, Lanie a strapless gown in white silk with long opera gloves covering her arms. They were holding hands, their joint smile a stab wound for anyone who knew her fate. Rachelle's fingertips lingered on the image before she passed it over, eyes wet with unshed tears. I gave her a moment to collect herself before diving in.

Rachelle had met Lanie less than a month after mustering out of the Coast Guard, at the coffee shop where Lanie worked as a barista. Though Rachelle didn't come out and say it, I got the general impression that courtship hadn't taken all that long. Several months later they had joined hundreds of other couples in tying the knot after gay marriage had been legalized in Washington. They had lived together for a little over a year after that. She was less than forthcoming with any details of that time. I could already tell that prying information out of Rachelle about her relationship would be a struggle.

She'd been at work when the sheriff's office had phoned her with the bad news; her wife had been found in the woods a few miles from their apartment, hanging from a noose. More tears slid down her cheeks when she described the moment she'd been notified. I gave her another couple of minutes to collect herself. After she nodded I continued.

"Minor question," I said. "Did Lanie know how to tie a noose?"

"I spent an afternoon showing her knots," Rachelle said. "She was curious."

"Was a hangman's noose one of them?"

“I don’t remember,” she said. “I don’t think it was, but I’m not sure.”

I wrote that down. "Did the police have an explanation as to why she was out in the woods?"

Rachelle nodded. "It was in her note," she said. "Lanie didn't want me to see her...like she was."

"Do you have the note?"

"The police do," she said. "It was on her cell phone."

More scribbling. "Is that something Lanie would have done?"

"What do you mean?"

"Hiding her death from you like that. Do you think that was something Lanie would've done?"

The banked fire in her eyes flared once again. "Killing herself isn't something Lanie would do," said Rachelle. “Lanie talked about future stuff all the time. She was happy. She wanted to live."

I didn't wish to argue against my client's convictions so I changed tack. "According to Andersen, the police questioned you as a possible suspect."

Rachelle snorted in obvious disgust. "Interrogated is more like it. Two big white cops put me in a room and kept asking me over and over where I'd been that day. I told them I'd been at work, had been since seven that morning. They could have called my job anytime, but they kept at me instead - saying they had evidence I was at the scene, all this other stuff that wasn't true. Took four hours before they let me go. Then I found out they'd called it suicide."

She leaned forward, stabbing the picture with a fingertip. "Four hours. Four hours and they give up. Lanie deserves better than that, Ms. Eckart."

"I'll do my best to give it to her," I said.

Another hour of questions and deal-making minutiae passed quickly; I didn't learn much more, but I had enough basic information to begin my hunt. After an elaborate three-way handshake I left Andersen's office, detouring to borrow his restroom so I could check my grooming. It didn't matter all that much as I would be heading home after leaving Andersen's but staying on top of how I looked was a habit I'd attempted to cultivate. I'd let myself go hoydenish far too often during the previous year and that just wasn't professional. Looking one's best is part of business and doing so requires constant attention.

As I refreshed my lipstick my phone rang. I capped the stick and answered the phone; according to the screen it was my office.

"Talk to me," I said.

"Hey boss," Julian said. "How'd it go at Andersen Law?"

"We have a new case," I told him. "Start a new file, label it 'Andersen-Hooper'. I've got a couple of names I need Izzy to do full bios on...Rachelle and Elaine Hooper. Elaine's maiden name is Jennings." I spelled it for him and read off their social security numbers. "Tell her to dig."

Keys tapped in the background. "We get a client with deep pockets?"

I smiled. "Something like that." I did not feel much guilt about raiding Kevin Andersen's wallet on this case. If he wanted to politely exploit Rachelle's plight for political gain that was his business, but he'd have to pay what it cost to solve her problem. As the lead investigator I could make sure of it, and I planned to.

"How's your report coming?"

"Almost done," he said. "I still would've preferred the peril."

"Did Miss Nightingale call?"

"We have a date Saturday." A slight pause. "Her place."

I grinned. "Outpatient therapy?"

"I think so," he said. "She told me she's a yoga instructor in her spare time."

I laughed as I walked out of the bathroom, startling the secretary. "Sounds perilous." I shouldered my purse and smiled at her.

"I'll see you two tomorrow," I said. "There isn't much point in coming back when I can work just as easily from my apartment. Hand Izzy the info I just gave you and finish your report. Then you can go home and dream of flexible redheads to your heart's content."

"You got it boss."

We traded good-byes and I hung up as I pushed open the door. When I reached my car I found my new client standing next to it, arms folded against the cold.

"Figured this one was yours," she said.

"How?"

She shrugged. "I saw the gym bag in the back seat. You shake hands like you know how to throw a punch, and no offense but I couldn't picture a lawyer driving it."

"True on all cards." I nodded appreciatively. "Well-played, Rachelle."

"My friends call me Shelle," she said.

"May I?"

She raised one eyebrow. "Y'know, I don't think anybody's ever asked me that before."

"I try not to assume," I said.

"Me either," she said in a soft tone.

She turned her head to gaze at the passing traffic, eyes narrowed against the wind. "I've never done anything like this before, Ms. Eckart. I might end up spending money I don't have to do it. So, I want to know...do you work for him, or do you work for me?"

"He writes my check, but you write his," I said. "Be sure to remember that."

Her eyebrows quirked together. "And by that you mean ..."

"I mean don't let him push you around," I said. "He'll try."

"I've dealt with bureaucrats before," she said. "I know how they like to play. Anything else I should know?"

"This won't be pleasant for you," I said.

"It already isn't," she said.

"I'll only get worse from here," I said. "To find out what happened to your wife I'll have to gather as much information as possible. Part of this means questioning you about all aspects of your relationship with her - and you telling me everything you know. I'll do my best to be respectful, but I can guarantee there will be a few questions you won't want to answer. I'll need you to do it anyway."

Shelle stood straighter. "You ask, I'll answer. No exceptions."

I believed her. "I'll contact you. First I need to go over what I already have, so I know what to ask."

"Anything else?"

I took a deep breath. "There is always the chance that Lanie did commit suicide."

"She didn't," Shelle said, with the tone of someone quoting physical laws. "How long you plan to look?"

"As long as I'm paid to," I said.

The coals in her eyes flared once more but I read the emotion more clearly. It wasn't anger. It was determination, leashed by pragmatic focus. "In that case I suggest you get comfortable."

"I guess I'd better."

Chapter 6

The consultation had lasted well past six and it was pointless to go back to the office so I headed home instead. Andersen's office was a good deal further from my apartment than my own office was, so it was after seven before I pulled into my apartment's parking lot. The rain had turned the lot's ever-present coating of pine needles into a fibrous goo with the bonding power of rubber cement. I tried not to get too much of it on my shoes.

The rain continued its sullen drizzle as I walked from my car to my front door, drops beading on my trench coat and dampening my hair. Zork the cat joined me halfway across the parking lot and fell into step beside me. Since I'd fished him out of a Dumpster a few years ago he had grown from a scrawny creamsicle kitten-puff into a twenty-five pound mass of muscle and claws capable of fending off a raccoon. While I fished for my keys he batted at the hem of my coat and favored me with a huffy *mrowl.* I didn't blame him; my normal office hours were eight to five thirty. I was late and he was hungry.

"Sorry buddy," I said as I unlocked the door. "Long day at the office." I talked to him in the habit of cat owners everywhere, but never in baby talk. I respected him too much for that sort of nonsense. If he appreciated my efforts he gave no sign. He was after all a cat.

My apartment looked as it usually did; clutter that threatened chaos but didn't quite have the guts to cross the line. Books lined the walls, jammed onto on shelves fashioned from particle board and Home Depot brackets. Last month I'd added another row across the living room wall and it was already half-full. I can't bring myself to get rid of books unless I don't care for them and I've always been far too easily amused by pulp fiction.

Zork got his dinner before I got mine, but that was just for reasons of practicality. His came from a can and mine required preparation time. I'd done my best to extend my health and fitness kick into the arena of my diet, but there was no such thing as prepared health food. I'd had to learn to cook better as well. That night I topped several handfuls of spinach and cucumbers with leftover shredded chicken and added a light dressing to the mix, careful to watch the portions. I left the wine in my fridge alone and poured a glass of lemonade instead; I needed to work after dinner.

My phone chimed as I sat down to eat, the *plunk* that signified an incoming email. I dug it out with one hand while attacking my dinner with a fork. The email was from Izzy. It was loaded with attachments, a preliminary summary of Rachelle and Elaine's lives. I smiled, amazed as usual by Izzy's thoroughness. A preliminary report from her was often more detailed than full reports I'd purchased from data brokers.

Rachelle Hooper's record was immaculate, not even a speeding ticket. She'd graduated from an Everett high school and joined the Coast Guard right after, having been turned down by the Air Force due to her vision being just below par. Fifth in her class, she'd been assigned to a rescue cutter working the fishing lanes. In her second tour her boat had encountered a burning trawler during a storm, an event which had warranted several news articles. I scanned them between bites of dinner.

It'd been a two hour battle to save the crew of the *Far North;* Rachelle had been first on the deck, pulling three crewmen to safety. Despite the fire she'd then ventured below deck in search of a machinist's mate other crewmen had insisted was trapped in the engine room. She'd found him, and despite taking wounds when a fuel line exploded she'd managed to carry him to safety. *I did what anyone else would have done,* she was quoted as saying. *It's the job I signed up for.*

The Coast Guard had decorated her for valor, but for her cost had been dear; a blow to the head had resulted in three rounds of surgery. That plus numerous other injuries kept her off the water. Rachelle had done most of her last year of service from a hospital bed.

A month after mustering out she had met Lanie, whose record was a great deal darker.

Elaine Laurel Jennings had been born in a Kansas town so small, "You'd blink and miss it, but be happy you did" in Izzy's words. Details of her time there were sketchy due to said town not having computerized records, but I found a trail of arrests leading from there to the Northwest, the first at fourteen. Vagrancy, possession, disorderly conduct, assault, prostitution; by the time she'd turned sixteen Lanie had been arrested almost twenty times, spending more time in juvenile detention and rehab than out of it. I shoveled the last of my dinner into my mouth and wondered how much of this Rachelle knew about...not to mention how much she'd want to.

According to Lanie and Shelle's Facebook walls they had dated for eight months before getting married. The tone of the posts Izzy had transcribed made it sound like the marriage was Rachelle's idea. Shortly after they had begun dating Lanie had stopped working at the coffee shop; Izzy had found no other evidence of employment before her death.

Izzy's report concluded with her theories.

I've got a string of addresses for her before she met Rachelle, but they are all sketchy at best. My guess is that Lanie was a professional couch-surfer, shacking up with whoever would keep a roof over her head. There are always plenty of people who will fall for that. Her possession charges were for heroin, but they just kept letting her go or sticking her in rehab. It sounds like she was a real head-case, and I'm not surprised.

Anyway, I'll keep digging. I've got a couple of addresses where Lanie definitely lived before she met Shelle and I'm gonna track those down. If she was murdered, it sounds like there was plenty of stuff from her past that could've killed her.

Keep you posted,

~Izzy

I cleaned up the remains of my dinner and unfolded my laptop so I could examine Izzy's source material on a larger screen. I started with their Facebook archives; I've always been shocked by how open people are online compared to real life even though the Internet is both more public and permanent, but I'd never hesitated to take advantage of the behavior. On my end the only reason I had active social-media accounts was so I could read those of other people. Like examining a living room, I'd found I could learn a great deal about a person by how they update their social media.

Rachelle's reflected what I'd already observed in her; her posts were infrequent and practical, largely devoid of politics or personal confessionals. It was the account of a quiet, private person who didn't have much to say to people she didn't personally know.

I did find a lot of pictures of her and Lanie, as well as the names of her parents. I Googled them both. Shelle's mother had died of breast cancer when Shelle was in middle school; her father had never remarried and still lived in Everett. There were no posts from him on her wall. I checked; they weren't friends.

"Interesting," I said aloud.

Lanie's wall was a much different animal, a wealth of personal information and social-activist screeds. However Shelle was right; Lanie talked a good deal about beating her demons, about the future, and how much she loved her wife. In the context of her death it was not easy to read. I left her wall and worked my way through her pictures.

One of the nice features of social media was the

permanence of connections between accounts. Unlike human recollection the Internet was a permanent web of trails to follow. In my field I appreciated it like I appreciated any other labor-saving device.

In Lanie's case I found a picture from three years ago, tagged by a somewhat older man who wasn't on her friends list. Though his name was obviously fake - nobody names their kid "Spider John" - I was sure Izzy could winkle his real name out for me. I studied the picture.

Spider John was an angular man in his late twenties with broad shoulders, a blond ponytail and high sharp cheekbones. Tattoos crawled across his muscled forearms. Drop a decade and change from my good sense and I might've swooned over him. He had the bad-boy look, the kind who knows how to be romantic when it suits him but only then. In the photo he had his arms around Lanie, low on her hips. She was leaned against him, back arched and head resting on his collarbone. It was a lover's pose.

"Plot thickens," I murmured.

Next I checked the timing on Lanie's arrest records and compared it to the time stamp on the picture. The arrest records dropped off to nothing a month before the picture was taken, then climbed again a few months later.

I copied the picture and the name and emailed them to Izzy, along with a description and context. *Find me a real name on this guy,* I wrote at the end. *I've got a hunch. I'll be out of the office tomorrow visiting the scene so you're in charge; make sure all the Is are dotted on the Darrington and Copeland cases. My work up there might take me a couple of days but if you need me don't hesitate to call.*

I fired off the email and picked up my phone. An old friend of mine lived up on Whidbey Island; she had a sideline as a blogger on local issues and kept herself plugged into as many rumor mills as she could find. I got few enough excuses to see her and working a case in her neighborhood would have to serve. I dialed her number from memory. The phone rang five times before it was answered.

"Fawkes residence," a familiar smoker's rasp said.

"Hey Mattie," I said. "It's Amber."

"Kiddo!" her voice brightened. "I'll be damned, I was just thinking of you." I heard the scratch of a Zippo. "How you been?"

"Bit of this, bit of that," I said. "I'll be up your way working a case, you mind if I stay with you for a couple of days?"

"Is this a trick question, girl? I haven't seen you in...damn, how long *has* it been?"

"Too long," I said.

"You said working a case," she said. "Tell me you still have your firm."

I grinned. "Yep," I said.

"Good to hear," she replied. "What are you working on?"

"It's a wrongful-death investigation," I said, before launching into a brief no-names-given explanation of the situation. Mattie had spent decades in various journalism fields and had worked with PIs many times. She knew the game and her perspective would be helpful.

"That poor girl," Mattie said when I was finished. "Both of them."

I fed the last of my dinner dishes into the machine. "You heard anything about it?"

"Local papers didn't run anything on it that I saw," she said, "but it might be too early yet."

"Hmm." I paused to think. A suicide wasn't a huge deal, but Oak Harbor was a sleepy town; even in a big city like Seattle a self-inflicted hanging was at least worth a paragraph on page six. I made a mental note to check the paper when I got to Oak Harbor. "Mattie, you have any friends at the *Whidbey Times?*"

"There are a couple people I can talk to," she said. "Want me to poke?"

"Please. I can pay you -"

"Oh hush, kiddo." I could hear Mattie's grin through the connection. "I'm bored anyway. I'll ask around, no charge."

I grinned. "You're a peach, Mattie. See you soon."

"Look forward to it," she said.

We exchanged good-byes and I signed off. As I did my email box chimed once more. I moved back to my computer and gave the screen a glance. The email was from Drake Albie. I took a deep breath and opened the message.

Amber,

I just wanted you to know that things are going better than they have in a while. I'm in Ogden right now, working as a cook - the guy is paying me cash under the table, and I'm living in his garage, so it'll be damned hard for anyone to track me down. I paid attention to some of the stuff you told me in our last exchange. Wanted you to know it was working. :)

Ogden's not a bad place to live; don't believe everything you hear about asshole Mormons, most of the people I've met down here are downright civilized. I've even managed to save up some money; not as much as I would need to take on Halcourt but it's a start. I have also done some homework on attorneys who might be able to take my case. Maybe in another year or so I can drop-kick that wrinkly bastard out of my life.

To say I miss you, well...that would be an understatement. I wish I could see your face, but my webcam is busted. Guess I'll have to settle for my memory banks.

Yours,

Drake

I let out the breath I hadn't realized I'd been holding and drummed my fingers on the desk, trying to think of how to reply. Drake Albie and I had a strange history, capped off with a whirlwind relationship prematurely truncated by the reality of his financial situation. We'd kept in touch with email, but it was always strained on my end; I never knew what to say. I'd never been good with relationships, especially the talking part.

I put my fingers on the keys and tried to compose a reply. There was a good deal I wanted to tell him but I couldn't put the words together right. After three false starts I gave up and sent him a generic update of my last month, with hints included regarding how I missed him likewise. It was clunky and awkward, but about as good as my brain could do. With a sigh, I hit Send.

"He's going to wander away," I said to myself. "He's going to think you don't care and he'll find somebody new."

If he hasn't already, the irrational part of me hissed.

I went to the kitchen and poured myself a generous Riesling nightcap. Other than the distant blare of traffic my apartment was a quiet, cold place. Zork hopped up onto the table and I petted him. He butted his forehead against my cheek while I sipped wine and ruminated on dead girls, missed chances and the justice of the world.

Chapter 7

The drive up to Whidbey Island was pleasant once I got out of the city proper. I caught the ferry at Mukilteo and prepared for a long drive north. Whidbey Island was a gangly landmass tucked into the crook of Puget Sound; read by square miles it didn't appear all that large, but on a map it comes off as massive. It was trees and winding roads with one small city, Oak Harbor. About the only other noteworthy feature on the island was a naval air station.

A quick phone call to my apartment manager solved the problem of Zork's care and feeding while I was out of town. We had a deal on the matter; I'd run the occasional background check on potential tenants for him, he'd make sure my cat didn't starve when I needed him seen to. After that I took a brisk turn around the ferry deck for some exercise. I hadn't gotten in my jogging that morning and ever since I'd made it into a habit I grew restless when I missed out. My phone rang while I stretched my legs. It was the office.

"Talk to me," I said.

"I got your email, boss," Izzy said. "I'm working on matching a name to the photo you sent."

"Good," I said. "Call me when you find something."

"So, you aren't coming in today?"

"Yep, and you're in charge while I'm gone." I suspected that was the reason for her call.

"Why me?"

I shook my head. "Why not? You have seniority and you know at least as much about how to run that place as I do."

Her voice was brittle, uncertain. "Well, yeah, but..."

"Izzy, Julian's advancing out of just being a secretary. I need you to do the same. The firm's reached a place where we need to either grow or fold...We're running too lean on just the three of us. I'll be hiring at least two new people, provided I can find good ones."

"How can we afford that? I mean, we don't even have the money to move."

"Having as few employees as we do is *why* we can't afford to move," I said. "We can't take enough cases to make enough profit to shift locations. It's a nasty catch twenty-two, and I need to break us out of it. Which means I'll need somebody I can trust in the office while I'm out in the field. That somebody is you."

"Boss, are you promoting me?"

I smiled. "Yes."

"Oh."

Silence reigned on the line. Fifteen feet ahead of me a pair of teenaged lovers held hands and whispered at each other with furtive abandon. The ferry was a favored place for illicit dates.

"I trust your judgment, Izzy. I need you to start trusting it too. So, take messages. Get Julian to do what he's good at. You get seriously out of your depth, call. I'll have my phone on me always."

"Okay, boss." I could hear that she was nervous, but less so than she'd been a minute ago. "I'll...be in touch."

I signed off. "You can do it, girl," I said to the gray water as the ferry sliced through it.

Managing Izzy and Julian was a study in contrasts; Julian had the initiative and cleverness to be a good field investigator...but he needed brakes, direction, and the occasional admonishment not to go too far. Izzy was all but Julian's direct opposite; she needed shelter, encouragement and prodding, reminders that she was indeed good enough at what she did to work for me. Balancing both was a challenge on the best of days but the results were worth it. I hoped, as I usually did, that my read of the situation was right and Izzy was ready. I'd never been formally trained in how to manage people or run a business.

Hiring new people would be a challenge all on its own. A good many private investigators were retired police officers, and a good many of them were male. Such individuals were often uncomfortable with the notion of taking orders from a woman young enough to be their daughter with a fifth their experience, one who also lacked any law enforcement background beyond having a cop for a father. I'd hired and fired two such individuals over the years, both for repeatedly refusing to follow my instructions.

I'd gotten lucky with Izzy and Julian, which led to my idea of hiring youngsters and training them myself. It was more responsibility and two other licenses to maintain but it had resulted in fewer ego clashes. For a boss, every decision involved at least one trade-off.

A garbled PA message crackled in the air. I couldn't understand a word of it but its timing meant the ferry was about to dock. I pocketed my phone and walked quickly in the direction of my car. After a short wait in concrete silence the ferry docked and I pulled out onto highway 525.

It had rained the previous night and the trees were

that fresh green color plants display after a good dose of water. There was a light mist on the road and more clung to the forest. I could've parked my car by the highway and ended up in a fairy-land after twenty paces.

My first priority would've been examining Lanie's body, but I needed Rachelle for that and according to her schedule she would be at work most of the day. Ditto for the apartment, so I drove to Mattie's place instead.

Mattie lived up at the north end of the island near the Deception Pass Bridge on several acres of wooded property. Her house was much the same as it had the first time I had been out there; a stout single-story cabin with shingled walls and a sharply peaked roof. A wraparound deck gave a stunning view of the water. Mattie's late husband had built the place himself. He had taken twenty years at it, and the workmanship showed. So did the additions Mattie had made for security; heavy shutters hung next to the windows and a blackened iron wreath which contained a security camera sat above the door. Mattie had spent almost thirty years at the sort of hard-biting journalism that had sometimes resulted in ruffled feathers and death threats. She lived out in the boonies for a reason.

The yard was more overgrown than it'd been last

time I'd been out, but the deck was still swept clean as an operating table. An olive-green Land Rover was parked near the barn. I could hear the clucking of chickens. I walked up the steps and knocked on the big wooden door. It opened almost immediately.

"Hey, Mattie."

"Damn but it's good to see you, kiddo," she said, leaning out to give me a hug. Marian Fawkes was plump, gray and wrinkled and didn't give a damn about it. Fey green eyes sparkled behind clunky bifocals. They gave a clue to the lascivious beauty she had once possessed. She had on a flowing hippie skirt and a patterned sweater and a worn-looking apron. I hugged her back. She smelled of woodsmoke and fresh bread and lavender.

"Good to see you too," I said. We walked inside.

Mattie's house was cluttered with the touchstones of two long and colorful lives. The walnut gun cabinet in the front room and wall full of military plaques were from her late husband. A shelf lined with trophies was hers, fencing awards from her teen years. She'd had dreams of the Olympics until a missed step had bent her knee the wrong way back. Front and center on the shelf was a faded black-and-white photo of a curvy girl in fencer's gear, hair feathered like Farrah Fawcett's. Next to the trophies was a pink mirabou boa mounted on an oak placard. Only a few people knew the story behind the boa. Books from all manner of subjects and genres lined the rest of the space on the walls. Like me, Mattie was a voracious reader.

We sat at her splintery old driftwood kitchen table and caught up with each other. It'd been four years since I'd seen her in person and a good deal had happened to both of us since then. After coffee and conversation Mattie fetched an unlabeled bottle of purple-tinged liquid and two glasses. I smiled.

"It's eleven o'clock in the morning, Mattie," I said.

"This is just to try," she said. "Latest batch, and I'm damn proud of it."

"Oh my," I said as she poured a quarter inch in both glasses. I could smell it from where I sat, blackberries and the cool-hot fire of high proof alcohol. I braced myself and sipped. A berry-coated thermonuclear warhead went off on my tongue. I coughed and waved my hand in front of my mouth.

"That's...like getting your face punched with delicious," I said when I could speak.

"Like I said, damn proud." Before liquor had been privatized in Washington, Whidbey had been a moonshiner's mecca. It was the real explanation for the dozen "craft distilleries" which had opened up since the law had changed. Mattie hadn't bothered, as for her it wasn't a business so much as a family tradition. Five generations of O'Learys had brewed moonshine in the Ozarks, and Mattie had brought the family secrets with her when she'd moved west.

"I did the poking you asked for," Mattie said after downing her portion.

"And?"

Her grin was crooked. "You're walking into a hornet's nest, dearie."

I sighed. "How bad?"

She reached into her apron and dug a pack of Camel Wides from the pocket. "I spoke with a friend of mine in the Sheriff's Department," she said. "Terrence Stone, he's a deputy there. He was one of the responding officers and was supposed to be the one to question the spouse. Unfortunately, some fool kids got themselves into a wreck near the Pass Bridge and he had to oversee the cleanup. By the time he was done two other officers had already ruled the case a suicide."

"That fast?"

"Yeah." She stuck a cigarette in her mouth and lit it. "Island County doesn't have any interest in pursuing the matter further...they want it forgotten, and soon."

"Sounds like I might need another drink later," I muttered. "The Sherriff's office did a good job trampling over my client's sensibilities, by the way."

"I heard that," said Mattie. "Stone isn't happy about it. It's why he's willing to talk to you."

"Well, that's something," I said. "What do you know about him?"

"Stone? He's a good cop." Mattie blew twin streams of smoke out her nose. "Honest and fair. You'll like him." She winked at me. "Just remember that he's married."

I let that last remark pass. "How do I find him?"

"I gave him your number," she said. "Department keeps him pretty busy, but he'll call."

"Does the Sheriff's Department know I'm coming?"

Mattie grinned. "Stone doesn't plan on mentioning it to them."

"I like him already," I said. Technically the police weren't allowed to interfere with my investigation, seeing as they had already ruled and I had the cooperation of the spouse...but the reality was that there was plenty they could do to obstruct me if they decided I was a headache. It would be best if I more or less stayed off their radar.

"What's your next move?"

"Getting in to see the body," I said. "Since the cops termed it a suicide they won't have done an autopsy. I need the wife's approval for that and she's at work right now. Then I check the apartment, and go knock on all the neighbor's doors and see what they say. After that, check the crime scene."

"Do you think it's a suicide?"

"I think I don't have enough evidence for a guess yet," I said.

"Atta girl," Mattie said.

Chapter 8

My next port of call was Rachelle's neighborhood for a long session of knocking on doors and seeing who had what to say. PIs called it "doing a neighborhood" and it often yielded a wealth of information. Little old ladies with nothing better to do than snoop on their neighbors might be annoying to the people they lived next to, but they're worth their weight in gold to investigators like me.

In Shelle's neighborhood I didn't luck out all that much. A good many knew about Lanie's death and all thought it a tragedy, although most people were convinced that Shelle and Lanie were "roommates'. Plenty of people wanted to talk to me but nobody had much to add beyond that. I wrote down what I did hear anyway. I never knew what could become important.

The last apartment I tried was the unit directly below Shelle's. My knock was answered by a sparsely-built boy still in his teens, with acne-spotted cheeks and hair that fell across his eyes in a smooth wing. "Uh, hi," he said in a cracked voice. "Did Mark forget to pay the power bill again?"

I resisted the urge to ask for his parents. "I don't

know," I said, passing him a business card. "My name is Amber Eckart...I'm a private investigator and I'd like to ask you some questions about your upstairs neighbor."

His eyes widened. "Wow. Uh, sure, okay. Come on in." He paused, then stuck out his hand. "I'm Dave," he said.

We traded grips. "Nice to meet you," I said.

The apartment turned out to be crowded with teenagers; from the mess I deduced that no adults lived there. The air smelled of pot and stale food and incense, with an undercurrent of cheap perfume from the two girls. A complex mess of greetings and questions followed. Somebody asked if I had a gun and I ducked the question. There was no unoccupied seating that I trusted. I leaned against a wall instead.

"So what's this about anyway?" A girl with blond stripes in her hair, speaking around a wad of gum.

"You guys know your upstairs neighbors, right?"

"Yeah," said the girl. "The lesbians."

"Lanie and Shelle," said the other girl, a tiny dark-skinned pixie with a spiky brush cut. "They're nice. I like them."

"And hot," chimed in one of the guys. "Really really

hot."

"Oh shut *up,* Todd," said Pixie.

He grinned and shrugged. "It's true," he said.

"Why do you want to know?" Dave, speaking from a corner of the couch. "Are they in trouble with somebody or something?"

"No," I said. I took a deep breath. "There's no easy way to say this, but...Lanie died a few days ago." The news quieted them down like a switch.

"Oh my god," said Pixie after a moment, her eyes wide. "What happened?"

"That's what I'm trying to find out," I said. "Anything you can tell me will help me do that."

What followed was less a conversation and more a five-way explosion of disconnected facts. I didn't have to ask much; it was work to keep my scribbling paced with their babbling. I deflected any questions about who I worked for and kept them talking. Lanie and Shelle had been popular with the teenagers in the apartment. The girls liked them because Shelle "knew how to fix stuff", and the boys for reasons having to do with hormones, though they all hastened to assure me that they "were totally cool with the lesbian thing". All of them also informed me how there'd been a domestic squabble between Lanie and Shelle two weeks before.

“There was a lot of yelling," Dave said. "One of them, I think it was Lanie, was crying...like, really loud. I almost called the cops, but Selena told me not to. I went for a walk instead."

"Lanie came down to hang out with us for a while after it was over," Selena the pixie said. "She was crying, but she wasn't, like, hurt or anything."

"Did she say what the fight was about?"

Selena shook her head. "We just smoked a bowl and watched a movie. She didn't really want to talk about it, y'know?"

"I bet it was about the drugs," Todd said. Selena glared at him in a way that said 'shut up'.

"What drugs?"

"Todd," Selena said, warning in her tone.

"I'm not a police officer," I said to Selena. "And anyway, Lanie's beyond everyone's jurisdiction now." I looked back at Todd. "Please go on."

"Lanie asked me if I knew anyone who had any heroin," he said.

"Did you?"

He shrugged. "I asked around some, but nobody I

know had any. Smack's heavy stuff, y'know? I found her some E once, but then Mark told me she was in rehab. I didn't get her any more after that, but she kept asking."

I asked him for dates and names and after some prodding he gave them to me. I scribbled them down after promising him I wouldn't get any of his friends in trouble. I asked a few more questions of the group but did not get anything further, so at length I excused myself.

"God bless talkative teenagers," I said under my breath after the door closed. A glance showed a light on in Shelle's apartment which hadn't been there before. It had been a long day and I was hungry, but work beckoned. I climbed the catwalk and knocked on Shelle's door. It opened after less than ten seconds.

"Sorry to just drop in," I said to Shelle as she opened the door.

"It's okay," she said, stepping aside to let me in.

The Hooper residence was a good deal like my own; secondhand furnishings, cluttered but not messy, with a large number of books and a kitchen too small for any real cooking. The row of military awards and photographs of people on boats were Shelle's, the Emilie Autumn posters and dream catcher hanging in the window likely Lanie's contributions. The Gibson twelve-string propped on a stand in the corner could've gone either way.

"Can I get you something, Ms. Eckart?" Shelle wore a black skirt and gray blouse, unbuttoned at the neck; from looking at her background I knew she worked as a secretary. A gold cross hung from a short chain at the base of her throat.

"I wouldn't mind a cup of coffee," I said.

Shelle walked into the kitchen and got a coffeepot going with the mechanical movements of habit weighed down with grief. "Do you know anything yet?"

"Not yet," I said, "but I do have more questions for you."

"Okay," she said, pushing the START button on the coffeepot.

"Your downstairs neighbors said that you and Lanie had a fight recently," I said. "Bad enough that one of them almost called the police."

Shelle flinched. "Yeah, we did."

"What about?"

She sighed and drummed her fingers on the counter.

"I warned you about this," I said.

"I know," she said.

Another pause. I waited it out.

"Lanie had a lot of problems," she said.

"Drugs, abuse, and a nasty past," I said. "I've seen her record."

"Yeah. Well, I told her when we started dating that I wanted her to stay clean. I don't like drugs, and I didn't want them in the house. She said she would. She promised me she would."

"And then she didn't," I said.

Another sigh. "At first it wasn't a big deal...she would go and hang out with Selena and Dave and they'd smoke pot or drink. I didn't like it, but when we talked it had been about the harder substances she'd been hooked on, so I didn't say anything." She paused, fidgeting. "But she started doing it all the time, on days when she was supposed to be looking for a job. I'd come home from work and she'd be drunk or high more days than she wasn't. It got hard to take. Then I found some stuff."

"Found what?"

"Needles, powder and a burned up spoon," she said.

I scribbled notes. "So you confronted her, and there

was a fight."

She looked up. "Ms. Eckart, I paid a lot of money to put her through rehab. I know people can't just quit heavy drugs without help, but getting her that help..." She shook her head. "I'm still paying it off. So yeah, we had a fight."

The coffee pot dinged. I walked into the kitchen and Shelle handed me a mug. "Did she say where she found the drugs?"

"No," Shelle said. "I pushed her about it but she wouldn't say. If those kids downstairs got it for her..." Shelle's eyes narrowed.

"According to them, they didn't."

"I'd give a lot to know who did," she said.

"So would I," I said as I doctored my coffee. "What happened after the fight?"

"Lanie went for a walk, came back a couple hours later wanting to talk. She smelled like pot and I told her we'd talk when she was sober. Then -" Shelle paused, and her dark skin darkened further with a blush. "Well..."

I put the pieces together. "Then you two had makeup sex," I said, "and the next morning you had work and didn't want to have another argument."

"Yeah. It was Lanie's answer to most problems." Shelle fingered the cross at her neck. "I've never been with anyone but her," she said. "Is that normal?"

I smiled. "Shelle, my career is digging into private lives. I can tell you with certainty there's no such thing as 'normal'. Just varying degrees of 'common'."

"How common is it?"

"Very," I said. "I've been on both ends of that exchange more than a few times." How it'd been with partners I very much wished I could un-date was a detail I chose not to mention.

"Oh," she said.

"The drugs," I said. "What did you do with them?"

"When we fought I dumped the powder down the drain," she said. "After Lanie left I smashed up the rest and threw it out. It wasn't the smartest thing, but I was mad. It's what caused her to storm out." She flinched and looked away, eyes glistening. "It was one of the last times we really talked."

I did my best not to flinch in turn. I'd never lost anyone, but I'd walked enough miles in Shelle's shoes otherwise. Upset and alone, surrounded by problems needing to hold it all together when what

I wanted to do was curl up and cry. I wanted to reach out to her, but I could tell she had too much pride to weep on a stranger's shoulder. I let her keep that pride; she needed it. I had a better picture of the Hooper marriage than I had before, but it wasn't one I liked.

"May I look through Lanie's things?"

"What would you be looking for?"

"If Lanie bought drugs, she would have a number somewhere for her dealer," I said. "She wouldn't have put it in her cell, because she'd be afraid you'd look there and find it. Addicts sneak around a lot - they have to. Thus, they assume everyone else does too." I paused. "I'm sorry about violating your privacy like this."

Shelle shook her head. "I want you to find out what happened. Look wherever you need to."

I dug a pair of disposable Nitrile gloves out of my purse and put them on. If I found an item that needed fingerprinting I didn't want to contaminate it. Then I cracked my knuckles, and started in the living room, drinking Shelle's coffee while I worked.

In the movies when people search a living space, they toss everything everywhere and make a huge mess. That doesn't work too well in reality, as any college kid who has ever looked for their car keys in a messy dorm room already knows. Instead I worked carefully from one end of the room to the other, putting things back where they were after inspecting them, asking Shelle what was Lanie's and what was hers. I could tell it was hard on Shelle to do and I wished I didn't have to, but it was necessary. There was nothing clue-ish in the living room, so I checked the office.

Lanie's desk was cluttered and dirty, but there was a clean space about a foot square at one end. A black smudge on the edge of the desk drew my attention; an oil stain, recent. I ran a finger through it, held it under my nose and sniffed. I looked back at Shelle, leaning against the doorway.

"You own a gun?"

Shelle's face jumped in surprise. "No - well, yes," she said.

"Please explain," I said.

"I own one, but it isn't here," she replied. "The idea of having it around made Lanie nervous, but it belonged to my grandfather's and she didn't want to make me get rid of it. It's in a safe deposit box. Why do you ask?"

I held up my gloved finger with the smear on it. "Solvent, lubricating oil and burnt gunpowder," I said. "It's distinctive. I smell it after I go to the range, three times a week."

"Lanie hated guns," Shelle said.

I bent down and dug through the trash can. Sure enough, there was a square of ragged jersey knit and several wadded-up paper towels, all with oil stains on them. "And yet she cleaned one," I said, pointing at the spot on the desk, "right here."

"What the hell," Shelle said.

"Good question." I stood up. "Where does Lanie keep her backpack?"

"In the closet - wait, how'd you know -"

"-That she had one?" I shrugged. "She doesn't have a car. People who don't own cars carry backpacks." I walked back out to the hall closet and opened it. Sitting on the floor was a battered pink bag with black zips. I picked it up. There was a second bag stuffed behind it, a worn out blue nylon number, something a kid would take to school. "You recognize that bag?"

"No," Shelle said, voice heavy with suspicion.

I set the pink bag aside and opened up the blue one. "Bingo," I said, reaching in to extract a battered .38 revolver in a worn shoulder holster.

"Jesus," Shelle said, "that's granddad's gun. What's it

doing here?"

I flicked open the cylinder. It was loaded with five rounds, one chamber empty for the hammer to rest on. I dumped the shells out into my palm. "Winchester Silvertip hollow-points," I said. "Man killers, and they're loaded the smart way. Somebody gave her good advice."

Shelle turned away, eyes wide, running her hands over her cornrows. "What the hell is this?"

I set gun and cartridges aside and dug through the rest of the backpack; I found a change of clothes, three Powerbars, a box of ammunition and fifty dollars in mixed bills, along with Lanie's state ID card and a cheap cell phone. "This," I said, "is a bug-out bag."

Her eyes went wider in disbelief. "Lanie planned to *leave me?"*

"I don't think so." I opened the cell and turned it on. There were two numbers programmed into it, both with no names. One number had been called several times, the other only once. The last date for the first number was the day before she'd died. It was incoming. All of the times were between the hours when Shelle would've been at work.

"First rule of investigation," I said, "is that conclusions aren't to be jumped to. You sneak up on them, real slow, one fact at a time." I looked up at Shelle. "Lanie had personal effects she valued from before you met, right?"

Shelle took a deep breath. "Yeah, she has this little box of trinkets and jewelry, ticket stubs, stuff like that."

I nodded. "If she was going to leave you, why isn't that in here?" I pulled out my phone.

"That makes sense," she said, relaxing some. I hit the speed-dial for the office. It rang twice.

"Eckart Investigations, this is Elizabeth," Izzy, shaky with nerves.

"Izzy, it's Amber. I've got some phone numbers for you to break," I said. "There's a better-than-even chance they're for go-phones but I want you to try anyway."

"Okay," she said. I rattled them off and waited while she read them back to me. "I still haven't put a name to Spider John."

"Break the numbers first," I said. "Lanie was talking to somebody before she died, and I want to know who."

"You got it boss," she said. I signed off.

Shelle cocked an eyebrow at me. "What was that

about?"

"Breaking a phone means connecting a number to a name," I said. "My researcher is going to do that with the two in Lanie's cell. If the owners are up to anything illegal the phones they go to are likely the cheap disposable kind." I held up Lanie's. "Like this. Lanie wouldn't want you picking through her phone and finding the numbers and asking about them...thus the second phone."

"If you probably won't get a name, why bother?"

"That's the second rule of investigation," I said. "Play every card you're dealt. People are careless sometimes, especially criminals. It's how the cops catch them."

Shelle nodded, folding her arms across her stomach and staring out the window while I rooted through the bag again, seeing if there was anything else. There wasn't. After a moment she turned back to me. "Ms. Eckart, I need something to do. No offense, but I can't just sit here and wait."

"Glad you mentioned that," I said. "I need you to contact the funeral home tomorrow and arrange for me to see Lanie's body." I put all the stuff back in the bag except the gun and ammo. "The cops didn't do an autopsy, and I'm guessing they didn't really look her over either. I'll need to."

"Okay. Then what?"

"Depends on what I find," I said.

Shelle scooped up the revolver and the cartridges and put one into the other the way they'd been before, one chamber empty beneath the hammer. Then she snapped the cylinder shut.

"Keep me informed," she said.

Chapter 9

I checked the rest of Shelle's apartment before leaving; I didn't find anything else of note but it paid to be sure. Shelle let me take Lanie's backpack, less the gun. I plugged the phone into my cigarette lighter. If somebody called it, I wanted to know. I also didn't want Shelle answering it and maybe taking up the hunt on her own hook. I'd seen the baleful look in her eyes when she'd loaded the gun.

If Lanie had been murdered, I did *not* want Shelle and whoever had done the deed to end up in the same room. I knew a want for vengeance when I saw it.

In the parking lot I did a Google search for the closest gun range. Lacking a car, Lanie would've likely done the same. There was one a little south of Oak Harbor. I checked the time and distance; I could get there easily within their stated hours of operation, and I did.

The Firing Line was similar to other ranges I'd visited; a windowless block of concrete, with a big sign and a parking lot full of shiny pickup trucks and SUVs. My ratty gray Golf fit in like a street pigeon at a peacock convention. I walked inside.

There was a store out front for ammo and guns,

rows of rifles and pistols, ammunition stacked behind locked Plexiglas. Through the wall I could hear the muted *pop* of gunfire. The front desk was manned by a beefy gentleman in jeans and a black t-shirt, head shaved shiny. His face sported the biggest, bristliest reddest mustache I'd ever laid eyes on. The angular shape of an automatic's handle showed on the left side of his waist.

"Hail to the fellow southpaw," I said.

"Well hi there, miss," he said in a surprised tone. "How'd you know?"

I pointed. "You're printing on the left side, butt backward," I said.

I opened my jacket to show him mine.

"Nice rig," he said with a smile. "Glock?"

"P7 nine millimeter," I said. "Heckler and Koch."

"Another fine choice," he said. "It can have fouling issues, though."

"I only feed it jacketed ammo," I said. "That way the gas system doesn't fill up with lead dust."

I watched as his first impression of me climbed several notches, which had been the entire point of talking shop with him for a few. Gun enthusiasts were like every other insular community in that one needed to establish *bona fides* to attain cooperation.

"Good plan," he said. "What can I do for you?"

"My name's Amber Eckart," I said, passing him a business card. "I'm curious to know if this girl came in here recently." I set the wedding photo on the counter and pointed to Lanie. "She would have had an old Smith & Wesson thirty-eight with her and wouldn't have known how to use it. Probably nervous about learning, too."

He studied the picture. Recognition dawned in his eyes.

"Yeah, I remember her," he said. "She came in here a couple weeks back. Wanted some pointers. Didn't know one damn thing about guns. I worked with her some, and after a couple boxes of ammo she had it down okay. Nice girl, too...a little jumpy, but a lot of ladies get that way around guns." He flinched. "No offense."

"None taken, it's true more than it isn't. Did she say why she wanted to learn?"

"Said somebody in her apartment complex was hassling her." He scratched the back of his neck. "A young lady's got the right to protect herself. She in some sort of trouble?"

"Serious trouble," I said. "She's dead."

His head rocked back. "Jesus," he murmured.

"I'm trying to figure out how it happened."

He shook his head. "What a damn shame," he said in a tone that told me he meant it. "I got a daughter 'bout her age. They get the sonuvabitch that did it?"

"The cops claim it was suicide," I said. "Other people don't think so."

He took one of his business cards off the counter and handed it to me. "My name's Kurt McConnell, and one thing I don't care for its sons of bitches who hurt young ladies," he said. "If you need anything, go ahead and call."

"Time and date she came in here would be most helpful," I said.

"Miss, I'll give you everything I've got," he said.

Twenty minutes later I bid goodbye to Kurt McConnell with a sheaf of paper under my arm. He'd been nice enough to give me photocopies of Lanie's receipts, range scores and even a few stills of her shooting from the security footage. He kept the originals, but promised to lock them in his safe. I kept his card in my case of good contacts. Friendly people are always useful to me.

It was past seven and fully dark and my stomach rumbled, reminding me that lunch had been a long time ago. I gave Mattie's cooking a serious thought when my phone rang. I checked it; I didn't know the number but it was a local prefix. I punched the button and pressed it to my ear.

"I'm looking for Amber Eckart." A man's voice drawled into my ear, deep into the bass register and smooth as marble. I pictured a young Barry White.

"This is she," I said.

"I'm Deputy Terrence Stone, Island County Sheriff's Department. A Marian Fawkes told me that you and I have mutual interests."

"We do," I said, "and I'd like to meet with you as soon as possible."

"So would I," he said. "Would you like dinner? My wife can set a place for you."

"I'd love it," I said.

Stone rattled off an address and I wrote it down. "I'm at the Firing Line gun range at the moment," I said.

"I know it. That's about twenty minutes from my home. I'll see you soon, Ms. Eckart." Thanks to a faint Louisiana drawl it came out *Miz.*

"Looking forward to it," I said.

A quick use of my phone's GPS navigator gave me a

map, and a text to Mattie explaining where I was going made sure she wouldn't cook for me. Then I sat in my car and brought my hair and cosmetics to business-meeting standards. After that, I put my car in gear and followed the nice voice from my GPS, hoping that Deputy Stone was reasonable and that his wife could cook.

Chapter 10

Deputy Stone's house was a ranch-style rambler clad in shingles and surrounded by trees, with a yard as neat as a parade ground. A sheriff's cruiser, a Jeep and a candy-colored Jetta took up most of the driveway. I parked on the street and stashed my H & K under the seat, as I didn't know how a sheriff's deputy would feel about an armed civilian in his home. My hip was light without the gun as I walked up the drive. When I'd first started carrying the weight of my gun had been as obtrusive as a boil. After a year, every time I took it off I felt its absence like a knocked-out tooth.

Thirty seconds after pressing the doorbell the door was opened by a teenage girl fully six inches taller than me, with dark olive skin and the athletic figure of a volleyball player. "Hi," she said, and then over her shoulder, "Dad, the private detective lady is here." She stepped aside to let me in.

I walked into a wall of warmth, cooking smells and joyous noise; in the living room I counted four children from toddler to teenager and none of them were being quiet. The aroma from the kitchen made my stomach growl like a junkyard dog.

"I'm Amber," I said to the gorgeous young giantess

in front of me. Her parents would have their hands full once she discovered dating.

"I'm Julie," she said. "Dad's in the dining room." She pointed and I started to walk that way, but a khaki-clad thundercloud turned the corner and I stopped.

Deputy Sheriff Terrence Stone was the archetypical lawman departments loved to put on recruiting posters and criminals tried to pretend they weren't terrified of, six feet and five inches of barrel-chested brawn with a Burt Reynolds mustache and skin as black and tough-looking as biker leather. Even teeth flashed at me in a gleaming smile. "Ms. Eckart," he said, extending a hand. "Terrence Stone."

"Pleased to meet you," I said. I let my hand be swallowed up by his while I resisted an irrational urge to curtsy. Terrence Stone had the salty charm hard men over forty sometimes developed, an aura that often made teenage girls giggle and women of my vintage check their grooming in the nearest mirror.

"So, business first or dinner first?" His voice was deeper in person.

"Dinner, please," I said. "Lunch was a while ago, and whatever your wife is cooking smells delicious."

"I hope you like salmon," he said.

"Consider me charmed," I said.

He laughed and made an after-you gesture at the hall. I walked down it, giving my reflection a quick glance in a nearby window. My hair and cosmetics were in fact still up to par. I gave my silly monkey brain a stiff swat and told it to stop entertaining half-formed fantasies about the nice married lawman.

There followed a complicated six-way introduction; Stone's wife, "Genny with a G, short for Genevieve" was a willowy French-Canadian with laugh lines on her cheeks and a thick blonde braid reaching past her hips. The children were as awkwardly polite as children could be; I shook their hands and returned their courtesies as we sat down to eat. Dinner was fresh greens and baked garlic with French bread and salmon swimming in butter; after the second bite I decided I would've married Genny Stone for a nightly dose of her cooking. It was an effort to remember my table manners.

"Just curious," Stone said as we ate, "are you by chance related to a James Eckart?"

"My father," I said with a faint pang. "You knew him?"

"Only by reputation," he said. "Jim Eckart was a hell of a cop from what I hear. He doing all right?"

"He passed away four years ago," I said. "Heart attack."

Stone flinched. "I'm sorry."

"So was I," I said.

I hoped the conversation would move away from the topic of my father. Dad and I had a complicated history, most of which I had no wish to share. I was saved from elaborating by Julie bouncing up from the table.

"Gotta go, I've got practice," she said.

"You have fun," he said.

She gave her father a kiss on the cheek before jogging towards the front door.

I glanced at Genny Stone. "Volleyball or basketball?"

She shook her head with a smile. "Lacrosse."

"That's like rugby," I said, "but with sticks."

Deputy Stone grinned. "My baby likes to play rough," he said.

"I guess so," I said. Apparently it would be the boys who would have *their* hands full when Julie Stone discovered dating.

After the meal Stone and I retreated into his den, me with my pages of notes and him carrying two bottles of Stella Artois. The walls were lined with photos and books. Hanging near the coat rack was a framed ticket. I glanced at it; an indecent-exposure citation, issued twenty-one years ago by Patrolman Terrence Stone to one Genevieve St. Croix.

I cocked an eyebrow at Stone. "That's one way to meet your future bride," I said.

"She was sunbathing nude in a public park," Stone said with a grin. "Tried to flirt her way out of the citation, too."

I had to laugh. "And you gave it to her anyway?"

"Let's just say I did not at all object to continuing that conversation," he said as he sat down behind his desk. "Now, you are a private investigator hired by Elaine Hooper's wife because she does not believe the police report."

"Correct," I said, taking a seat across from him. "You were the responding officer?"

"I was," he said. "A hiker saw the body and called it in. Right away it looked wrong for a suicide. I wanted to check it out proper." He took a sip of beer. "But then some dumb kids in funny costumes got themselves in a wreck up by the Pass Bridge and I had to go sort it out." His expression turned dark with anger. "By the time I got that mess cleaned up, Deputies Strandell and Peters had declared the case closed."

"They jumped the gun," I said before giving Stone a brief description of what I'd uncovered.

"I thought so," he said. "Unfortunately I can guarantee Strandell and Peters won't willingly re-open the case."

I took a sip from my bottle. "And they won't re-open it because..."

"Ma'am, are we off the record?"

I nodded and made a zipping motion over my lips.

"They won't re-open it because Rick Strandell is a ladder-climbing shitbird who thinks closing cases is a numbers game," Stone said.

"I take it you don't have the clout to object," I said.

Stone shook his head. "Unfortunately, Strandell's a ladder-climbing shitbird whose daddy happens to write my paycheck."

I rolled my eyes. "Ah, nepotism. Is there anything it can't screw up?"

"Nothing I know of." Stone reached into his desk drawer and came out with a file folder and a plastic bag.

I glanced at the folder. "That's the report on Lanie's

death," I said.

"And the personal effects Elaine had on her when she died," he said. "Rachelle Hooper requested it, and Strandell sandbagged on the paperwork. I applied some elbow grease. I figure you can deliver them to her."

I decided to put my cards on the table. What I was about to tell Stone was a technical violation of the rules but when someone scratched my back, I always tried to return the favor.

"Deputy Stone, there's something you should know." I took a sip of beer. "My direct employer is not Rachelle Hooper."

Stone's head cocked in surprise. "Who is it?"

"A jive-talking yuppie attorney with political aspirations," I said, "who wants street cred with Seattle liberals and intends to get it by saving the poor black lesbian from the hick racist cops." I took another sip of Stella. "I'd appreciate your help, but I'd rather not thank you for it by giving your department a black eye."

Stone leaned forward. "Miss Eckart, there is every chance Elaine Hooper did not put her neck in that noose. When I put on this uniform I swore an oath to keep people from getting away with things like that in Island County. If Strandell and Peters dropped the ball and that makes the department look bad, so be it. I frankly do not give a damn."

"The guy I'm working for will try and take Island County for every cent he can," I said, "spinning the racism and gay-bashing angles for all they're worth - which will be a lot. Heads will roll by the time he's through putting your department through the wringer. I don't want one of those heads to be yours."

Stone sighed. "One of these days," he said, "I'll get a case where money and politics do not get in the way of enforcing the damn law."

"Anything's possible," I said. "It's important to have dreams."

He chuckled. "So what's the solution?"

"The solution is for this conversation to never have occurred," I said. "You keep the lazy deputies out of my hair by staying silent, and I keep the greedy lawyer out of yours by handing him the right facts. I find out how Lanie Hooper *really* got herself strung up, walking on tippy-toe the whole way like a good PI should, and toss the facts in your direction."

"Tricky, but doable," Stone said. "What then?"

"I leave by the back door while you collar the bad guys and take the credit and glory. If there is a murderer, you having them in cuffs on what'll likely become a *very* public case means your superiors won't dare discipline you, no matter how badly Andersen kicks them in the balls. If we play our cards right, the only people who'll be at risk of losing their jobs are the people who deserve it."

He steepled his fingers. "So, you bird-dog and I play Dudley Do-Right."

"Yep," I said. "Credit's all yours. As long as the bad guys go down and my bill is paid, I'm happy."

"There's about a half-dozen ways that plan could go wrong," Stone said.

I finished off my beer. "More like a dozen," I said, "but is there a second choice?"

"No, I don't believe there is."

I set the bottle aside. "Well then Deputy, what do you say?"

He winked at me. "Play fetch, ma'am."

"Woof," I said, and picked up the file.

Chapter 11

By the time I pulled into Mattie's driveway it was past nine. The lights were still on, and Mattie came to the door with a drink in her hand. "How'd it go?"

"Beautifully," I said.

I sat down at the kitchen table and stretched. Mattie mixed me a cocktail while I gave her the rundown. Her blackberry moonshine went exceptionally well with Dr. Pepper and ice. I approached the drink with slow caution and declined a second. I wasn't done with work yet and I needed my brains to stay unscrambled.

"I told you Stone was a good cop," Mattie said. "Quite a looker too."

"Genny Stone is a lucky woman," I said.

Mattie laughed. "So what's your next move?"

"I've got to get my employer a report, delivered with a tag that says 'top secret', and I've got the police report to go over. Tomorrow, I go examine Lanie's remains."

Mattie sipped at her drink. Despite it being her fourth she was still more or less sober. Thanks to thirty years of boozing with journalists Mattie could out-drink Hunter Thompson and Archie Bunker back-to-back. "You ever done that before?"

"Yeah, twice. I didn't enjoy it, but I could handle it."

I pulled out my laptop and fired it up. Twenty-five minutes of typing later, I had a cohesive report of my progress for Kevin Andersen, along with a warning to keep the situation quiet.

"Question," Mattie said as I closed my laptop. "Do Lanie's parents know that she's dead?"

I cocked my head. Whether anyone had placed a call to Kansas to reach Lanie's birth family hadn't occurred to me. The more I considered the situation, the more I doubted anyone had thought to.

"I don't know," I said. "As far as I can tell Lanie wasn't on speaking terms with them."

Mattie lit a cigarette. "Somebody ought to make sure they know before that lawyer splatters her name all over the front page."

I sighed. "You're right. I'll go call them."

Mattie held up my empty glass. "Want another drink?"

"We'll see," I said over my shoulder as I stepped out onto her porch.

Outside the sky was black with low clouds, the moon a faint suggestion of glow behind them. Only the rush of water and the occasional fleck of white from below me let me know I was at the edge of the ocean. From below there came a faint bumping as Mattie's launch, rubbed against her dock.

I dug through Izzy's emailed report on my phone until I found the Jennings' home number, then punched it into my phone. It rang seven times before somebody picked up.

"Hello?" The voice was female and roughened with sleep. I flinched as I remembered that not everyone lived under Pacific Standard Time.

"I'm sorry to wake you, ma'am. Are you Gloria Jennings?"

"I am," she said. "Who am I speaking to?"

My name is Amber Eckart. I'm a private investigator from Seattle. I have some unfortunate news for you."

There was the rustling of cloth; sheets, I guessed. "And what might that be?"

"Something's happened, Mrs. Jennings. Your daughter Elaine has been killed. I'm sorry to -"

The voice that walked over mine was cold as Arctic ice. "I have no daughter by that name."

"Ma'am, I'm sure that-"

"I have no daughter by that name. Do not call here again." There was a loud *clack* and the line went dead.

I stared at my phone for five long seconds before shoving it back in my pocket. Around me the ocean swished and the wind muttered in the pines, playing at my hair like a child's fingers. I gripped the railing and took a deep breath of sea air.

"Jesus Christ," I muttered.

Professional detachment is a hard thing to cultivate, but it is necessary when one's living is made digging into the bad things people do to each other. I'd seen a lot and I'd done a fair number of things I wasn't proud of in the pursuit of my trade. Most days I could keep the evil outside where it belonged. Once in a while a piece of ugliness made it through my defenses. The coldness ringing in my ear had done just that.

I walked back inside.

Mattie had the case file open, photos scattered across the table. "This is nowhere near complete," she said. "There isn't even a medical examiner's report."

I glanced over at the photos; a dead girl with a half-lidded eyes stared back at me, hanging from a tree like a side of beef. I turned my head and closed my eyes.

"Put it away, Mattie," I said. "Please. I can't look at it just now."

Papers shuffled, and then there was silence. I felt a hand on my shoulder. "What happened?"

I told her.

"Good God," Mattie said softly.

"I'll take that drink," I said.

I sat down at the table and waited. The folder sat in the middle of the table and I stared at it, but made no move to open it. Mattie came back with a two-liter of Dr. Pepper, a glass with ice and the bottle of moonshine. I combined the liquids and drank from the result. Mattie's pack of Camels sat next to the file. I took one and lit it with her Zippo.

"I thought you quit," she said.

"Nobody in this business ever really quits," I said.

"What makes a parent write off their own child?"

"Maybe they couldn't stomach her being bisexual," I said. "Maybe she got in trouble one too many times. Maybe they caught her smoking pot behind the school or making out with a girl. It doesn't matter." I drank more and smoked more. "What matters is a fourteen year old girl wound up on the street, and the street chewed her up and spat her out. Then she tried to save herself and died hard anyway. Now there's a long list of people who want to either pretend it didn't happen or use it for their own ends." I looked up at my old friend. "And I'm one of them, Mattie. I'm one of them and it's bothering me."

Mattie shook her head. "You're trying to find the truth, kiddo. Nobody likes it, nobody wants to hear it, and there's always been a reason why."

My laugh was a bitter thing. "Whoever said 'the truth will set you free' clearly never went hunting for it."

"I have an idea," she said. "Let's get tipsy and talk about something else."

I raised my glass. "Please," I said.

So we did. We smoked cigarettes and drank Mattie's moonshine while she told me funny stories about her family in the Ozarks; I laughed at them and got silly-drunk and forgot about my troubles for a little while. Eventually I stumbled into the spare room and stripped off my clothes, crawling under the thick quilt and pulling it over my head like I'd done back when I as a kid, when the other kids were mean and made me cry. Sleep found me before the evil could come back.

Chapter 12

When my phone's alarm went off the next morning. I was greeted by a headache, a stomachache and a fuzzy feeling like swamp moss on my tongue. I mumbled some incoherent profanity, but peeled my butt out of bed all the same. A cold-water face rinse and some vigorous tooth-brushing dealt with two of the problems, and I accepted the rumbling in my guts as fair consequence for staying up late smoking cigarettes and drinking white lightning.

"You aren't twenty-five anymore," I muttered to myself.

I struggled into jogging shorts and a tank top. The last thing I wanted to do was go on my morning run, but I knew I needed to. It was a pretty morning when I stepped outside, birds singing, the leaves beaded with dew. I went through a brief stretching routine, plugged an ear bead into one ear, queued up Iron Maiden and off I went.

The first mile is always the hardest, especially on a hangover, but I stuck with it. Halfway out the hangover drained out of me along with a goodly portion of sweat. On the return leg the galloping double-bass of "Two Minutes to Midnight" thundered in my ears and I took the last half-mile at a dead sprint, heart pounding in my ribs and cold air burning my lungs.

Mattie was still asleep when I returned so I quietly made my own coffee and breakfast after showering off the sweat of a vigorous run. Scrambled free-range eggs and garlic toast settled my stomach and two cups of strong java brought me all the way awake. I cleaned up the kitchen and started a second pot for my still-sleeping friend, leaving a note stuck to the refrigerator. *Had to get to work. Your moonshine is evil stuff. Thanks for everything.* I left a check for a hundred dollars with the note. Mattie wouldn't ask for it, but she also knew I wouldn't take it back. Besides, I could bill Andersen for it as lodging expenses.

Thanks to my usual gift for packing I'd grabbed the wrong bra. It was one I'd been meaning to throw out couldn't yet bring myself to, a once-comfy mess of frays and stains about two years old. The underwire had worked loose and kept poking me in the boob as I did my makeup. I swore about it, but didn't have time to change again. I grabbed my purse and the police report and headed out the door.

My phone buzzed as I walked to my car; Andersen's office. "Talk to me," I said.

"I got your report, Amber." Andersen's warm voice filled my ear. "Great work, as always."

"Remember to keep it quiet," I said. "If the police get wind of me sniffing around, they'll likely start getting in my way."

"We've almost found enough for a case," he said.

"No we don't," I said. "I haven't entirely ruled out suicide, and then there's the complete lack of a foul-play suspect to consider."

"If the Sheriff's department is obstructing you, that's grounds for a suit right there. My client has a right to the truth." I caught the note of excitement in his voice.

I sighed. "That means I need to find it first. Patience, Andersen. If the media gets wind of this now it'd be flying on rumor, not fact. That'd hurt more than it'd help. You'll get your big hero moment, just let me work."

"Last thing," he said. "There's the matter of poor Lanie's next of kin..."

"Not an issue," I said. After I explained, Andersen whistled.

"Wow, that's...I'm not even sure what to call that," he said.

"Go with tragically commonplace," I said. "I'll be in touch."

After signing off I paused, wondering where it was I thought I was headed to. Rachelle had yet to contact me about the body, Izzy didn't have a name for Spider John and for the moment all my leads were played out. I shrugged, walked back up Mattie's porch, sat in her swing and dug out the police report.

Mattie had been right; the file was a perfunctory exercise in police work, lacking even a coroner's report. The photography could charitably be called "spotty", done by somebody who didn't know how to shoot a crime scene. The pictures were gruesome, but I made myself look at them closely.

Lanie Hooper hung from a fir tree, her neck at an angle no living human could manage. She'd dressed for death in sneakers, skinny jeans and a black hooded sweatshirt, all soaked through from rain. Her thick hair was half-tangled in the noose, obscuring the rope around her throat. I raised an eyebrow at that. I'd had waist-length hair in high school and remembered how keeping it from getting tangled in things became an unconscious habit. I noted it down and moved on.

There was no clear shot of the wound the rope had made in Lanie's neck. I flipped through the pictures several times before giving up with a sigh. The only other unusual detail I noticed was how one of her shoes was untied. I noted that down as well.

The written report covered two single-spaced pages of chicken scratch. Slowly I puzzled it out. The investigators had found no sign of a struggle, no evidence of injury other than the wound in her neck, no forced entry in the home and no suspects for a case of foul play. It mentioned Lanie's struggles with depression and drug addiction, as well as a previous hospitalization from a suicide attempt four years prior. Lanie had slashed her wrist with a broken bottle during a bout of withdrawals and almost bled to death in an alleyway.

The report surmised that she must have climbed the tree, tied the rope to a branch, put the other end in a noose around her neck and jumped off; the cause of death was listed as cervical fracture, helped along by a crushed trachea. A transcription of the note in her phone was also included.

Shelle, I read, *I know you love me but I can't stay here. I can't be here anymore. I hurt all the time. I can't stay off the drugs. I can't make you happy. I can't make anyone happy. i tried but I can't. try to forget about me. I hope you dont have to see me like this. I love you.*

Lanie

Conclusion; suicide.

I set the report on the seat next to me and considered. Lacking the facts I'd uncovered, the report made a more compelling argument than I'd thought it would. It was sloppy and incomplete, written by somebody out to support a pre-existing assumption, but I could see a jury buying it. Especially once the police trotted out her record for prostitution, her history of drug abuse, and her previous attempt to kill herself. All I had was a bunch of stray facts any competent attorney could explain in the context of suicide.

I needed more. A suspect, and some evidence of foul play that wasn't acutely circumstantial. I hefted the bag of Lanie's possessions.

My phone buzzed. I set aside the bag and checked the screen. Izzy, calling on her cell.

"Talk to me," I said.

"You're gonna love this, boss." Her voice bubbled with excitement. "I broke both those numbers you gave me."

"And?" I stood and made my way to my car.

"One was a go-phone, just like you thought it'd be. Whoever bought it took more than the usual set of precautions to prevent being made."

"Well, that's something all by itself," I said. "And the other?"

I could hear her grin. "Spider John's home number."

"Hell yes," I said with a laugh. "I love it."

"His real name's Alexander Harkness. He owns a house in Greenwood, near Aurora Avenue. I poked around a little...he has a record for disorderly conduct, assault, public intoxication and possession. Likes motorcycles, beer and girls. Not in a biker gang that I found, but he hangs out with them."

"Sounds like a couple of my ex-boyfriends," I said.

Izzy laughed. "Wow, okay. Anyway, his address is in your email along with all the other stuff I found. Figured you'd want to know pronto."

"Your timing is impeccable as always," I said, firing up my car. "I had just run out of leads."

"Boss, you used to date bad boys?"

"Of course," I said. "It's why I don't fall for them now."

"How does that work?"

I grinned even though Izzy couldn't see it. "Izzy, when it comes to dating the rule is learn young or pay later."

"I'll have to remember that," she said.

I signed off and pointed my car in the direction of Aurora Avenue. It would be a long drive to a destination I tried normally to avoid, and I wanted plenty of time to prepare for it.

Chapter 13

It can be hard for outsiders to spot the scummy neighborhoods in Seattle. The signs they're used to looking for just aren't there; even in the bad part of town the lawns are green and the trees have leaves, legacies of the good soil and never-ending rain. But there are signs and they're still readable.

Greenwood had them; peeling paint, outdated vehicles, overgrown lawns and a general feeling of order kept more by the business end of a policeman's truncheon than civic-mindedness on the part of the residents. I followed the voice from my GPS and did my best to look like I knew where I was going, keeping an eye out for tailing vehicles in my rear view mirror.

I reached under my jacket and loosened my handgun in its holster, partially for reassurance and partially to keep it from conspiring with the loose underwire to skewer my left breast. Carrying a gun is hard for women, and not just for the reasons people think. Contrary to what the movies preach a gun needs a holster and the self-defense industry and the fashion industry aren't on speaking terms; most carry options aren't practical for women. Strong-side waist carry? Fashion belts are never sturdy enough and I'd yet to find a skirt with enough loops. Inside-the-waistband? Doesn't work with stretch jeans. Shoulder rigs? Uncomfortable with a bra. Fanny pack? Screams 'off-duty cop' to anyone with street smarts and makes an individual wanted for questioning by the fashion police unless they're jogging.

The options designed with women in mind don't work much better either. Purse carry? Lose your purse, lose your piece. Bra Holster? Works only as long as she always wears loose tops, never tucks them in and didn't mind going about her business with a loaded gun pointed at her breast.

I made do with a lot of comparative shopping, rudimentary sewing ability and the occasional lucky find. My H&K rode in a modified reverse-draw shoulder rig under my right arm, two spare magazines under my left. Considering the neighborhood I drove through I was glad to have it, however much two sets of straps and a loose underwire conspired to create an annoying distraction.

The GPS instructions led me to a battered doublewide in serious need of six kinds of maintenance, with cracked dusty windows and a sagging porch. The plethora of oil stains kept the weeds from growing in the cracks on the driveway. Parked in it was a gutted Camaro, several milk cartons full of rusted auto parts and a gleaming Harley with more chrome than paint. A figure sat on the porch, bottle in hand. Even at a distance I recognized my quarry from his Facebook page.

"Help you?" He said with a grin.

"Alexander Harkness?"

"You're either a cop, or a reporter," he said.

"Neither," I said, closing the distance between us with brisk steps.

The grinning man who stood and met me at the foot of his front porch stair all but stepped out of my adolescent fantasies; tall, broad-shouldered, beardless but with a hint of stubble. He had enough muscle and roughness to his features to indicate he could handle himself in a bar brawl and enough passion in his eyes to say he knew his way around in the bedroom. The tight jeans and leather jacket and long blond hair helped the image along.

Teenage me would have taken one look and drowned in naughty unrequited wants from across the street. Current me saw a grown man with nothing better to do than drink beer at noon on a weekday.

"Xander Harkness," He said, offering me a hand. His eyes went from the tops of my shoes to my hairline in one swift motion, taking in the salient features along the way; hips, tits, lips and eyes with a brief detour for my ring finger. He had the action down pat; process without lingering and get it done in a jiffy. At least half a decade had passed since I'd been the recipient of such a skillful ogling. I was almost flattered.

"Amber Eckart," I put my hand in his and waited for the rest of the routine. "I'm a private investigator."

He didn't make the expected 'investigate my privates' joke and he didn't kiss my hand, but rather clasped it firmly and gave it a shake. The first surprise of the day.

"You have some ID?"

I already had it out. People usually wanted to see it. Harkness didn't just nod at it the way most did, but rather held it up to the light and examined the State seal before he handed it back. Only two people other than police officers had ever thought to do that before.

"It's legit, all right." He gestured to the porch and the cooler of beer. "So, Miss Private Eye...why don't we sit and have a brew and you can tell me what kinda trouble I'm in now."

"None at the moment," I said.

"Hard to believe." He dug into the cooler and held out a damp bottle of Corona. I shook my head.

"It's hard to like a lady who don't drink beer," he said.

"I do," I said, "just not on the job."

He laughed. "Okay, so...what's this about?"

"You knew a girl named Elaine Jennings." I didn't make it a question.

His grin slipped a few degrees and shutters came down over his eyes. He held off replying by digging a Marlboro out of a pack on the railing next to him and torching it with a Zippo.

"Maybe," he said in a cloud of smoke. "I've known a lot of girls."

I reached into my purse. He tensed, hand dipping below the table towards his calf. I glanced down; a Bowie knife handle protruded from the top of his right boot. I took my hand out of my purse, slowly. "You can relax," I said and held open my jacket, so he could see where my piece was stored. "We're in Seattle, not Tombstone."

He chuckled, a laugh which died as I held up a printout of the Facebook photo with him in it. I set it on the table with Lanie's wedding photo next to it.

"That's you," I said, "and that's Ms. Jennings. She was Mrs. Hooper until recently."

Harkness gave the photos a scan. "Divorced?"

"Dead."

His head snapped up, face a mask of startled shock. "What? How?"

"I thought you didn't know her," I said.

He grimaced and leaned back, smoke rushing out between his lips with a sigh.

"You aren't a cop," he said.

I headed off the I-don't-have-to-talk-to-you train before it could gather steam. "Nope, but the real ones will get interested in you at this rate." I leaned forward. "There's compelling evidence to suggest Lanie might have been murdered, and an ex-boyfriend with a rap sheet who probably lacks a good alibi would be Suspect Number One as far as they're concerned. Especially when you throw in the matter of her age."

"Now just hold on a fucking second," Harkness said. "Lanie was nineteen when I was with her."

I shook my head and dug in my purse again, coming up with a photocopy of Lanie's state ID card. I tossed it on the table next to the photos.

"Jennings, Elaine Laurel. Born February 24th, 1994," I said. "You dated her three years ago. Do the math."

He picked it up and read it. His face screwed up in a wince. "Son of a bitch," he muttered.

"So," I said, "do you want to talk to me for-real or is a charming stonewall your final answer?"

"Depends on where you're going with this," Harkness said.

I sat down across from him and leaned forward. I'd gotten through with a stick. It was time for a carrot.

"Harkness, you have it right," I said in a friendly tone. "I'm not a cop. From reading up on you, I know that you like to drink and brawl and screw girls on the young side. I'm pretty sure you also deal drugs and get up to various other things society says you shouldn't."

I reached into the cooler, came up with a Corona bottle and opened it using the heel of my hand and the table edge. He noticed.

"Not being a cop means I don't give a damn about any of that," I said. "My interest is in finding out what really happened to Lanie Hooper, and from the look in your eyes a second ago I think you want to know too." I swigged from the bottle I'd opened.

"Thought you didn't drink on the job," he said.

"I do make exceptions." I clinked my bottle to his. "Tell me a story. When you're done I'll tell you one."

"You wired?"

I shook my head. "Wouldn't be admissible if I was. Mind if I take notes?"

"Only if my name don't come within a mile of them," he said after a pull on his bottle. "I'll tell you what I know. In exchange I want what you know."

I nodded. "That's the deal. Go ahead."

Harkness flicked the dead cigarette into a coffee can at his feet and opened another beer the same way I had. "I met Lanie a few years back at a party I was at - lots of drugs, lots of people I didn't know. A guy name of Joey Briggs brought her."

I scribbled while he talked. "Who's Joey Briggs?"

"A nasty piece of white trash from Spokane," he said. "Liked wiring runaways up on meth or heroin so they'd make movies for him. Specialized in the gay kids."

"Why?"

Harkness shrugged. "Families aren't in the habit of missing 'em."

"He had them doing porn?"

"Yeah," he said. "The sort that's real hard to find."

Scribble, scribble. "And Lanie was with him?"

Harkness snorted. "Being pimped by him is more like it. Briggs brought her 'cause he knew I'd like her and he wanted on my good side. Well I did like her, but what can I say...I got a preference for the girl being fully conscious." A grin lit his features like a power plant, but the glow didn't go near his eyes. "I'm old-fashioned like that."

"Nice to know chivalry still means something," I said. "So what happened then?"

"We talked for a while, just stoner conversation really, and then she left. I gave her my number. Two days later she calls me from jail, says she's been popped for possession and doesn't know what the hell to do...says its serious this time 'cause of her record. I tell her to turn State's evidence on Briggs."

I stopped scribbling. "Did she?"

"Sure. Got dropped charges and sealed proceedings out of the deal. Turned out SPD had wanted his ass for months. They were generous."

"Could Joey Briggs have killed Lanie?"

"Would he? Sure." Harkness took a pull from his bottle. "Did he? No."

I sipped from mine. "Why not?"

"When the cops grabbed Briggs he had the body of a fourteen year old girl in the trunk of his car. Judge refused to plea-bargain and threw the book. Joey's doing thirty-some years down at Skagit, won't be out til he's pushing seventy...and that's assuming another convict doesn't take a shank and play mumbly-peg with his intestines during yard time."

"Nobody likes a child killer," I said. "So, Lanie came to live with you?"

Another shrug. "Sure. She was messed up, still all wired on junk, but I weaned her off it and she got better some. The next thing I know she's climbing into my jeans. Which was damn fine far as I was concerned."

I scribbled some more notes. "And you did all this to get laid."

"Crazy in the head means crazy in the bed." His sly grin didn't convince. Some part of me wanted it to but I didn't listen.

"That's not all," I said.

"No it wasn't," he said, "but I don't feel like giving you the rest."

"You did your best for her," I heard myself say.

"For all the good it served," Harkness said after a long silence.

"More evil than the sinner is the indifference of decent folk," I said.

"If you can sell that line to an actual sinner I'll be real impressed," Harkness said with a bitter smirk.

"What happened after that?"

"After a few months of turbo-powered fucking she dug through my wallet for loose bills and took off. I haven't seen her since. Always looking for the angle, that one."

"She called you," I said," a couple of weeks before she died. What was that about?"

Harkness drained his beer, arms thick with tension. "She wanted to score. I told her I wasn't holding any. I was, but she'd ripped me off once before. I didn't trust her not to do the same again." He reached into the cooler for another beer. "So tell me, Miss Private Eye...how did she leave this world?"

"At the wrong end of a noose," I said. "Cops ruled it suicide."

"Bullshit," he said without hesitation.

"How so?"

Harkness cracked open his beer with more force

than necessary, eyes locked on mine. The sly sleaziness had fallen out of his stare, and in its place was a naked intensity which bordered on compelling. I wasn't sure what Harkness had felt for Lanie, but he'd felt *something.*

"Lanie didn't like things around her neck, Miss Private Eye," he said in a dark tone. "She had a real problem with anything she thought might strangle her. She wouldn't even wear necklaces. I asked her why once. She told me her daddy liked to choke her out when he thought she was being bad...which was apparently quite often." He paused to drink some beer. "The only way anyone would get a noose around that girl's neck is if she weren't conscious for it."

"Noted," I said.

A sliding glass door opened to my left and I turned my head. A young girl wearing nothing but a man's gray denim shirt stood in the doorway. She had tousled hair with highlights in it, cheerleader's calves and freckles mixed with acne. A sullen weight sat in her eyes where life ought to have been.

"Who's she?" Her voice grated like a scrape from a dull razor.

"My parole officer," Harkness said.

"Hi," I said, waving.

"Whatever." She stumbled out onto the porch. "You got a cigarette for me?"

"Sure, baby." Harkness handed her his pack. She lit up, gave me a withering look and walked back inside, leaving the door open behind her. Harkness got up and shut it, then settled back into his chair.

"Cute," I said. "What's her name?"

"Can't remember just now," Harkness said, picking up his half-empty beer and staring into it like it had an answer for him. "I'm sure it'll come to me."

"You know, once you forgot I had tits you were pretty likeable."

He smirked, the slyness returning. “Yeah?”

“Yeah.” I set my beer on the table half-finished. "But here you sit...old Spider John the robber man, long tall and handsome, taking ransom."

He looked up at me in surprise.

"Willis Ramsey, *Ballad of Spider John,*" I said. "I'm a country girl by birth."

Harkness gave me the first honest smile I'd seen from him. "Would you marry me, Miss Private Eye?"

"Ask again later," I said.

His face was wreathed with smoke as he lit up another Marlboro. "How much later?"

"When you've grown up," I said over my shoulder as I walked off his porch and back to work.

Chapter 14

I made it back to Whidbey Island and the funeral home where Lanie's body waited with just enough time to grab a cup of coffee. My stomach wanted lunch but I decided against it; I hadn't gotten nauseated looking at bodies yet, but there is always a first time for everything. After acquiring a single-shot mocha I dialed Shelle's work number.

"Blythe Insurance, Rachelle speaking."

"Shelle, its Amber. Did you speak with the funeral director?"

"I did," she said. "My boss is okay with me leaving early but I've got some work to finish up. I'll be there as soon as I can be."

"See you then," I said and then exchanged good-byes before hanging up. I was relieved Rachelle wouldn't be present for the examination. I'd been worried that she would want to be in the room while it was conducted, and watching her dead wife's body be prodded and poked at would've like been too much for her.

Northwest Funeral Services turned out to be a church-like edifice painted bright white, with a neat lawn and well-kept flowerbeds. A small sign on the door barred the carrying of firearms, concealed or otherwise. I took a moment to divest myself of my shoulder holster and stashed it under the seat in front of me before entering. My pepper spray stayed in my pocket.

The waiting area was arranged somewhere between a doctor's office and a church foyer; nice potted plants, comfortable chairs, a table with pamphlets and expired magazines. Standing near the receptionist's desk was a man in his fifties wearing a crisp black suit, dark red tie and matching pocket square. He looked up and extended a hand as I approached.

"Amber Eckart?"

I nodded and took his hand. "Thank you for meeting with me."

"Doctor Anwar Shahiristani," he said. He was compact and dusky, with a silver brush of hair matched by a well-kept goatee. "Rachelle Hooper informed me of your coming." A faint Persian lilt reached my ears, all but buried beneath the clipped tones of British education. "I have some paperwork for you to sign."

"Of course."

It took only a few minutes for me to deal with the bureaucracy of Dr. Shahiristani's profession. Afterward he led me towards the preparation room.

The coffee was not sitting well in my stomach and I did my best to ignore it. He pushed the door open and held it for me. I stepped inside.

The preparation room resembled a surgical theater, all white plastic and stainless steel, not a speck of grime anywhere that I could see. The air was cold and dry, heavy with the smell of disinfectant. Under that I caught a faint sickly sweet odor; decaying flesh. Nothing in my experience could ever cover that up completely. My stomach roiled some more as I took in the place where people go after they die.

"Has the body been altered at all since its arrival here?"

Dr. Shahiristani shook his head. "I was about to begin the preparation when her widow informed me there was to be a second investigation. Aside from washing and undressing the remains nothing else has been done." He paused to adjust his glasses. "I have to say, Ms. Eckart...already I have noticed several irregularities. Would you object to discussing them first?"

"Not at all," I said. Curious people are worth their weight in gold in my profession, especially curious people with relevant skills. I pulled out pad and pen.

"When I undressed the body, the first irregularity I

noticed was the state of the deceased's clothing. It was clean."

I cocked an eyebrow at the funeral director. "I saw the crime scene photos," I said. "Lanie's clothes were soaked and muddy."

He held up a finger. "Yes, but not as they should have been." I knew what would come next. Inside every professional lives a frustrated teacher. "When the body expires the muscular tissue relaxes, voluntary and involuntary. This includes the sphincters which control the bladder and bowels. Hooper's trousers should have contained body waste. They did not."

"So, perhaps the clothes aren't the ones she died in."

Shahiristani took two steps towards a cabinet and opened it, drawing out a steel tray about three feet long. On it was a heap of garments. "This is the clothing Hooper was wearing when her body was delivered to me." He set it on one of the steel tables. "If I may beg your indulgence, please tell me what is missing."

At my point and his nod I pulled a pair of latex examination gloves from a nearby box and put them on before touching the clothes. I recognized the jeans, shoes and hooded sweatshirt from the police report photos. The only other item was a violet tank top with a silk-screened butterfly design. After a quick dig-through I looked up.

"Undergarments," I said.

"Exactly," he said. "No panties, no brassiere. Also, when I undressed the corpse I noticed three other points of interest. Her trousers were fastened but not zipped. She was not wearing socks. And one of her shoes was not tied. All of which are possible indicators of forced dressing."

"Somebody redressed her after she died."

"Correct," he said. "A possible sign of foul play."

I smiled. "I'm going to make a leap here and say you weren't always a funeral director."

His expression was a pleased, inscrutable expression. "In my youth I was the assistant medical examiner in Cork, Ireland."

"If I may ask -"

"Why am I not still there?" He spread his hands. "I am cursed with an inability to stay silent, even when I hold an unpopular opinion...especially in the face of rank stupidity from superiors."

"I feel your pain," I said, giving the pile of clothes a second glance. "I could believe no underwear...Lanie had spent time as a runway, and runaways don't always get to bathe or wash their clothes regularly. I could almost buy no bra for the same reason. No socks, that's just plain suspicious with the weather as cold as it is...and a girl going around without panties wouldn't forget to zip up her jeans."

"Indeed, Ms. Eckart."

"Was there anything else?"

"All else concerns the body," he said.

"Then let's get started," I said.

Dr. Shahiristani bade me put on a mask and a scrub smock. After I had finished he put his hand on one of a set of coffin-sized steel drawers and looked at me.

"Ms. Eckart, before we begin I must ask. Have you examined a corpse before?"

"I have, Doctor," I said. "I won't faint on you."

He nudged a steel can sitting on the floor at his feet. "If you must," he said.

"Thank you. Please proceed."

He nodded and pulled open the drawer. Lying on a metal slab was a slender shape under a white sheet. At my nod he removed the sheet with a practiced flick of his wrists. The hairs on the back of my neck stood straight up as the smell of decay grew stronger. I'd never been particularly squeamish or superstitious. It didn't matter.

Death doesn't give a damn what you believe.

A corpse is a corpse, there can be no mistake. Elaine Hooper's body didn't resemble a sleeping girl at all. Instead a naked, anatomically-correct mannequin molded from marbled wax sat in front of me. The lips were bloodless and dry, stomach bloated, eyelids sunken and held closed with surgical tape. On a corpse eyes won't stay shut without help. I fought my roiling stomach and won, but it was a near thing.

Here and there I saw evidence of Lanie's short sad life. Track marks spotted the inside of her left elbow, along with a jagged scar that ran parallel to the big vein on her arm. Her right nipple was pierced with a steel ring and a crude tattoo of vines encircled both ankles, a small pink butterfly scribed on her left hip. The remains of eyeliner clung at the corner of her left eye; another vine pattern, I judged. I'd seen young girls sporting them.

Her legs were swollen and purple from the thighs down; lividity, caused by dying in an upright position. The same condition was present in her hands. Her hair was bundled along the right side of her body, permitting me to see the wound on her throat.

Or rather, the pair of wounds.

I raised an eyebrow. "That's not right," I said.

"No, Miss Eckart, it is not." He pointed with a finger at one mark, a reddish-black crevasse in her neck almost an inch deep surrounded by bruises. "This is the wound which killed her," he said. "Bruising and blood loss indicates an antemortem injury. This," he said pointing at the second mark, "is a postmortem abrasion caused by the same rope as it shifted locations. Help me roll her over."

I nodded and screwed up my courage, putting my hands on her shoulders; her flesh was as cold as the room around me and yielded under my grip in a way that made my skin crawl. As we started to roll her Lanie's head fell to one side in a sickening motion. I jumped back, almost dropping her on the floor. I gave the doctor an apologetic glance.

"Jesus, I'm sorry," I said.

He patted me on the arm. "Unlike others in my trade, Ms. Eckart, I recognize that you don't handle human remains on a daily basis. Please, take the time you must."

"Thank you," I said.

After several deep breaths I managed to help him

enough. It wasn't a memory I'd cherish but we got her turned over. Both marks on her neck continued around to her spine, but in opposite directions. The first wound went almost parallel with her collarbone, terminating in an ovoid bruise at the base of her neck. The other faded out as it marched into her hairline. I stared at the marks. "That's...that's not-"

"Correct, Miss Eckart. The wound which killed this young woman is inconsistent with death by hanging. Had I seen this wound absent of any context I would have concluded foul play." A frown crossed his features. "The Sheriff's department termed this a suicide?"

"They did."

"Tell me...was the investigating officer visually impaired?"

"No," I said, "just in a hurry."

I probed the first wound with my fingers. It was deep all the way around; the stippling in the bruise at the base of her neck indicated something which was not smooth. I made a fist and pressed it against the marks. Although the bruise was much bigger than my fist, the marks were consistent.

"Oh my God." Hot sickness blossomed in my stomach as the facts came together. I stepped back, resisting the urge to put my hand over my mouth.

"Find something?"

I stripped off the gloves and glanced around. "Take off your jacket and tie."

He blinked. "Excuse me?"

"I'm begging your indulgence," I said, spying a dry-erase marker sitting on a whiteboard shelf.

I grabbed the marker as Shahiristani did as I had instructed. "Might I ask what you are doing?"

"Testing a theory. Lift your chin, please." He did so. Slowly I drew a double line around his neck in the same fashion as the mark on Lanie's, checking the original to make sure I got it right and being careful to avoid getting marker on his starched dress shirt. With two buttons of it undone I could see an ivory crucifix dangling from a chain. Once the mark was completed, I stepped back.

"Let's assume for the sake of argument that Lanie didn't die by hanging - that ligature mark is consistent with strangulation from behind, so let's go there." I stepped behind him. "You're about her height. However the mark angles downward, with abrasions almost to her collarbone."

"Correct," he said.

I glanced around and found a measuring tape. "So that doesn't work either," I said, slipping the measuring tape around his neck and pantomiming - gently - a choking attempt. "Unless our hypothetical killer was three-foot-six, the mark is in the wrong place for that. And leave us not forget, there's no sign of a struggle."

"So what then?"

I pointed at an unused lab table. "Bend over," I said.

He glanced over his shoulder at me.

"Please keep indulging," I said.

"As you wish," he said, bending over the table. I stepped behind him and placed the tape around his neck. Slowly I drew my hand into a fist and pressed it against my drawn-on bruise. It matched. To get the mark to line up with the tape I had to press my hips against his.

"Now," I said, "look where we are."

"Merciful God."

I released him and stepped back. The sickness in my gut pounded against my ribs. *Clinical,* I told myself. *Be clinical.* "Did you check her for sexual assault?"

There was a long silence. "I can," he said.

"Please do," I said. "I'll wait out in the hall." I took a deep breath. "We've reached the limit of what I'm willing to observe."

"I understand, Ms. Eckart." Beneath his dusky complexion his face had gone pale. I stripped off the gloves and mask and smock and left the room without looking back. The door to the front was glassed in and looked out into the reception area. Rachelle sat in one of the chairs with a magazine in her lap, flipping through the pages without reading them. I closed my eyes and hoped against hope that I was wrong. After fifteen long minutes of pacing and waiting the door opened and Dr. Shahiristani stepped out, face grim.

"I really don't want to be right," I said.

"You are," he said.

My face twisted up as though I'd tasted something vile.

"Son of a bitch," I muttered. "How bad?"

"Bruising and tearing of the vaginal canal, consistent with forcible penetration," he said. "No semen. Do we phone the police?"

"No," I said, mind shifting gears even as a dark part of my thoughts gibbered in white-hot anger. "At this point their slipshod investigation all but crosses the line into conspiracy. Can you do an autopsy?"

"More or less," he said. "But that really is a matter for the country coroner."

"Decay waits for nothing, especially not bureaucracy," I said. "Her remains are degrading as we speak...by the time the keyboard jockeys at the sheriff's office get done dickering the body will be in even worse shape. If an autopsy is going to be done, it needs to be done now."

"I do not possess the capacity for anything beyond the most rudimentary testing," he said.

"Do what you can with what you have," I said. "Pretend it's for the police. What you can't test, prepare a sample of and freeze. Follow chain-of-evidence procedures as well as you can. Your work may well end up in the courtroom."

His face took on a strained, uncomfortable expression. "I hate to sound mercenary, but..." he trailed off, and I took his meaning.

"...but you have a business to run," I said.

He winced. "Correct."

"It's okay, doctor. I do too and I don't expect charity." I pulled a business card from my jacket and held it out to him. "Document your hours and expenses, then send the invoice to this address. I'll see to it that you're paid for your work."

He took the card. "I shall begin immediately." He glanced down the hall to where Rachelle sat waiting. "What are you going to tell her?"

"The truth," I said. "She's paying for it."

Dr. Shahiristani fingered my card before pocketing it. "Indeed she is," he murmured.

Rachelle stood up as soon as I came through the door, face a mask of curiosity. "Did you find anything?" Something in my face must have showed through; her eyebrows came together in concern. "Ms. Eckart," she said, "What is it?"

"I think you'd better sit back down," I said.

Chapter 15

An unpleasant part of my job is giving bad news to people who often don't deserve it. I don't enjoy it but it comes with the territory. I've told partners of cheating spouses, businesspeople of crooked employees, relatives of suicides that the death was wrongful...each reacted differently to hearing that which they did not wish to. Some yell, some cry, still others deny what I tell them or blame me for the occurrence.

Rachelle did nothing of the kind. She sat upright and rigid as I laid out what I'd discovered, hands clenched in her lap, face frozen in a mask so still it could have been carved from wood. From a distance we were having a tranquil conversation.

From a distance.

"Who did this to her?" Rachelle's voice was a strained whisper.

"I don't know," I said, "but I mean to find out."

"What about the police?"

I shook my head. "Their investigation was so incomplete...in light of what I just found, it raises the question of complicity."

"Are you saying a cop -" she turned away, choking

on the words. "Are you saying a cop did this to her, that they're covering for somebody?"

"It's possible," I said. "Bad things have been hidden behind the thin blue line before." At her scowl I spread my hands. "I said it's possible, but nowhere near certain. But I need to *be* certain before I take my case to the Sheriff's department...if an officer did do this and somebody's covering for them, they'll make everything I've found disappear. If it isn't so and I push that angle, I could find myself in a big pot of hot water." I sighed. "All I've established here is the certainty that Lanie didn't commit suicide. I still have to put the rope in somebody's hand."

Rachelle nodded slowly, eyes wet. "I...I need to go. Call me when you know something more."

"I'm sorry," I said. The words were trite on my tongue but I couldn't think of anything else to say.

"I know," she said.

"Where do you plan on going?"

"To church," she said. "I want to pray."

I nodded. "I'll keep in touch."

"Please." She stood and collected her purse, wooden stiffness in every gesture.

"Rachelle," I said before she could leave. She turned

to face me.

"Yeah?"

"Be careful," I said.

"Already am," she said, and walked through the door.

After she had gotten in her car and driven off I sat for several long minutes with my eyes closed, hands clenching and relaxing. "One," I whispered on the clench, "two, three, four..."

I was far from calm. My discoveries in the mortuary room and the theories they'd spawned had planted a scene in my head, a powerful, visceral one that played over and over again like a film clip. In my mind's eye, Lanie Hooper was bent over and naked and terrified, fighting for air. Some anonymous man defiled her, choked her life away and left her in the woods like roadside trash, over and over and over again. I could see it, clear as an Arctic sky. Based on what I'd found, it was an easy scenario to imagine. It felt like truth.

That didn't make it factual. Belief was poison to objectivity. I wasn't calm...but I needed to be.

I swallowed down the images along with my disgust and my outrage. No crime had ever been solved with those tools and they wouldn't serve me no matter how tempted I was to indulge. Once my breathing had steadied and the sickness had faded I pulled out my phone, punching in Andersen's office number. A perky secretary answered; it was several minutes of waiting on hold before I heard my employer's friendly voice.

"I've got something," I said. It didn't take me long to explain the situation.

"Jesus," Andersen said. "And the cops *missed* that?"

"Easy to miss what you aren't looking for," I said.

"Does Rachelle know?"

"I told her," I said. "She took it about as well as can be expected." I walked in the direction of my car, phone still pressed to my ear. "We need to keep this quiet."

"Are you kidding? What you've just given me is negligence, pure and simple."

"Andersen, you keep forgetting I don't have a suspect. Without one there are a whole bunch of ways a competent attorney could poke holes in this."

"Amber, Lanie Hooper was sexually assaulted and the police straight-up missed it. I'm not asking you to solve a crime. That's the DA's job."

"Fair point," I said, "but the easiest way for me to get you what you *do* want is to find *all* the things the police missed. If I can find enough it won't matter if Lanie did or didn't kill herself - negligence is negligence, right?"

"You still think she did?"

"Lanie has a record for prostitution," I said, "and I've already found evidence she'd fallen off the wagon with her heroin habit before she died. Maybe she decided to turn a trick for cash her wife wouldn't know about, got overcome with guilt and hung herself. After all, no semen means whoever did it wore protection - how many violent rapists take the time to put on a rubber?"

"That's pretty cold," he said.

"Rape's a hard crime to prosecute," I said, "but negligence isn't. Like I said the best way I can get you what you want is to do the police's job for them, so you can march into court with a big stack of evidence they didn't discover and make them look like bigoted oafs to a jury."

"You really think we need a suspect?"

"Somebody forced themselves on Lanie, and quite likely the same somebody strangled her," I said. "If I can find out who did what on a citizen's credentials, the cops will have a real hard time proving they did their due diligence."

There was a pause. "That would play, all right," he said.

"Look at it this way," I said. "Now we know *something* happened."

"I suppose that's true," he said. "So what now?"

"You," I said, "do your best to be patient, same as before. I'll go over all the evidence again and find the pieces I'm missing. I'll also need more money soon...your retainer's about to run out."

"Already?"

"Two full days on a three-day retainer," I said. "Truth is expensive. I'll call you again when I have more."

"Find it soon," he said, hanging up before I could reply.

I slipped my phone into my purse and dug under the seat for my shoulder holster. Once it was in place I drew my pistol and did a press-check on the chamber. A round was in it just like that morning when I had first loaded it, but I made sure anyway. The pistol went back under my arm. Then I fired up the engine and pointed my car in the direction of the place where Lanie's corpse had been found. I glanced at my mirrors, looking for familiar faces or cars lingering too long. There weren't any of either.

I was certain of that because I checked every fifteen seconds for the length of my trip, regular as the ticking of a clock.

Chapter 16

Stone had been kind enough to scrawl the GPS coordinates of the crime scene in the report he'd given me. That was good, because it would've been difficult to find otherwise. According to the coordinates it was about an eighth of a mile from any roads. On a whim I checked the location relative to the Hooper address. Four miles, a hell of a hike for a sick addict without socks and suicide on her mind. I noted that down, then prepared for some woods walking.

After a quick glance to make sure I was alone I jumped into the backseat and wiggled out of my skirt and hose, swapping them for the jeans and sneakers I kept in the backseat pocket for such occasions. Anyone watching would have giggled at the show, but I went to some length to avoid ruining my wardrobe and backseat clothes-changing was one of my secret weapons. My blazer got exchanged for a faded Patagonia fleece. The good clothes I hung from the garment hook. Only then did I brave the mud pit that was the woods of Whidbey.

At the scene the police had strung yellow CAUTION tape between the trees. Most of it had blown down but the fluttering strips made finding the right spot easier. I dug a pair of latex gloves out of my purse and gave the area a wide slow circle.

The tree Lanie had allegedly died on was a thick Douglas fir with hardly any branches for the first five feet. There was a scuff in the bark where the rope had been, along with a streaking scar where the police had cut through it to get Lanie down. I did a rough calculation; a difficult climb for someone of Lanie's height and build, but a plausible one. The height was correct for what executioners used to call a short-drop hanging, an event which could indeed result in trauma to the neck. There were scuff-marks on the bark, ones I could easily believe were caused by shoes.

The ground was too disturbed from police work to be of any use, and twenty minutes of searching told me nothing. I didn't have much light left, so I widened the search, drifting out from the scene in a careful spiral. I wasn't looking for trace evidence; places where investigators got lucky enough to find fibers stuck to branches or the wrong kind of dirt on a leaf existed only in movies and television.

I did, however, have a different kind of luck.

Several hundred yards southeast of the scene the forest opened up into old farmland long since reverted to waist high grass, the twin ruts of a service road looping first towards, then away. Near the loop, the grass had been beaten down by tire tracks. The damage was recent and caused by two vehicles with wide wheel-bases and prominent treads. I pulled out my phone and took pictures before getting any closer; something told me the cops hadn't found this particular gem. Upon closer inspection I found the faint but definite traces of yet more beaten down grass, heading in a trail back towards the crime scene; it headed north and west.

The path was intermittent but wide enough that a group of people moving together would have been the cause of it. I followed alongside it, taking pictures all the while. The trail died at the treeline, but twenty yards ahead I saw the yellow streamers of police CAUTION tape flapping in the breeze. I did a quick bit of by-eye estimation; somebody could've parked at the service road, dragged Lanie's body up into the trees and strung her up, all without being observed from the main road as long as they were careful.

"Interesting," I said to the trail. I pulled out my phone to check Google Maps, but Whidbey's spotty cell coverage defeated me. I wanted to know where that service road went, but the light was fading and my car would in all likelihood get stuck if I tried it.

I also didn't want to be out alone after dark even though I was armed. I found my car and drove back to Mattie's place.

A wall of heat and cooking smells greeted me, and my mouth watered. Skipping lunch and then hiking in the woods had left my stomach empty, and freed from the clinical horror of the mortuary I was ready to eat just about anything. Mattie looked up from her labors and instantly knew. At her question I explained what I had found out while I helped her get dinner on the table. She took the news about the case with somber pragmatism and I was not surprised. A few years of working crime scenes beat the hand-wringing horror out of anyone.

Before I sat down to eat I drafted a sizable email to Izzy, letting her know what I'd uncovered and asking her to do a more thorough check on Harkness' location at the time of Lanie's death. My gut told me he wasn't her killer, but guts don't play in a courtroom. I needed to eliminate his involvement with facts.

After two helpings of chicken and dumplings and a good deal of conversation Mattie leaned back with a cigarette in her hands and thought. My eyes drifted to the pack of Camels on the table. I didn't grab one but I wanted to.

"So," Mattie said, "Time to sum up. What's the timeline?"

I shuffled my stack of notes. "Lanie starts using again. Shelle catches her, they have a fight. Lanie talks to some of her old drug buddies, her ex-boy toy Harkness and somebody else. I don't know who that is yet. She goes and gets Shelle's heirloom revolver out of the safe deposit box, puts together a bug-out bag...only she doesn't have time to use it, because she disappears from her apartment and turns up four miles away in the woods dangling from a tree." I sighed. "And somewhere between disappearing and getting strung up she gets raped."

"From what you told me, the rape and the strangling happened at the same time."

"Supposition," I said, eying the pack of coffin nails again. "It's a theory that happens to fit the facts, nothing more."

Mattie nodded. "Still, sounds like the ex boy-toy is Suspect Number One."

"I doubt it," I said. "Izzy's going to run that angle down tomorrow, but I don't think he's the one. I talked with the guy. Men like him...oh sure, they'll break a girl's heart. I can't see this one breaking a neck." I said to hell with it and stole one of Mattie's cigarettes. She lit it for me. "He's a bastard, but he's the wrong species of bastard." I took a deep drag and tried not to cough.

"What's eating you, kiddo?"

My smile came out crooked. "You mean other than the obvious?"

"Other than that," she said.

"Nothing fits," I said, dizzy from the hit of smoke. "If Lanie's death was suicide, why two ligature marks, the hike in the woods? If somebody was stalking her, why didn't she go to the cops? If it was a cop doing the stalking, why didn't she tell her wife? And if somebody killed her for something she saw or heard from back in her drug days, why the rape, the hasty cover-up? No matter how I arrange the details they just don't add."

"That means you're missing an integer," Mattie said. She swept my notes up into a neater pile. "Put all the evidence you have on the table, right here. Let's look at it again. There has to be something you didn't check."

We did so; the police report, all my notes, the photos I'd shot of everything, Lanie's possessions -

-I stopped. I'd never opened the bag.

"I love you Mattie," I said.

I broke the seal on the black plastic and dumped the contents on the table. There wasn't much in it, a late-model cell phone, some pocket change and the wrapper from a Snicker's bar.

"No wallet," I said. "No purse. No house keys. No cash. No jewelry." I flicked ash into the Campari ashtray in front of me. "Hell, she didn't even have her wedding band on."

"I don't think this girl left her apartment voluntarily," Mattie said.

"No forced entry," I replied. "No witnesses."

Mattie snorted. "Kiddo, the cops probably just glanced at the door and window frames and checked a box on their form because nothing was broken. The lock on most apartments can't even keep out a college kid with a credit card."

"Fair point," I said. "Witnesses?"

"Do *you* remember every coming and going where you live? Especially during business hours?"

"True," I said, remembering a time I had been walked at gunpoint through a crowded hotel without anybody noticing. I did keep track of the people in my vicinity most times, but that was due to me going armed out of habit. Most people didn't have that extra responsibility cluttering up their life.

I glanced at Lanie's phone. "I wonder if that has prints."

Mattie grimaced. "It isn't bagged separately, which means they either already did it or chain-of-evidence is broken."

"Sucks, but that means we can play with it." Lanie's phone was a new one with a universal charger. It was the work of a moment to get it plugged in and powered on. I found the suicide note easily...and after digging through her pictures I found something else. A video clip, shot on the day she died. I got a tingle.

"I think I've got something," I said.

I stubbed out my cigarette and connected Lanie's phone to my laptop. There were predictable compatibility issues and I swore about them but after ten minutes of fiddling I got Lanie's media onto my laptop. I brought up the clip and hit play, Mattie leaning over behind me.

A shiver went up my back as I took in my first view of Elaine Hooper in living motion.

The lighting was bad and the footage was cell-camera grainy; only Lanie's head and shoulders were visible, the wall behind her some shade of white. A bathroom, perhaps. Her nose was red underneath and her eyes were glassy, but she was still beautiful in a frayed, feral fashion. It was several seconds before she spoke.

"Hi Shellie," she said with a sad smile. *"God, I don't know what to say...I thought I did, but y'know, that's always the way isn't it? We want to talk and then the words just don't come out."* She ran her hands through her hair. *"If you're watching this, it means things went bad. It means they got me. I...*she turned away and a tear ran down her cheek. *"I haven't been good to you, Shellie. I thought I could be. I* ***wanted*** *to be. But the bad shit, it just keeps coming back. It hurts me so much, that I can't be good to you the way you are to me."* Lanie made a frustrated gesture, sloppy with intoxication. *"Christ...I'm high right now, y'know? I promised you I wouldn't and look at me, spiking my arm again. I love you, but...it's* ***too good****, Shellie. It's like...like the mom I never had."* More tears. *"I tried to make things right, Shellie. I want you to know that. I wanted to make things good. I just couldn't. I* ***don't know how****."*

There was a long moment where Lanie sat with her head bowed, shoulders shaking. Then she looked up and the haunted eyes in the clip struck me like ice water. *"Don't come looking for me, Shellie. Don't ask. Don't reach. If I don't come back,* ***let me go****. You're too good to get mixed up in this. They'll hurt you, Shellie. They'll make you* ***disappear****. You don't deserve that. Please."* Lanie wiped at her nose and sniffed. "*I love you, Shellie. I always did. You were the best thing that ever happened to me. Be the best thing that happens* *to somebody else."* She touched two fingers to her lips, and my throat caught as the clip went black; Elaine, touching her fingers to the lens in a farewell motion. "*Goodbye, Shellie."*

The clip ran out, and silence reigned.

I stole another smoke from Mattie and lit it. I didn't cough that time.

"Holy Moses," Mattie said softly.

"Yeah," I said. "This isn't a suicide, and it isn't some random sex crime. Lanie was into something. She was into something and it got her killed."

Mattie drew on her cigarette and gazed at the screen. "Poor thing," she said.

"I'm not sure about that anymore," I said.

Mattie blinked. "How so?"

"She was already doing drugs behind her wife's back, refusing to look for work, and now this," I said. "Sure it's a sad tale, but there comes a point when somebody's making their own bed."

Mattie's eyebrows went up. "You think she deserved this?"

"Deserved it? Hell no, but I'm starting to think she had a hand in it."

"She certainly did," Mattie said, "but I still feel for her." She turned to stare out the window. "You forget, kiddo...I worked the reporter's beat back when nobody did drug tests. I watched a good many bright young men burn themselves out trying to be the next Hunter Thompson. They were good people before the dope got them, and bad people after it did." She pointed without looking at the cigarette burning in my left hand. "Besides, you aren't in a position to judge somebody going back to old habits under stress."

I blushed. "I could say it's different, but I won't."

"There's a fine line between objectivity and cynicism, kiddo."

My phone rang. I jumped and answered it without even looking at the screen. "Amber Eckart," I said.

"Boss it's me," Izzy said. "I got your email about the Harkness guy."

"And?"

"He's in Harborview."

"What?" I came out of my chair. "How? What for?"

"Hit and run, earlier today," Izzy said. "I found the article five minutes ago."

"He going to live?" I was already reaching for my

coat and shoulder holster.

"Listed as stable," she said. "Police are calling it an accident."

"I bet," I muttered. "Izzy, I want you and Julian to buddy up. Don't go anywhere without each other, understand?"

"Boss, I -"

"That's an order," I said. "I'll run this Harkness thing down myself. Keep on the media about the accident. I'll be in touch."

I signed off before she could protest further. Mattie watched me from her seat, cigarette smoldering forgotten between her fingers.

"What was that about?"

"Lanie was into something that got her killed," I said, "and we have no idea what it was."

"So where are you going?"

I checked the magazine on my pistol, shoved it into its holster and slid into my coat. "To talk to somebody who *does* know before he has another accident."

Chapter 17

I drove within the law all the way to the hospital, checking my mirrors continually and going over my list of possible questions. It was a long shot that Harkness would be available, but I needed to play it. If something happened to him before we could talk my only link from Lanie to her phantom killers would be cut and I would be dead in the water. I cursed myself for not being pushier with him the first time around, but only a little; after all, the circumstances had been much different then.

His choices hadn't been reduced to 'cooperate with me or get squashed' the last time we'd talked.

I'd asked Mattie for a small favor before I'd left. She'd hemmed and hawed some but in the end had capitulated to my pleading. I resolved to pay her back for all her help, with interest. Her favor rode at the bottom of my purse along with a few other things I stopped along the way to acquire. My next move would involve bending some rules, but it was time. The bad guys had roused themselves and people were getting hurt. I pulled off Interstate 5 and negotiated the side streets.

Harborview Medical Center took up the block of Alder Street and 9th Avenue, a set of ultramodern cubes in concrete and gleaming glass. I pulled into a visitor's only parking space and reached for my phone. Harkness' number was still in it. I dialed and waited. No answer. I tried again, same result.

On the fourth time it rang twice and a ragged voice answered. "Who the fuck *is* this?"

"One guess," I said.

"Oh shit, not *you."*

I grinned. "Whatever happened to 'will you marry me'?"

"That was before talking to you put me in the damn hospital," he growled.

"I know. I heard. I'm sorry. I'm also in the parking lot."

"Figures," he muttered. "Look, lady, I don't know a damn -"

"Lanie was raped," I said.

Silence on the other end of the line.

"Kidnapped, raped and strangled to death," I said. "Somebody wants to cover it all up."

"Who?"

I glanced around. "Maybe you can tell me."

Another long silence. "Go to the front desk," he said softly. "Tell 'em you're my fiancée. I'll have the nurse let you in."

"You won't regret it...honey," I said.

"I already do," he replied before hanging up.

There was a bottle of water in my center console. I grabbed it and rubbed my eyes as hard as I could with my knuckles. A few splashes from the water bottle onto my face made what was left of my makeup run in streams; to the casual observer I'd been crying recently. With that I hurried up the walk, putting my face into a mask of frantic worry.

Inside the reception area was just as cool and angular as the outside, manned by polished youngsters in immaculate blue scrubs. I made myself fidget and glance around as I waited in line. Presently it was my turn.

A soft-featured boy with red hair smiled at me. "Can I help you?"

"Alexander Harkness," I said. "A friend called me and said he was in a wreck. Can I see him?"

"Are you family?"

"He's my fiancée," I said. "Please, I just called him...he said I could see him."

The boy glanced at his watch. "Visiting hours are almost up," he said.

"I just want a few minutes with him...please?" I gave him my very best kicked-puppy look. It earned me a sigh, some directions to wait for a nurse to lead me back and a clipboard to sign. I scrawled something unreadable on the sign-in sheet and waited. Presently a nurse in her fifties with a professional frown walked through the big swinging doors. "Somebody wanted to see a man named Harkness," she said.

"Me," I said.

The nurse jerked her head in a follow-me gesture. I did. She led me up an elevator and down a hallway without saying a word, dull cynicism layered on her face like armor plating. I followed and didn't try to make conversation.

"You get fifteen minutes," she said as she opened the door.

"Thank you. Can we have some privacy?"

She shrugged. "Fifteen minutes."

I stepped inside and shut the door.

Stretched out on a hospital bed, swathed in bandages and bereft of his tough-guy clothes Harkness was thinner and younger, almost vulnerable. His cheeks were sunken, eyes bloodshot and glassy from drugs and tension. Where his skin wasn't bruised or bloody it was gray-pale, disturbingly like that of the corpse I'd looked at earlier. One leg was elevated in a thick cast, the other wrapped in a layer of gauze. When I entered he grinned, revealing smashed lips and a big gap where three teeth used to be.

"Hey there, Miss Private Eye," he said, waving the one hand that had escaped major injury. His voice was worse in person.

"Jesus," I said. "Who hit you?"

"Like I told the cops," he rasped, "I didn't see shit. Somebody clipped me and the next thing I know I'm face down in the median with half my fucking limbs bent the wrong way back."

"I'm not a cop," I said.

"You're close enough," he said.

I grinned and reached into my purse. "Would a cop do this?" I pulled out the biggest sandwich Arby's made, wrapped in paper.

"Lady, you do *not* play fair." He reached for the sandwich. I handed it to him, along with a 20 ounce bottle of Coke.

"Eat, drink and listen," I said. "Then I'll want you to

talk."

He dug in, eating from the side of his mouth that didn't sport knocked-out teeth. I sat in the chair next to his bed.

"I examined Lanie's remains. She didn't die from hanging - she died from being strangled while somebody raped her. Before that happened, she composed a video message to her wife, telling her not to look for her if she didn't come home, telling her 'they' would make her disappear if she did."

Harkness kept eating. He didn't look at me.

"I know she used to live with you, I know she called you before she died. You said last time that she was looking to score. Well, I think she was...just not dope." I leaned forward. "I think Lanie was trying to do some kind of deal, and whoever she was dealing with killed her. Then this morning they came looking for you."

"That's a good story," he said. Like the sleaze and the apathy before, his bleak cynicism didn't convince.

"It needs a bunch of blanks filled in," I said.

"Christ, lady," Harkness muttered. "I'm all out of friends. You know how dead I'll be if I do that?"

"It is, indeed, dangerous to go alone." I dug in my

purse and came up with something that made Harkness' eyes widen. "Take this."

Mattie's other favor was a Raven Arms .25 automatic in a plastic bag. It was cheap, ugly and tiny, with a business end about as intimidating as a spitball straw...but it was still a handgun with six rounds of ammunition, and in the close quarters of Harkness' hospital room could be as deadly as desperation needed it to be.

"I'll be damned," he said, taking the bag from my hand and dumping the pistol out of it.

"It's unregistered, clean and disposable," I said. "Keep it. Say it was yours. You have to use it, ditch it. You try and say I gave it to you and I'll swear I never saw it before."

"Why give it to me at all?"

I leaned forward. "Harkness, whoever ran you off the road might make a stab at you while you're laid up. I don't want that to work out for them. That makes me just about the only friend you've got."

"What do you want from me?"

"A name," I said. "Anything else you want to share would be nice, but I need a name."

Harkness hefted the .25 in his good hand and stared at the empty Arby's wrapper, the cynicism in his gaze melting into something soft and oddly sad. "Calloway," he said. "William Calloway. Goes by Billy." He tucked the pistol underneath his body. "He's a rich brat, late twenties by now, likes weights and guns and the kind of porn Joey Briggs used to make. One of those wannabe mall-ninja types. Used to buy his steroids from me until Briggs moved into that market. I didn't miss him."

"What's he look like?"

"A Brinks truck," he said, "of the Anglo-Saxon persuasion."

I scribbled notes on my trusty pad. "Context?"

"A month after Lanie shacked up with me Billy comes back. Had a bunch of other clean-cut Anglo boys with him. They had a deal he wanted to offer me as apology for not buying from me no more. I didn't give a fuck, but I figured sure, I'd hear 'em out. Billy's friends lay it on the table...they've got a bunch of heroin they want to unload and they want me to do it for 'em."

"How much is a 'bunch'?"

Harkness wasn't smiling. "A thousand keys," he said. "Uncut."

My eyes widened. "Damn." A thousand kilograms of pure heroin translated into a large fortune in street drugs. It was more than enough to murder over. "And you said..."

"I said go to hell, politely." He shrugged and winced. "I don't move on that scale. A ton of pure...shit, that's a magnet for trouble."

I smiled and moved from the chair to the edge of the bed, reaching out to adjust his pillow. He blinked at me in surprise. "In case the nurse comes back," I said. He relaxed and I kept talking.

"My dad was a cop, twenty years with Seattle Police. He worked narcotics for a while. I heard all about it. A score like that is not something a guy like you would walk away from. Would you move it? Hell no...like you just said, it's too much for a lone operator like yourself. But you know people who know people who *would* and *could* move that much merchandise. So you'd make a few calls, play middleman in exchange for a small finder's fee. Which would be pure cream for you and chicken feed to the buyer and the seller. Except something didn't go right, and the deal never happened."

"I passed on it," he said. "Billy's friends were amateurs. They made me nervous." He grinned and squeezed my hand. I let him. "You catch on quick, Miss Private Eye."

"Did you get any of their names?"

"Nope," he said. "But here's the thing. They all looked like military-types...and the stuff they were trying to move was brown."

"Brown?"

"Afghan heroin," he said. "Golden Crescent shit. You can either purify it for shooting or sell it as-is for smoking. Makes it real versatile, 'cause ever since AIDS a lot of newbies don't like the notion of putting a needle in their arm. At least at first." Another bloody grin. "Guys figured they could corner the market."

"And Lanie overheard this," I said.

"She was in the other room with Billy playing host while I did business," he said. "Who knows what he told her. Guy's dumber than he is mean, and that's saying a lot." Something moved beneath the painkiller-glazed surface of his grinning bravado, something black and sad and ugly. The pieces were drifting together, in my mind and in his, and neither of us liked what we saw. "Then just this morning a big shiny pickup truck ran me off the freeway...looked an awful lot like the big shiny pickup truck Billy's friends drove up in."

"I see," I said. "And when Lanie called you, she wanted -"

"Calloway's number," Harkness said.

The ugly emotion moved to the surface and I saw it plain as a sunrise; grief and guilt, the kind that packs a rusty knife to twist.

"You gave it to her," I said softly.

Harkness didn't speak. He simply nodded, eyes closing on tears. Maybe at another time and place he could have swallowed it down and hid it like the tough man he thought he was, but broken on a hospital bed and doped up on painkillers he wasn't up to the task. But he faced it square, the place his choices had put him. I liked him better for it.

"I got her killed," he whispered. "Jesus fucking Christ, I got her killed."

I reached out and laid my hand flat against his cheek. A tear rolled over my fingers. It started hot but was cold before it dripped off my pinkie knuckle.

Harkness met my eyes. "In case the nurse comes back?"

"No," I said.

The nurse did come back a few minutes later; Harkness, sobbing into my jacket, never even knew it. It wasn't the cynical old lady, but a plain-faced woman about my age with round eyes that grew wide when she looked in the room.

Give us a minute, I mouthed at her.

She gave us five, long enough for Harkness to slip off to sleep. I thanked her for it on the way out.

Chapter 18

I made it back to Mattie's cabin at one in the morning and passed out for five hours of sleep, barely enough to call a nap. I woke with something like a mid-grade hangover, a blurry feeling even a hot shower and three cups of black coffee couldn't shake off all the way. I did my best to put it aside. I had serious work to do.

My first action was to call Shelle. I got lucky and caught her as she was preparing for her day. "You know something?" her voice was still rough from sleep.

"Lots," I said. "Take the day off from work. Pack up a few days' supplies, anything you can't live without. I'll give you an address. Get there as soon as you can."

"I can't just skip work, Ms. Eckart."

"Shelle, a contact of mine on Lanie's death came within a hair of getting murdered yesterday. He might still. You'd be next on somebody's accident list. Please, do as I'm asking. Neither you or I have time to argue."

"Okay," she said after a short pause. "When I get there I'll want answers."

"You'll have them," I said. We signed off.

I flipped speed-dials and hit Julian's number. Several rings went by. "Hmyeah?"

I poured myself a fourth cup of coffee. "It's Amber. Izzy there with you?"

"Jeez, boss, do you ever sleep? She's on the couch. What's going on?"

"Nothing good," I said. I explained about Harkness and the threat to everybody's lives.

"Yuck," Julian said. "This is like that thing that one time."

"Worse," I said. "You and Izzy stay together. In fact, take a cab to work - company will pick up the tab. These assholes already ran one biker into the dirt. Have Izzy call me, pronto."

"Boss, can I go back to bed now? I've got a deposition today for the Copeland thing."

I smacked my forehead with my hand. "Shit, I'm sorry. All this other nonsense...yes, and good luck."

"Don't need good luck," he grumbled. "I need good sleep."

I signed off and stood holding my phone wondering where to go next. Izzy had been up until the wee hours researching already and wouldn't be available until later. I shrugged and reached for my laptop. "Guess you get to do your own dirty work this time," I said to myself, firing up my laptop and opening my browser and a Word document. I also dug out a scratch pad and pencil. Izzy ribbed me mercilessly about my anachronistic tendency to scribble on things when Copy and Paste were a click away, but I'd grown up in the era when notes were taken on paper. It was how I rolled.

Once I had a search bar I typed WILLIAM CALLOWAY WASHINGTON into it. Predictably Google came back with over two pages of search hits, but I had a few other data points to work with thanks to Harkness; twenty-something, rich, Caucasian and a bodybuilder, along with an address somewhere in the Seattle area. With these I eliminated an elderly gentleman from Marysville, an African-American teenager living in Bothell as well as several others who did not fit the profile. Forty-five minutes later I had the image of a booth-tanned male with a shaved head and a body like a sack of watermelons.

I cracked my knuckles, and dug into his life.

In a world where all manner of data points are logged anonymously more often than not, most American citizens live larger lives than they realize. Our day-to-day existence creates a trail for someone to follow and most people help this along by talking about said existence in a multitude of places. My quarry didn't have a Facebook page, but what he did have was a membership at a gym where he competed in power-lifting competitions and an account on the gym's forum. I checked the forum, and posting was gym members only but viewing was there for all to see. It is a common misconception that forums with limited membership are private, and people in my profession were in no great hurry to correct it. I punched Calloway's screen name into the forum's search bar and gave the results a scan.

"Dumber than he is mean, and that's saying a lot" was how Harkness had described this young man and from his posting I could see it was an apt description. His grammar wouldn't have passed muster in the eighth grade and his attitudes about women wouldn't have gotten him a date at that age either; I did not find a reference to my gender without the word "bitch". I stopped reading after post five and nosed around the gym website some more. After twenty more minutes I had his birthday, phone number and home address. Calloway was twenty-nine, lived in a Kirkland condo and rode a Harley Fat Boy. All useful, but what I wanted was his Social Security number. I opened a new tab and started again.

One of the nice things about working in a tech-friendly state was how government records were online and easy to search through. I started with incarceration records and after filtering for age and race found my quarry's. Calloway had a history of violence; assault and battery, six counts, along with a squalid assortment of possession and vandalism charges from his teenage years. A quick scan of his DMV record netted a perennial habit of speeding, but no DUIs or accidents. Thanks to the records I got the first five digits of his Social, but thanks to security the last four were truncated. I scribbled the first five down anyway. There were other ways to get the last four.

I nosed around Calloway's court documents for a further thirty minutes and dug up another interesting fact; each time he was charged, his counsel was a defense attorney from a firm I knew...Burton, Cameron and Clive. In most of the charges, the sentence had involved community service, fines or counseling; despite a rap sheet as long as my arm William Calloway had spent less than six weeks total behind bars, all soft time.

I leaned back and twirled a pencil while I pondered this development. BC & C had some of the best attorneys in Washington working for them. That they were expensive was an understatement. I checked my notes; no employment history for Billy Calloway had shown itself.

Where did his money come from?

"Mornin' kiddo," Mattie said from behind me. I turned to see her stumbling into the kitchen wearing a floral print nightgown and a slit-eyed grimace. Her hair was a steel-wool explosion. "Workin' already?"

"Got a line on a suspect last night," I said. "Now I'm going fishing into his life. Guy's got a record, but somebody rich is paying his legal expenses...guy's never had a job that I can find. Trying to figure out who."

Mattie poured herself a cup of coffee and sipped at it black. "Where's he live?"

"Condo up in Kirkland," I said.

"Check the property records," she said. "If he's sponging somebody else would have signed the loan."

I sighed, favoring her with a rueful grin. "I've got to stop being lazy and letting Izzy do this for me," I said. "I'm forgetting how it's done."

Mattie smiled back over her coffee cup. "Delegation will kill you, kiddo. Also, ten bucks says it's a parent."

"No bet here, but we'll see."

While Mattie puttered in the kitchen I dug into Calloway's finances. Property was a matter of public record; a quick search netted me the actual owner of the condo, one Cynthia Lewis. I followed that trail into the Pierce County courthouse website and came up with a marriage license to a Francis X. Calloway, filed two months before Billy was born. Two years after that the couple divorced. A check of Francis Calloway in the same database found a total of eight marriages and divorces over the sixty-five years of his life.

"You'd have made the ten bucks," I said over my shoulder.

"Mother or father?"

"Mother," I said. "Looks like his dad's into serial marriage."

"Let me guess," Mattie said. "Marry them when they're pretty, deck them in jewels, kick them out when the flesh starts to droop?"

I flashed her a sarcastic grin. "Gee, how'd you know?"

"Not being born yesterday might have something to do with it."

I paused as a thought struck me. "Mattie, you ever

heard of a man named Francis Calloway?"

She blinked. "You haven't?"

"Educate me," I said.

"Frank Calloway was one of the owners of Weiss & Calloway, at one time the biggest shipping company in Seattle," Mattie said. "Up until the late seventies nothing entered or left the ports around here without Weiss & Calloway getting a cut."

"So what happened?"

Mattie shrugged. "The business got unreliable. The hippies got uppity, Japan started doing its own shipping, the longshoreman's union got greedy...Calloway saw the writing on the wall and sold his part of the company. Without him it puttered along for another decade. Now it's owned by somebody else."

"So what did Calloway do after that?"

"Invested the profits from the sale into some tech startups," she said.

I fidgeted with my pencil some more. "And those were..."

"Microsoft, Compaq and Dell," Mattie said with a grin.

"Maybe after this case is done I'll break into

Calloway's home and steal his crystal ball," I said.

"Lots of people have said the same," she said with a grin. "Why'd you ask?"

I shrugged. "The suspect I'm researching is his son."

"In that case I'd be careful," she said. "Frank Calloway has a lot of influence in Seattle."

"Joy," I said. "Guess that's one more reason to make sure my client stays safe." I sipped at my coffee. "Which reminds me, I'm bringing her here briefly until I can figure out where to stash her. If the bad guys got to Lanie at her apartment they by default know where Shelle lives."

"So stash her here," Mattie said.

"Mattie, you've done enough."

"Nonsense, kiddo. Besides, could you name a safer place? I'm all but off the grid, Island County's records aren't computerized, my mail goes to a private box and unlike a hotel I have security systems that work." She hooked a thumb in the direction of her gun cabinet. "And then there's the matter of Eddie's collection."

I reached for my purse and dug out my checkbook. "In that case -"

"Kiddo, keep your money."

"Won't be my money," I said. "This is for a case. I'll be passing the cost onto the client."

Mattie perked up. "The lawyer?"

"Yep."

"In that case, gimme."

I laughed while I wrote out the check. It was for a reasonable amount; Andersen was already growing squirrely about the bill and I didn't want him to refuse to pay - something clients attempted to do on occasion despite contracts and guarantees.

"Advice time," I said as she pocketed the check. "What should I do about the video clip?"

"Show it to the client," Mattie said.

"You sure?"

"She's paying for it, kiddo. The moment you start cherry-picking the facts you aren't an investigator, you're a politician."

I sighed. "How much more ugly truth am I going to have to hand this poor girl?"

"As much as you find," Mattie said. "As much as there is. It's the job."

I nodded. "You're right," I said. "Momentary lapse."

"They happen." She patted me on the shoulder.

"Good luck with your work. I need to go feed the chickens."

"One of these days I'm going to pay you back all the way, Mattie."

Mattie shook her head. "Kiddo, one of these days you're going to learn that some things aren't paid back. They're paid forward." With that she went to feed her chickens, leaving me to my work.

Chapter 19

Building up a background on a member of the rich and famous is easy in today's world, thanks to bloggers and electronic news. Everything they do is photographed and commented on. Sifting out relevant truth from salacious rumor can take some doing, but it is normally a matter of comparative analysis and fact-checking. In less than a half-hour I had a clear picture of Frank Calloway - and Steven Weiss. Further connections appeared; Weiss' son had attended high school with Billy Calloway, same year and many of the same classes.

Instead of becoming a trust-fund brat Peter Weiss had joined the Army, doing a tour in Afghanistan before mustering out and taking a job at McKnight Industries, a private military contractor. That had sent him back to Afghanistan for a further two years. Online information on him was spotty, even in places where it shouldn't have been. I saw evidence that Peter Weiss had exerted some effort in covering his tracks and that made me more curious about him.

I had just finished compiling a report for Andersen - less my suspects but including the video clip - when the door opened and Mattie walked in, followed by Rachelle. She had a military duffel slung over her shoulder and a guitar case in her hand. I stood up. "Any trouble?"

"Not a bit," said Rachelle. "Mind telling me what's going on here? My boss is hacked off at me big-time."

"Somebody who gave me information on what happened to Lanie was nearly killed yesterday," I said. "The people who did it might be the same people who came after Lanie."

"You're going to have to start from the beginning," she said, setting down her duffel and guitar case.

"Lanie was into some kind of scheme," I said. "She had information on a big drug deal and I think she tried to use it to blackmail the dealers. Only something went wrong for her and they killed her. Same people tried to whack my contact."

"And you think they'll come after me," said Shelle, "because I'm paying you to find out what happened to her."

"That, or Lanie might have told you about it."

"She didn't," said Shelle.

"They don't know that," I said. "For all they can be sure you might have been in on it with her." I paused, noting an angular bulge under Shelle's left arm. "I hope that isn't what I think it is."

Shelle opened her jacket and proved my suspicions correct; her grandfather's .38 was tucked under her arm in the same worn-out rig I'd seen in Lanie's backpack. "You said to be careful."

"You don't have a carry permit," I said. "Even a clear-cut case of self-defense would be suicide in the courtroom if you use that."

Shelle's eyes narrowed. "What good is following the rules if I get killed doing it?"

I turned to Mattie. "You still licensed?"

She snorted. "Does Dolly Parton still sleep on her back?" She hiked up the hem of her sweater, revealing a snub-nosed Colt Python .357 Magnum in an inside-the-waist holster. Its nickel plating gleamed. "I never leave home without it."

"Feel like playing bodyguard?"

She grinned and nodded to Rachelle. "I'll drive you to work tomorrow, dear."

Rachelle looked at Mattie and then me. "I can handle myself," she said.

"Nobody's saying you can't," I said. "But we still have to do this right."

"What do you mean?"

"Shelle, the bad guys know where you live. If they

did their homework at all they'll know your name, what you look like, where you work and what kind of car you drive. We can't help the work thing, but they'd have to be pretty damn stupid to come after you in such a public location. All the rest is another matter. That's why you're here and Mattie's going to drive you to work. Please Shelle...take off the gun. It'll only create more problems than it'll solve."

Shelle took a deep breath and let it out slowly. "All right," she said. She slipped out of her pea coat and unfastened the shoulder holster. "What happens if these people find their way here?"

Mattie walked over to her gun cabinet. "They'll regret it," she said, opening the double doors. "And then, they'll tuck tail and run."

Mattie's husband Edward had been a fan of firearms and so had several of her late relatives and their combined collection was a sight to behold. Stuffed into the double-door cabinet were twelve rifles, three shotguns and more pistols than I knew the names for. Shelle's eyebrows got lost in her cornrows as Mattie pulled a long, slender magazine-fed rifle out of the cabinet along with a box of ammunition.

"Holy crap," Shelle said, eying the rifle as Mattie stuff-loaded one of its magazines, tucking the gun in the crook of her arm. "Is that what I think it is?"

"Springfield M-14 semi-automatic conversion," Mattie said, slapping the loaded magazine into the receiver and working the bolt. "Belonged to my Eddie. He bought it before the ban in '68. I still have the papers on it."

"I shot one of those in boot camp," Shelle said. "I was better with a shotgun, though."

"Be useful, if the time comes." Mattie slung the rifle over her shoulder. "We hope it doesn't get to shooting at all."

"I know," Shelle said softly, but she eyed the guns all the same.

"I'll let you to argue over who gets the couch and who gets the spare room," Mattie said. "I'm going to go check the generator." With that, she closed the cabinet and slipped out the front door.

"You have interesting friends," Shelle said softly.

"Mattie's a spitfire," I said.

Shelle set her revolver on the kitchen table reluctantly. "She isn't one of those paranoid survivalist-types is she?"

I laughed. "Mattie was a reporter in several capacities for thirty years," I said. "She ended up covering militia movements in the nineties, did a big expose for *Time* magazine. The militiamen took exception to what she published about them."

Shelle eyed the gun cabinet again. "Took exception to it?"

"One of the leaders ended up in prison thanks to what Mattie found out," I said. "He got in touch with some of his more serious supporters and put a forty-thousand dollar bounty on her head. Far as I know, it's still active."

"Wow," Shelle said.

"That's why she lives out here. When I met her she was teaching political science at Western Washington University. A year after I graduated a would-be hitman took a shot at her while she was leaving work." I didn't tell her what Mattie had done in response. "Her department asked her to retire, so she did. She didn't want some poor college kid getting hurt on her account."

Shelle nodded. "So, in order to be safe from the survivalists..."

"...she has to live like one," I said.

"That's irony for you," Shelle said.

I nodded, then took a deep breath. I was putting off the video clip and I shouldn't have been. "Shelle, there's something you need to see," I said. "You won't like it, but you're paying for it."

Shelle tensed. "What is it?"

"A video clip Lanie recorded before she died," I said. "It's for you."

I queued up the clip on my laptop, unplugged it and handed it to her. "The spare bedroom's at the end of the hall if you want some privacy."

"Thank you," she said, walking down the hall and disappearing into the spare bedroom. I waited, fidgeting, then sighed and sat down to work some more. I didn't have my laptop, but I could sort through the paper trail.

Twenty minutes later the bedroom door opened and Shelle walked out into the living room. Without a word she opened the door to the back deck and stepped through, closing it behind her. My chest got a pang at the tear stains on her face but I didn't follow I could see her standing at the railing and staring out at the water. She just wanted some air and I resolved to let her have it. I went back into the bedroom, collected my laptop and got back to the boring-yet-necessary grind of my profession. Several minutes later Mattie stepped through the front door.

"Generator's fine," she said. "So are the floodlights and the sprinkler system."

"Good to hear," I said.

Mattie eyed Shelle, standing out on the deck. "She see the clip?"

"Yeah. She took it about as well as I thought she would."

Mattie's eyes narrowed in thought. "Where'd she watch it?"

"Back bedroom," I said.

"How long's she been out there?"

"About fifteen minutes," I said. "Why?"

Mattie turned to me. "Go out there, kiddo. Go talk to her."

I blinked. "Mattie, the girl needs her privacy."

"What she needs," Mattie said, "is a *friend.* If she wanted privacy, why didn't she stay in the bedroom? She walked out here so you could see her. She wants to talk....she's just too proud to make the first move."

I glanced at Shelle, standing rigid at the rail, backlit by the dull gray sky. "I'm not sure about that."

Mattie snorted. "You ought to be," she said with a crooked grin. "You've always been the same damn way."

I gave her a wry look, but didn't argue. "All right," I

said.

Shelle didn't look back as I slipped out the door onto the deck, but she did glance over as I came to stand next to her.

"Hi," she said softly.

"If you want to be alone, I can go back inside."

"No," she said and stared out at the water. "I'm tired of being alone." Her eyes were black with grief, voice ragged from the effort of holding back a sob. "I've been alone since this happened. Everybody's nice and nobody says anything. They're all afraid of saying the wrong thing, afraid of offending me, and so people just pretend it didn't happen. And I smile and nod and muddle through my day and pretend it didn't happen, too. I pretend so well, I get home and some part of me thinks Lanie's going to be there waiting. But she isn't. She isn't but all her things are there and then it hurts all over again." Her voice broke. "She's gone, Miss Eckart. It's worse than dead. It's like she's just...*gone."*

I put my hand on her shoulder, ready to take it back if I had to. She made no move towards or away from me.

"I don't - I mean, I'm not usually..." Under my hand the muscles in her shoulder were hard, tense and quivering like cable under strain. "I -"

I reached out and gathered her into my arms. It happened slowly, by degrees, but she ended up with her head on my shoulder and her arms tight around my back. Her body shook with sobs, the kind that come from deep down and hurt all the way through. I held her and let her cling to me and didn't say a word. As is the way of all things the storm passed and she stopped shaking, relaxed her grip on me.

"I didn't know what to do," she said into my shoulder. "I saw her fading away and I didn't know what to *do."*

"Nobody did," I said.

"I should have *done something,"* She whispered, voice ragged.

I let her go and stepped back. "You didn't fail her, Shelle," I said softly. "You lost her, but you didn't fail her. I know right now it feels like you did, but you didn't."

Shelle reached into the pocket of her coat and took out a small black box, opening it. There was a medal inside, nestled in dark blue velvet. Her Coast Guard Medal, earned for saving three lives from a burning ship. She traced a finger over the brass orb, looking at it without really seeing it. What thoughts passed through Rachelle Hooper's mind in those few minutes I couldn't begin to guess at. At length she closed the box and put it back in her pocket. When she looked up her eyes were still red and raw, but the conviction I'd found so striking when I'd first met her was back in them.

"Thank you," she whispered.

"Anytime."

Shelle gazed out over the water and folded her arms against her stomach. "That clip...I can't get over it. 'Be the best thing that happens to somebody else'..." she closed her eyes. "How could she think so little of herself?"

"Life like hers, it can kill a person before their time," I said.

Shelle ran her hands over her hair and composed herself further. "I'm okay now," she said. "I'd like to do something, anything. I don't care if it's about the case or not. I just need to do. I'm not good at sitting around, Ms. Eckart."

"My friends call me Amber," I said.

She smiled through her drying tears and offered me her hand. "May I?"

"Be honored if you did," I said, and clasped her hand in mine.

Chapter 20

We spent the rest of the day helping Mattie with chores around her property, discussing the case while we worked. Shelle threw herself into whatever she was given with a grim sort of zeal. I knew the look on her face quite well. It was somebody working to take their mind off ugly facts they couldn't change. I knew it because I was the same way. The teenagers at her apartment complex had been right; Shelle could indeed fix a good many things, likely a legacy of her time in the Coast Guard. Boats don't maintain themselves.

No breakthroughs happened during our discussion of the case, but Shelle was able to fill in some timeline issues regarding Lanie's disappearance and the events which led up to it. I also used the time to bring her up to speed on the suspects and where I stood with them. A quick glance at the photos of Weiss and Calloway proved that she hadn't seen either of them around the complex, but that didn't surprise me. Lanie would have been careful to keep them at arm's length. I wondered how they would have smuggled her out of her apartment without anybody noticing, but Mattie had a point there too; people could be amazingly oblivious in familiar surroundings.

We broke for dinner, all of us cooperating on meal preparation and cleanup. Neither Mattie or I went for the moonshine on account of us both being armed. Alcohol and firearms do not go together, period. However, Mattie did pour a portion for Shelle and shoved it across the table to her.

"You've had a hell of a time of it, dear," she said. "Have some general anesthetic."

"Thank you," Shelle said, and picked up the glass.

"Careful," Mattie said, "it's a tad-"

Without hesitation Shelle swallowed the portion, exhaled and set the glass back on the table, expression unchanged. Mattie glanced at me. I shrugged.

"In the Coast Guard we had a saying," Shelle said. "If it won't degrease an engine it's not fit for a sailor."

Mattie chuckled. "So, would my white lightning degrease an engine?"

"Might melt it," Shelle said, swallowing a second time.

We all had a good laugh before heading to bed; Mattie, I noticed, took the M-14 with her to her room. Shelle ended up getting the spare bed despite her protests.

"You're the client," I said. "I'm the armed employee. Me on the couch puts me between the door and anyone coming through it to hurt you."

Shelle glanced at Mattie's front door; one of the improvements since last time I'd been there was a stout oak two-by-six in a steel frame across the front of it as a primitive latch. The door itself was more oak, three inches thick.

"How's somebody supposed to pick that...explosives?" But she took the bed all the same.

The next morning I woke to find Shelle in the middle of the floor in jogging shorts and a sports bra, stretching. A pale caterpillar of scar tissue marched across the dark skin of her stomach; one of the several injuries that came along with her citation for bravery.

"I hope you don't mind running," she said. "I'm pretty sure you won't let me do it alone, but I need to move."

"I'll try not to faint on you," I mumbled, rubbing sleep out of my eyes.

Half an hour later we were pounding down the cracked asphalt, Shelle in the lead and me following behind. She set a pace somewhere between torture and murder; I doggedly kept at her heels as best I could and spent my non-breathing energy wishing

I'd taken up healthy habits earlier in life than I had. All the sitting I'd done and every cigarette I'd smoked since my first light-up at sixteen conspired to punish me. After a few miles of my heart trying to beat its way out of my ribcage, I called a halt.

Shelle turned, legs still pumping. "Only four miles?"

"Pass thirty," I said, "and get back, to me, with that." After a hard jog you speak only in fragments. I hadn't stopped moving since I didn't want my legs to seize up, but I couldn't keep up Shelle's pace without injury.

She grinned, sweat gleaming on her face. "We'll see," she said.

She did indeed slow her pace by several degrees. The new pace was only a little better than the old one and after another few minutes I slowed to a walk.

"Okay," I called, "you win."

"Sorry," she said, slowing down likewise.

"Don't be," I said. "I didn't think-"

CRACK!

The sound slapped my ears and left them ringing. *Bullet, high-caliber, close* my brain screamed as I dove forward, tackling Shelle into the ditch beside us as the echoing *BOOM* of the rifle's report crashed off the trees like a wild beast.

"Christ!" Shelle came up into a crouch, hugging the side of the ditch.

I tore my H & K out of my fanny pack. "Rifle," I whispered.

My right ear whined from the sonic boom of a bullet passing far too close. Whoever had missed me hadn't done so by much. Shelle went to peek over the edge of the ditch and I tugged her back down.

"You'll never see them before they blow your head apart," I hissed.

"What do we do?" Her eyes were wide, hot with tension but not panicked.

I glanced around. The road we were on was carved into the slope of a shallow hill; whoever had picked their ambush spot had done so poorly. In front of us the hill sloped up to waist height, on the other side it dipped off sharply, spotted with trees. "Roll across the road," I said. "Stay low and keep between the trees. Whatever you do *don't stop moving.*" I brought my legs up into a crouch and tucked my pistol away. It was useless against a high-powered rifle. "We stay in one place and we may as well dig a hole."

She nodded. "Ready?"

"Go!"

I skittered across the road, staying as low as possible -

-*BOOM* said the rifle, bullet kicking up a fountain of asphalt six inches from my leg -

- and got to the other side of the road. Shelle followed behind me, sliding down the hill in a controlled fall. Her lip and her knee were red with blood but neither wound was serious. "Keep moving!"

She did. I did. We ducked between the trees and ran faster than our way out here, adrenaline coming down on fatigue and sore muscles like a red-hot hammer. Three more shots rang out as we ran, one throwing up a cloud of splinters on a tree an arm's length from both of us. A branch whipped across my arm in a hot line, drawing blood. I ignored it and kept running, lungs and veins scorched with adrenaline and lactic acid.

No more shots rang out. Fifteen long and terrifying minutes after the first gunshot Mattie's cabin came into view. Mattie stood on the porch with her binoculars, M-14 cradled in her arms. Her expression relaxed as soon as we closed to ten feet.

"I heard the shots," she said. "What happened?"

"Somebody fucking tried to kill us," I gasped out, coming up the stairs at a half-sprint with Shelle at my heels. Mattie followed us inside.

"No chance it could've been an accident?" Mattie closed the door behind us and locked it.

"Five aimed shots," I snapped. "Neither of us looks *that* much like a deer." I glanced at Shelle. "You okay?"

"Functional," she muttered, bending over to cough. A fast jog out and a dead sprint back had left us both gasping and hacking. I sat on the floor and put my head between my knees as the nausea of adrenaline and exercise took my legs out from underneath me.

My right ear was still half-deaf. For that to have happened the bullet had passed less than a foot from me. *Less than a foot,* I thought. *Maybe one-millionth of an inch at the other end of a hundred-some yards. A gust of air, a heartbeat, that's it, that's all that saved your life...*

I made it to the kitchen sink in time to throw up.

"Are *you* okay, kiddo?" Mattie put a hand on my shoulder. I twitched.

"Adrenaline shock," I mumbled, shuddering. "I'll be

fine. What I want to know is who the fuck was shooting."

Mattie's face was grim. "Well I don't know who but I do know why," she said.

I looked over at her, wiping my mouth. "How's that?"

"Simple, dearie," she said. "You're famous."

Chapter 21

It was five full seconds before my mouth would close on words. "I'm *what*?"

"Somebody talked," Mattie said, "and they did it in the worst possible way. I found it when I went to check my internet sources this morning. Come see."

I got a sick little feeling in my stomach as I followed her. Once I got to within ten feet of the computer screen I saw it; Lanie's video clip, staring at me from Mattie's Facebook feed and bracketed by cap-smashed text. I stopped walking.

"Jesus crunchy corkscrewing Christ," I said, staring at the image.

"Like I said, somebody talked." Mattie lit a cigarette.

Shelle peered at the screen in disgust. "Who *did* this?"

"I've been tracking it since I found it," Mattie said. "I don't know who first put it up but it hit the blogosphere like a thermonuclear warhead. Tumblr's having a field day with it...so are the Huffington Post and about a dozen Facebook pages. Salon, Daily Kos and LGBT News have pieces each on it. All of them are angry as a kicked rattlesnake and *none* of them have their facts straight."

I buried my face in my hand with a loud smack. It hurt. I didn't care. "How far off are they? And how bad is the exposure?"

Mattie adjusted her glasses. "Terrible, on both counts. Your name and your firm are mentioned. And as far as the story, it appears your vague theory about police department involvement in Lanie's rape and murder has officially become Internet fact."

"Oh that's bad," I said, digging for my phone. "Real, real bad." I thought of Deputy Stone and how I'd promised to keep my investigation quiet. What had just occurred was the polar opposite. "How long before this hits the TV news?"

Mattie snorted. "Are you kidding? I'm surprised it hasn't happened already."

"But this isn't what happened at all," Shelle said, scrolling through one of the blog posts. "This is all bullshit...they didn't even spell Lanie's *name* right."

"A lie told often enough becomes the truth," Mattie said. "Nonsense like this is why journalists used to have ethics."

I pulled out my phone and speed-dialed the office. The line was busy, which meant three or more incoming calls at once. "Shit," I muttered and punched for Izzy's cell instead. She picked up in less than two rings.

"Boss, what the hell is going on? Our phone won't stop ringing. Julian's been fending off reporters calling about the Hooper case all morning."

I braced myself against the kitchen table. "Been online yet?"

"Haven't had a chance," she said. "Too many freaking phone calls."

"Somebody put Lanie's video on the internet," I said, "along with some half-assed bullshit about how the cops killed her and it's a coverup. Now every armchair social-justice warrior who can string two buzzwords together is howling about it."

"Holy hell," Izzy said.

"Yeah."

I closed my eyes. This was a violation of about six different rules, in my profession and in Andersen's, playing out where the whole world could read about it. My stomach was already empty from lack of breakfast and adrenaline-induced vomiting; now it churned like I'd swallowed a running blender. I would be lucky, very lucky indeed, to avoid a censure from the State over this. I winced, wishing the situation had a face I could punch.

"Find out where this started and who did it," I said to Izzy. "Every viral story has a Patient Zero."

"Won't be easy," Izzy said.

"That's why I pay you the big bucks."

"Okay," she said.

I signed off and scrolled through my phone for Kevin Andersen's cell number. I didn't even consider his office line. If mine was ringing off the hook his would be even worse.

Mattie lit a cigarette. "Considering the content it has to be somebody in that attorney's office."

"That's who I'm calling next," I said. "And if that smarmy yuppie jumped the gun for free publicity he'll end up wearing his ass as a hat."

"Doubtful he'd be that dumb," Mattie said. "This is a gross violation of confidentiality. Depending on how the Bar wants to judge it he could lose his practice."

Andersen's phone only got through half a ring. "Amber what the hell's going-"

"Shut up," I said. "Somebody in your office leaked Lanie's file and I'm real unhappy about it."

"Hey it could have been somebody at your -"

"Andersen," I snapped, "right now I really want an excuse to pound somebody's face in and if you jerk me around *at all* that somebody is gonna be you."

"There's no call for that," he said, affronted.

"Deep breaths, kiddo," Mattie said, passing me a lit cigarette. I drew on it until the cherry turned yellow and struggled to get a grip on my temper.

"Apologies," I said into the phone. "It's been a hell of a morning."

"There's still no need for that kind of talk," he said, voice sharp.

"Less than twenty minutes ago Shelle and I were being shot at," I said.

"Oh my God," Andersen said. "Are you two all right?"

"Fine," I said. "We got lucky. Now, just accept that nobody on my end leaked. I'm telling you, none of my people are that fucking brain-dead." I drew on the cigarette and sucked down another half-inch. "Besides, there isn't a copy at my office because I never sent one there. The leak's at your end."

"But the files are on the offline server," Andersen said. "The only people who ever saw them -" He stopped talking for a long second. "Oh damn," he muttered.

"What?"

"Let me call you back," he said, and hung up.

I resisted the urge to throw my cell against the wall. "It was one of Andersen's people," I told the other two. "He's going through who saw the files right now to figure out who."

Shelle rubbed at her temples. "Is there anything we can do about this?"

"Nope." I sucked down the rest of the cigarette and ground it out. "The cat is now well and truly out of the bag - there's no way on Earth anyone could cover the story up now, even if we got all the telcoms to cooperate in shutting off the goddamn Internet."

"This is disgusting," Shelle said.

"Yeah." I picked up my purse. "Right now, I need to drive down to the Sheriff's office and abase myself before them so that the nice deputy who's been trying to help me doesn't lose his job."

"No," Mattie said, "what you need to do is have a shower and change into your good clothes while I make you some breakfast."

"I don't have time," I snapped.

"Make the damn time, kiddo," she said in a lecturer's tone. "Look at yourself right now. You're dirty, frazzled and by your own words a half-inch from tearing somebody's throat out. You go down there like you are at the moment and you'll either burst into tears or get all up in the first face what looks at you funny. Neither of which is productive if you want to make nice. Take a moment and get a grip."

"She's right," Shelle said quietly. "No offense Amber, but she's right."

I gave myself a glance in a nearby mirror; Mattie had it correct on all cards. I wouldn't make much of an impression with dirt on my knees and tear-stains on my face, babbling at the speed of sound. "Okay," I said. "It isn't as if this can get any worse in a half-hour."

"I'll fix you some eggs," Mattie said. My stomach growled as I grabbed my day bag and headed to the bathroom, so I could prepare to face the music.

Chapter 22

It never ceased to amaze me, the healing power of a hot shower.

I stood under the spray and scrubbed off the dirt, letting my eyes bawl themselves out as my body shuddered and sobbed its way through the final stages of adrenaline shock. By the time I finished that plus the body-maintenance rituals that came along with bathing I felt a small measure of calm, as well as the willingness to negotiate with angry cops.

After ducking out in a bathrobe to wolf down a generous portion of coffee and eggs on toast along with another of Mattie's cigarettes I dug out my nice clothes. With as much efficiency as I could muster I donned them, feeling very much like somebody girding themselves for battle; hose, bra, blouse, skirt, heels, jacket, conservative cosmetics, 9-millimeter. The war paint helped almost as much as the pistol did.

Which was good as this wouldn't be a pleasant talk. The Island County Sheriffs had every reason to be upset with somebody, and since I was handy I'd get the brunt of it even when one threw in the attempt on my life. With a final smoothing of the hair I walked back out into the main room.

Shelle sat at the kitchen table, eyes leaking tears. I squeezed her shoulder. "You okay?"

"Yeah," she said in a bemused voice, wiping at her eyes with a tissue. "I'm fine, I just can't stop crying."

"Adrenaline," I said. "It does that. I had the waterworks going in there for a while too. It doesn't mean anything."

"Still feel stupid," she said.

"I'm the one who tossed my cookies," I said.

She laughed. "I guess."

"Neurotransmitters function no matter how tough you think you are."

"You need me to come too?"

I shook my head. "Better only one of us gets their head torn off."

"But I didn't do this," she said.

"Neither did I," I said. "Doesn't matter. You hired the law firm which made the boo-boo, and it was my report which got leaked. If this comes to a lawsuit, we could both end up as defendants."

"You're kidding," Shelle said.

"I wish." I lit up another Camel, resolving to buy Mattie a carton before this was over. Also to try and stop wimping every time things got worse. "Island County would be within its rights to press a libel suit. After all, thanks to Andersen's office dropping the ball the whole Internet is accusing its officers of conspiracy to commit rape."

"My God," Shelle said.

"Civil court's like the Mos Eisley spaceport," Mattie said from the kitchen. "You will never find a more wretched hive of scum and villainy."

I scooped up my purse. "Starting to see why I want to pound on somebody's face?"

"Right there with you," Shelle said, anger in her eyes.

"Good luck kiddo," Mattie said as I stepped out the door.

"I'll need it," I called back.

The drive to the Sheriff's office was an exercise in uneventful tension. I kept my head on a swivel the whole way but no suspicious vehicles followed me and no shots rang out. Underneath my blouse my heart beat a stressed-out tattoo; it was work not to duck every time somebody pulled up next to me at a traffic light.

There was already a small crowd of protesters in the parking lot when I pulled in. It was mostly teens cutting class and jobless twenty-somethings with nothing better to do, spiked with the same attention-whoring weirdos that showed up to every event which involved yelling and signs. JUSTICE FOR LANY, I read on one scrawled piece of posterboard.

"Idiots," I muttered, stashing my gun beneath the seat and grabbing my case files.

Nobody looked up as I got out of my car and walked a straight for the door, keeping my stride brisk but not hurried. Over the years I'd been scrupulous about keeping my picture offline and I blessed the time it had taken; everybody with an Internet connection knew my name but I was still faceless. I passed one sign which had AMBER ECKHART, HEROINE painted on it in blotchy red capitals.

No fucking H, I wanted to snarl at the girl with the sign. Every attendance sheet from kindergarten to senior year had made that mistake. I'd grown up hating it and I still did. It shouldn't have made me so annoyed, but in the context of the situation it drove home the stupidity of the whole nasty mess.

I pushed open the door to discover a scowling Deputy Stone walking towards me. I put on my best apologetic expression.

"May I ask what you are doing here, Ms. Eckart?" His stare was cold and closed-off. I did my best not to quail under it.

"Apologizing, a lot." I glanced over my shoulder at the angry crowd, visible through the glass double doors. "I didn't know they'd be here already."

"Well they are," he said. "What the hell happened?"

"Something really, really stupid. Exact words for it are being unearthed as we speak, but I can promise you, this was *not* me or anyone I employ."

"Don't think that's gonna help." He adjusted his Stetson. "Strandell told me to come find you. He wants somebody's hind end on a plate."

"Guess I draw the duty." I sighed. "Does he know this mess has already caused me to get shot at?"

Stone's eyebrows jumped. "No," he said.

There was a silence and I could all but hear the wheels turning behind his eyes. "No he does not. Don't tell him, if you please."

I raised an eyebrow at that, wondering what sort of move Stone was planning but knowing I couldn't ask. I nodded instead. "Let's go get this over with," I said.

Strandell's office was neat and well-ordered, bare of

books and overloaded with citations and pictures. The desk was arranged fortress-style; the man behind it sat with the posture of a king in his castle. My heart sank.

Deputy Sergeant Richard Sullivan Strandell had all the makings of a handsome man: above-average height, smooth skin, prominent features, sandy-brown hair cut in a style straight from the pages of GQ, along with deep blue eyes and a fit, muscular build. What ruined it was the surly arrogance that wafted off his expression like bad cologne. If somebody told me he was a Rotarian who beat his wife four times a week I'd have believed them on both counts.

Stone stepped through the door behind me and closed it. "You wanted me to find her, Sergeant," he drawled. "She came to us."

"So," Strandell said in a boyish tenor, "you're the heroine."

I winced, glancing over his shoulder out the window. The signs and the angry people were visible. "I apologize, Deputy Sergeant. Neither I nor anyone I employ was responsible for this mess, but that doesn't mean I like seeing it."

"So why are you here?"

"Amends," I said.

His smile was a nasty slice of bile. "Okay, Eckart. Let me explain to you what you're making 'amends' for. In the last twelve hours I've had one deputy spat on, two cruisers vandalized and more angry calls than our phone system can handle, as well as a crowd of dumb youngsters in our parking lot waving signs, of course. All because of a malicious report you filed with a law firm that I'm led to understand has every intention of making us grab our ankles in civil court." He waved his hand in a come-along gesture. "You got some 'amends' for all that? Let's hear them."

"I can assure you the report wasn't malicious," I said. "I don't know where the rumor about officer involvement came from, but -"

"I'll also add," he said, "that you've been walking around with one of my closed case files and having some funeral director do unauthorized autopsies. I wonder what the Department of Licensing would think about your conduct."

"The case was closed," I said. "Elaine Hooper's remains and the file are the legal property of her spouse -"

"- Who is lucky I'm not bringing her up on charges," Strandell said.

I torqued a few more turns on my temper's choke

valve. It wasn't easy but I'd had practice. I sat down across from him and pulled my case file out of my folio.

"I know everybody's unhappy with what happened here," I said, setting my case file on his desk and opening it. "I have uncovered some leads, and I'd like to apologize by helping you, if I may. If we can find out what really happened -"

"When I want advice from a failed cop," he said, "I'll ask for it."

His words went through my fragile calm like a wrecking ball. I sat back and clamped my teeth together before my mouth could write me a check for serious trouble.

"I made a few calls about you, Eckart," he said, smiling bigger now that he'd scored for points. "I guess you found out having a well-connected father isn't everything, is it? You still have to make the grade. And if you don't stop pissing in our soup you'll be the first Eckart in one hundred years to be arrested for obstruction of justice."

He leaned back in his chair. "You aren't a cop, and you never will be," he said. "So go back to peeping through windows and let the qualified folks handle the real crime, all right?"

I didn't leap across Strandell's fancy desk and go

for his throat but it was a near thing. My Scots-Nordic heritage might've been gentrified by changing custom, but any of my Gallowglass or Viking ancestors would've drawn steel and split Strandell's skull open over such talk. I felt the same basic urge but I didn't move a muscle. Instead, I coldly decided that if the opportunity presented itself to end his career I would do it. It wasn't nice or honest and I didn't care at all.

"I'll have that file," Strandell said, reaching for the folder in front of me. I brought my open hand down on it hard enough to sting. The sound made everyone jump except me.

"That," I said in a clipped tone, "is confidential."

"I can get a court order," he said.

"Go ahead." I pulled the file off his desk and stood. "In the meantime, good day to you."

"We're not done here," he said.

"You want me to stick around, Deputy Sergeant?" I leaned forward. "Book me."

Something in my stare made his smug grin slip, as though he wanted to get his teeth tucked away before I kicked them in. I stood and waited for somebody to do something. Nobody did and I wasn't surprised; Strandell hadn't a thing to hold me on and everybody knew it. I put my case file back into my folio, tucked it under my arm, turned on my heel and walked out the door.

"Christ, what a ball-breaker," Strandell muttered after the door closed. If Stone said anything I didn't hear it.

I was able to keep my armor up all the way out of the police station and into the driver's seat of my car. By then my hands shook and a lump of frustrated anger sat in my throat. I wanted a cigarette. I wanted to cry. I wanted to go back into that police station and start a fistfight. I didn't do any of those things, but rather stared straight ahead and listened to a knot of people-sheep shout about something they didn't understand.

"Prick," I muttered, flexing my hands.

Over several minutes I cursed him, the braying crowd in the parking lot and my own stupid temper, for letting a sexist ladder-climbing oaf get me riled up by throwing my childhood in my face. I used every swear word I knew in every way I could remember. It helped, but not by much.

There was a tap at my window. I jumped and looked over. Deputy Stone leaned down and tipped his Stetson to me. I rolled down my window.

"That could have gone better," he said.

"Come to finish me off?"

"No ma'am," he said. "Just asking you where you're planning on going from here."

"Back to work," I said.

"Strandell won't like that," he said.

"Deputy Stone, I don't give a rusty fuck what Strandell won't like."

"He catches you poking around, you'll find yourself on the wrong end of an obstruction charge," Stone said.

"He can bring the noise," I said. "I've got the attorneys of Burton, Cameron and Clive on retainer and Andersen Law champing at the bit to sue. If Strandell wants to play Lucky Pierre in a lawyer-driven clusterfuck, I'm all sorts of okay with that."

Stone tried not to smile and nearly succeeded. "Be that as it may, I still need to collect a statement from you regarding the shooting incident this morning."

I sighed. "I'm not really in a talking mood just now, Deputy. I'll call you."

"Ms. Eckart, thanks to your notification I am now officially the responding officer on that incident. If through the course of my investigation I happen to discover evidence pertinent to the death of Elaine

Hooper, her murder case will be reopened under *my* authority." He grinned and took out his notebook. "Now. Would you care to make a statement?"

A big chunk of my anger guttered out. *You beautiful, beautiful man,* I thought as I smiled back at him.

"When you put it like that," I said, and stepped out of the car.

Chapter 23

I sat with Stone in the parking lot of a nearby coffee stand and told him what I remembered of the shooting. It didn't take long because there was not much I could relate. Stone asked plenty of questions and I answered them as best I could.

"Tell me about the sound," he said.

"Loud," I said. "Big and powerful, whatever it was...the sonic boom left me deaf for an hour." I shook my head, remembering once more how close a bullet had to pass for that to happen. "Had to have been a semi-automatic though." I sipped at my coffee. "The last three shots were too quick for a bolt action."

"Semi-automatic, multiple shots...that means shell casings," he said. "I'll be sure to have a look."

"Good luck," I said. "Criminals don't pick them up because they're hard to find."

"Perps are in a hurry," he said. "I won't be."

"Just be careful," I said.

"Always am," he said. "As to the location, you say it happened about four miles north of the Fawkes residence?"

"So my legs keep insisting," I said, rubbing at my knee. The side effects of my desperate flight had caught up with me. My legs were twin columns of ache. "Shots came from my right as we jogged north. I never saw a muzzle flash or anything." I punched up a map on my phone and traced my route for him, pointing out the approximate location. "If it helps, there's a bullet hole in the road and another in a tree."

He nodded and took a sip of coffee, giving the surrounding area a scan. Strandell had said something about a deputy getting spat on and Stone quite likely did not want such an interruption, although I had to wonder at the stupidity of the person who would choose to assault a police officer Stone's size.

"I'll get on this, ma'am. In the meantime I suggest you try to be quieter about your investigation. I would hate to see you arrested for obstruction."

I snorted. "Obstruction, my foot. That was Strandell waving his wee-wee in my face."

Stone tried very hard to keep his expression impassive. "How so?"

"The case is closed," I said. "Fuck, he's the one who closed it. It's difficult for me to 'obstruct' an investigation that doesn't exist."

"So you weren't impressed," Stone said.

"You kidding?" I grinned and winked at him. "I saw bigger while studying Renaissance paintings."

Stone shook his head and laughed, unable to keep his facade. I took that as a win.

"The only reason Lanie's death isn't yesterday's news is because of my work," I said. "Strandell's explanation has blank spots big enough to drive a blimp through and he knows it. That's why he tried to take my files, and why he's threatening me."

"I hope you take this the right way, ma'am," he said, "but for a Gen-Xer with a fine arts degree you sure know how to play this game."

"What can I say...I am my daddy's girl," I said.

Stone's teeth flashed beneath his mustache as he grinned at me. "I'm pretty sure he'd agree."

Out of nowhere a blush bloomed on my face. I buried it by turning away and taking a sip of coffee. "I guess we'd both better get back to work," I said.

"Watch your step," he said.

"You too," I said.

We traded grips and parted ways. I got back in my car, mainly to avoid presenting a stationary target. As I pulled out of the parking lot my phone rang. I stuck my Bluetooth in my ear and punched up the call; Andersen Law.

"Talk to me," I said.

"Carla," Andersen said. "One of my interns. She was the leak."

"How does that even happen?"

Andersen sighed. "She was helping my paralegal arrange a large number of cases for filing and caught a look at some current matters. Technically she shouldn't have even been helping yet, but..."

"...but interns always do things they aren't supposed to do and see what they aren't supposed to see, because everybody's always five hands short," I said. "What possessed her to pull this nonsense anyway?"

"According to her, a bottle and a half of Merlot."

"Christ," I muttered. "You mean we're in this because a Tumblrina got tipsy? Tell me you've handled it."

"Dismissed her on the spot," he said.

"You are much nicer than I," I said.

"And you would have...?"

"I would've kicked that little bitch in her baby-box

'til her ovaries met her eyeballs," I said.

There was a pause. "Amber, have you ever considered anger-management courses?"

"Andersen, because of her drunken stunt I've been shot at, yelled at, threatened with felony arrest and had to bend a fistful of laws to keep *you* from being sued. Then there's the matter of your client almost getting killed and a very dear friend having *her* life put at risk. Sorry, but shit like that makes me cranky."

He sighed. "Believe me, I hear you. I could be disbarred over this. There's just nothing else I could do to her."

"Thus ovaries and eyeballs," I said.

"This is the twenty-first century," he said. "I'm not allowed to even *think* things like that anymore."

I laughed - then had a thought. It spawned several others and I had to avoid a sudden urge to giggle in glee. "Andersen, have you talked to the press at all?"

"Not a bit. Can't imagine what I would say to them," he said. "Why?"

"Give a statement and play crucify-the-ninny," I said. "Publicly state to a reporter that the video was leaked by an unpaid intern who wasn't authorized to even see it. You condemn the action and heavily imply that she did something illegal to get it."

"But she didn't," he said.

"Yes she did," I said. "She removed confidential client information from your office and made it public."

"That's legally debatable," he said.

"Andersen, you're an attorney. You know how to say something without saying it." I paused to negotiate a four-way stop. "Anyway, then you let her name slip to a print reporter in an 'off the record' conversation, maybe throw in some vague comments about how your client's life was put at risk due to the leak. Let the media's taste for salaciousness do the rest."

"That's pretty cruel," he said, but from his tone I could tell he liked the idea. "And anyway, how does that help us with all the Internet howling?"

"If you leak her name the press will want to interview her," I said.

"So?"

"So the average social justice blogger is a massive attention-whore, and I'd bet sex to doughnuts sweet little Carla is no different," I said. "The press will stick a microphone in her face and she'll 'tell her story', not realizing that by doing so she'll be catching the hot potato known as Internet fame."

"And if she wises up? Decides not to talk at all?"

"She won't," I said. "If she was stupid enough to do this she's too stupid to avoid the court of public opinion. Between your charm and her naiveté, we should be okay."

"This could get her in a lot of trouble," he said.

"Fuck the cat, raise the kittens," I said.

"I'll think about it," he said.

"Think quickly and act faster," I said. "Otherwise, *you* raise the kittens."

"You know Amber, there's a certain irony I'm savoring here."

"Which is?"

"A PI is telling a lawyer how to sleaze his way out of trouble, "he said, "and the lawyer is the one having a crisis of conscience."

I laughed. "Claws and horns, Andersen. I use them. It's why I'm still in business."

"I'll be in touch," he said.

We signed off and I pried my Bluetooth out of my ear. Despite his protestations I was pretty sure he'd go for it and even more certain it stood a good chance of working. Viral outrage didn't respond well being driven with a stick, but it could be easily led around with the right species of carrot.

I kept my car headed down the road to Mattie's house, occasionally reaching down to rub my thighs; the sprint plus a period of sitting had caused my legs to cramp up something fierce. I still kept an eye on the rear view but thanks to winding country roads and a sparse population there was no traffic for anyone trying to follow me to hide in.

I was grateful for small favors.

Chapter 24

I got back to Mattie's place early in the afternoon. Mattie was there, Shelle wasn't. Her boss had demanded she come to work and Mattie had driven her in. I wondered about a boss who didn't want to accept 'I was shot at' as an excuse for not showing up. Examples like that helped me remember I wasn't a bad boss. I gave my employees time off for getting shot at.

"So," Mattie said, "how did things go at the Sheriff's office?"

"They went all over the place," I said, and explained over several minutes.

Mattie chuckled as she fiddled with her current crochet project. "Stone's being his usual crafty self, I see."

"Pretty much," I said. "By the way, Rick Strandell's a right royal asshole. It's been a while since I've had that big an urge to punch somebody in the face."

"There's few enough who'd disagree with you," Mattie said. "His father's a popular man but the son, not so much. Sully Strandell made a mistake putting him on the force."

"Wonder how that'll play in the next Sheriff's

election," I said.

"At this point, all Island County is waiting for is somebody better than Sully," Mattie said. "He's popular, but not with everybody."

"Stone ought to put his name in," I said.

"Stone's got too much melanin and not enough friends," Mattie said with a grimace. "Remember kiddo, Island County is whiter than Rush Limbaugh's ass."

I feigned outrage. "Racism? In *my* Washington?"

"The hippies around here sure love to support Black America," Mattie said, "as long as individual black Americans keep deciding to live someplace else."

I laughed. I couldn't help it. "You know, I've always thought it was a shame how you had to quit teaching."

"Who said I quit?" She squinted at a recalcitrant strand of yarn, adjusting it with clever fingers. "I just stopped doing it out in public where idiots could shoot at me."

I chuckled and cracked open my computer.

When I checked my email I discovered Izzy had confirmed what I already knew, specifically that an intern at Andersen Law had leaked our information and caused the Internet firestorm. It took me a while to parse out her data trail but once I did it all made perfect sense. I sent her off a congratulation email, then spent a few moments cleaning up her work so that somebody who didn't live in her head could follow it. After that I drafted a message to Kevin Andersen, attaching Izzy's work to it.

In case you need it, here's proof that sweet little Carla's drunken blogging caused all the fuss, I typed. *It's on the house, courtesy of my pet devil. You're welcome.*

-Amber

Julian had likewise emailed me with more good news, namely that his deposition had gone better than expected. Ray Copeland's lawyer was now begging Ellison Shipwrights' counsel for an out-of-court settlement. I grinned; a move like that at such an early stage meant the opposing side had nothing and was scared into desperation. Julian's message bubbled with enthusiasm and I didn't blame him one bit. I drafted him a congratulatory missive as well before leaning back and punching the air.

Mattie looked up from her work. "Good news?"

"My employees, being awesome as usual," I said. "My apprentice aced his first deposition, and my researcher has drawn a court-admissible bead on our viral outrage Patient Zero."

Mattie chuckled. "Moments like this, I'm glad I never stopped teaching."

My phone rang, sparing me from replying. The number was unknown but a local prefix. I picked it up. "Amber Eckart," I said.

"This is Doctor Shahiristani," a familiar cultured voice said. "I have some autopsy results for you."

"Please," I said, grabbing a pad.

"Most testing was beyond my purview but I did manage a toxicology screening. Elaine Hooper had heroin in her system. I also found evidence of a recent injection, rather clumsily done."

"That's no surprise," I said. "Lanie was an off-and-on junkie."

"Ms. Eckart, what I mean is this...at the time of her death Elaine had enough opiate in her bloodstream to euthanize a family pet."

I stopped scribbling. "So, she couldn't have tied a noose and climbed a tree?"

"Hardly," he said. "She would have been unable to find her feet. I doubt she was even fully conscious when she expired."

I sat back as Xander Harkness' voice rang in my mind. *The only way anyone could've gotten a noose around that girl's neck is if she wasn't conscious for it.* Facts shook hands with other facts and coalesced into a picture, one that grew more complex as my brain spun its wheels. *Evidence of a recent injection, rather clumsily done.*

"It would explain the lack of a struggle," the doctor said as my brain kept spinning. *Afghan heroin. Golden Crescent shit. A thousand kilos, uncut.*

"It might explain a lot of things," I said. *Calloway's dumber than he is mean and that's saying a lot.* "Thank you doctor. I'll be looking forward to your full report."

"I'll be looking forward to a check," he said.

"You'll get it," I said and signed off, putting the phone down with a slow hand.

Mattie looked up from her crochet and saw the expression on my face. "Progress?"

"Let me tell you a story," I said, "just as soon as my brain finishes telling it to me."

Mattie glanced at her watch. "It's about time for Shelle to be off work." She tossed me a pack of Camels. "Write your story down while I go fetch your client."

I picked up the pack. "You do realize you're enabling me, right?"

"In all ways," she said.

She slipped out the door and locked it on her way out. Left alone with coffee, cigarettes and paper I sketched out the story of a murder. After eight pages, two bathroom trips and six cigarettes I had a sore throat, a cramped hand and a plausible scenario which fit all the facts. It wasn't nice, but such matters never are.

Mattie returned with Shelle as I put the finishing touches on my notes. Shelle nodded a greeting and slipped into the bathroom to take a shower. From the set of her face I deduced that her workday had not gone well.

"She almost got fired," Mattie said. "Her boss wrote her up for spotty attendance."

"Spends the morning dodging bullets and gets yelled at for tardiness," I said. "What is it with jerkoff bosses today?"

"She needs the money, and badly." Mattie said. "We talked a little on the way back. Between Lanie's rehab, her car and all the funeral expenses the poor girl is drowning in debt. That's leaving aside whatever this attorney ends up charging her, of course."

I looked up, thoughts centering on the here-and-now. Shelle's finances wasn't an angle I'd considered. "Think she'll drop the case?"

Mattie frowned. "She might have to."

I sighed. "She'll do what she has to," I said, "and so will I."

Mattie blinked at me. "You'd really walk away from this?"

"If somebody doesn't want to pay me, I have to walk."

"The truth is the truth," she said.

"Dollars are dollars," I said. "Lives are lives."

"Look, kiddo -"

"Mattie, in all ways I'm not the one paying the tab here," I said.

"So?"

"So somebody else is. So I don't get to decide the price tag. I'm not a crusader, I'm a mercenary." It was work to keep my tone civil. "I knew this job had limits when I took it on." I took a deep breath and faced my friend square, trying my best to keep old bitterness from becoming a fresh problem.

"I'm not you," I said softly. "I don't have the luxury."

Mattie adjusted her glasses and gave me a severe look. She and I had argued this point before. It was how we'd met, back in her classroom at WWU. I'd been raised in a cop family and knew intimately the reasons for the thin blue line, whereas Mattie came from a rough neighborhood where the cops and the courts were just another gang to be avoided or fought with. Though graduate school had polished her rough edges down, the chip remained. She lived for exposing corruption - to the point of risking collateral damage to others while doing so.

I'd called her out on her bias back then, she'd called me out on mine and we'd argued our points passionately. The subject had come up on occasion and in each instance it hadn't gone anywhere productive. Most times we agreed to disagree, I prepared for the current conversation to go differently.

"Ladies," Shelle said from the bathroom hall, "I'm not an abstraction."

I winced and turned to look. Shelle had changed out of her office attire and into jeans and a tight t-shirt; her cornrows were still damp from the shower. Her expression was closed, eyes full of the same banked fire.

"Amber, I told you once that I'd take this as far as I have to. That hasn't changed." She walked over to the table and sat down. "I want justice for my wife and I knew *that* would be difficult when *I* took it on.

I know what I'm doing...if I'm going to trust you, please trust me." She came up with a faint smile. "You said you had a theory. Let's hear it."

From the corner of the living room one of Mattie's computers beeped. She sighed and ambled over to it. "Sorry," she muttered awkwardly. "I turned the motion sensors for the cameras on this morning...damn things are always pinging at deer."

Mattie played with the keyboard while I wrestled with a big pile of social issues. At length I gave Shelle an abashed glance.

"I'm sorry," I said.

"Don't be sorry," she said. "Just believe I can handle what I've asked for. Stop being prepared to walk away. I'm not giving this up."

"Okay," I said.

"It'll have to wait, kiddo," Mattie said, voice serious.

I looked over. "What's going on?"

"Uninvited guests," she said.

Chapter 25

Mattie's property had a driveway of nearly an eighth of a mile with a sharp bend in the middle of it, the result of second-growth Douglas firs her late husband had been unwilling to cut down. This left the first half of the driveway concealed from the house; for this reason Mattie had installed motion sensors at the mouth of the driveway and a camera in the bole of one of the trees, pointed at the wide turnaround at the bend. It was that camera's feed we all crowded around to look at.

Nighttime made the picture hard to see details, but we could clearly make out five Harley-style motorcycles and five men. The bikes were laden with gas cans, the men clad in denim and leather. One of the bikers had what was unmistakably a large revolver clutched in his right fist. All moved with the furtive tension of people about to knowingly break laws.

"Jesus creeping shit," I said.

Mattie stood up and walked to her gun cabinet. "Shelle dear, you said you know your way around a shotgun?"

"Yes ma'am," said Shelle, slipping on her shoes.

Mattie gave her collection a quick survey. "Remington, Ithaca or Mossberg?"

Shelle tied off her laces and stood. "The Remington, please."

Mattie tossed her a Parkerized pump-action followed by a box of buckshot rounds. She caught both and began stuffing shells into the shotgun's magazine.

I drew my H & K and did a press-check on the chamber. "Do we have anything resembling a plan?"

Mattie smiled. "Dear, who do you think you're talking to?"

She scooped up her M-14. "You two slip out the back door and go over the corner of the railing. Circle around to the front. Get these yahoos to surrender if you can, shoot them dead if you can't. Whistle if you manage either, I'll come help out." She flipped off the room lights and opened a narrow slit in one of her storm shutters, cut for the purpose of shooting out of. "If things go bad, I'm your backup. Pull back and I'll cover you. Stay on the left side of the driveway so I know who not to shoot at. That all make sense?"

Shelle pumped her shotgun. "Yes it does."

"Good. Do it."

It wasn't often I felt like the least competent person in the room, but there were times.

"After you," I said to Shelle. She went out the back door and I followed her.

There is a special kind of excitement that comes from risking your life. It's potent in its delivery and almost sexual in its urgency. My blood sang with it as I moved from tree to tree, ears buzzing, every sense honed to a razor's edge, palms sweating into the polymer grips of my automatic.

I let Shelle lead the way, as she had the more effective weapon. I kicked myself for not grabbing one of my own but only for a moment; the last time I'd handled a shotgun or rifle I hadn't been old enough to drive. Accuracy was more important and I trained with my P7 three times a week.

Thanks to the spreading canopy of the trees there wasn't much underbrush to work through, allowing us to stay quiet. It wasn't long before I could make out the sounds of men over the noise of the night; the soft metallic clinks of zippers, the sloshing of liquid, male voices low and tense. After one more tree I caught a glimpse of two figures, one pouring a line of gasoline on the ground towards the house. Shelle stopped and gave me a questioning look. I pointed at her shotgun and pantomimed a blow to the head. She nodded and moved to my left, circling in the direction of the pair's slow movement. I went right to intercept their path.

Due to darkness and tree trunks I lost sight of my quarry; I fought a moment of panic and stayed patient. Sure enough, the one pouring the gasoline came into view followed by the other. The first was slender, the second built wide and beefy. I got myself behind a tree and raised my automatic.

"Hi," I said to Arsonist.

His head snapped around, revealing a young pale face and frightened eyes. "Shit!"

His partner scrabbled for something in his belt - then pitched forward on his face as Shelle stepped from behind a tree and tapped him neatly behind the ear.

Arsonist's eyes grew wide as Shelle leveled her shotgun at him. "Drop the can," she whispered, "and stay quiet."

"Fuck me," Arsonist whispered back. He was early twenties, beardless and skinny and not at all prepared to argue with the business end of a 12-gauge. He dropped the gas can with a slosh.

"Yo Andy," I heard from up the driveway, "You done or what?"

Shelle stuck the shotgun against the back of

Arsonist's head. "Call him over."

He swallowed. "Uh, Mark...come gimme a hand, willya?"

"Jeez, prospect, you can't even take a piss without help."

I heard the crunch of boots on gravel; I slipped back behind the tree and leveled my automatic at the direction of the sound, dropping to one knee. Shelle moved to use Arsonist as modified cover, keeping her shotgun trained on him.

A rangy, bearded man ambled around the corner with two younger men in tow; they stopped when they saw one of their comrades face-down in the dirt and the other with a shotgun to his head. Beard had a big revolver in his right hand and a face that said he was willing to use it.

"Don't think it," I said from behind the tree. "You'll live longer."

The barrel twitched as Beard considered his options.

"Blaze of glory or compliance," I said. "Your call."

His face turned ugly as he tossed the revolver into the gravel. "Son of a bitch," he said.

"All of you, hands behind your head." My heart pounded but I made sure my voice came out steady.

One of the younger men was the next to comply. "You cops or something?"

"Or something," I said.

A few minutes later we had four very disgruntled bikers kneeling in a half-circle near their bikes, stripped of weapons; the fifth I had dragged groaning to join his friends, taking more effort than I wanted to. A quick search and several pat-downs netted us Beard's .44 Magnum, Beefy's 9mm Glock and five hunting knives. A whistle alerted Mattie.

She walked up her driveway in her black drover's coat and wide-brimmed leather hat. The pockets of her coat bristled with spare magazines. The bikers all stared at the M-14 in her hands. Mattie grinned, but her eyes were full of fury. Somehow that worried me more than the bikers did.

"You boys picked the wrong damn house to burn down," she said.

"What do we do with them?" Shelle said from behind her shotgun. "Call the cops?"

"Not yet," I said. I nudged Beefy's moaning body with my foot. "Fetch me his vest."

"Why?"

"I wants it," I said.

Shelle pulled it off his shoulders while the rest stared goggle-eyed. "Got it," she said, tossing it to me. I gave it a quick inspection. It was a biker's 'kutte', a sleeveless leather garment adorned with patches; FREAK PATROL TACOMA was stitched onto the back along with a grinning death's head wearing a jester cap above crossed hatchets and a fan of playing cards. The rest of the leather was heavy with patches and pins. I'd seen the symbol before many times and I wasn't surprised to see it again; from what I knew the Freak Patrol had chapters all over the Northwest. I took a moment to examine the five men kneeling in Mattie's driveway and picked out Beard as their leader. I hoped I wasn't wrong as I dug out a business card.

"I want to talk to your chapter president," I said. "If you want the kutte and your weapons back, have him call me." I tossed my card in front of him. I was aware of both Mattie and Shelle staring at me and I ignored it.

"Irish Bob," said Beard, "don't talk to bitches like you."

I'd heard the name before, but I made sure to keep that recognition off my face. "In that case the kutte and the weapons have a date with the bottom of Puget Sound," I said.

Beard glared daggers at me, but picked up my

business card all the same.

"Bitch, this is a fucking act of war," Arsonist snarled, voice laden with brittle bravado.

"Oh really," said Mattie. "Well then, here's another."

She raised her rifle and flicked the safety off. I prepared for the worst.

A 7.62 millimeter hardball round packs quite a punch; the poor defenseless motorcycles parked in Mattie's driveway never stood a chance. She parceled out four rounds per engine compartment with a thunderous *BAM-BAM-BAM-BAM* that left my ears ringing. By the time she was done the machines were incapable of moving under their own power. The bikers stared at their destroyed vehicles with almost childlike dismay as Mattie reloaded her rifle.

"Jesus Mattie," I said.

"Holy *crap*," Shelle said.

"They tried to burn down my house," Mattie said. "I object."

"Lady," Beard said, "You're fucking crazy."

Mattie fed him a steel-shod glare. "Young man," she said, "I turned fifty-nine this last November and I didn't get there being frightened by the likes of you." She gestured at the bikes with her smoking M-14. "Get your trash off my driveway."

Nobody moved. Mattie pointed the rifle at the sky. All present quailed as another shot ripped the night asunder.

"That's one," Mattie said. "On three, I start shooting trespassers."

The bikers slowly began to get to their feet. Mattie pulled the trigger again. *BAM.*

"Two," she called out.

The bikers scrambled across the gravel in a chorus of frightened profanity, grabbed their bikes and pushed them down Mattie's driveway as fast as they could run; even the one Shelle had cold-cocked moved with a startling degree of alacrity. In less than two minutes they were too far down the road to make out. Mattie slung the rifle, dug in her pocket and found herself a cigarette. In the distance, sirens blared.

"Shelle, take the vest and the weapons and stash them in the house," I said. "Be quick."

She nodded, scooped up the items and sprinted for the house. The sirens grew louder.

"So," Mattie said, "we're picking fights with biker gangs now?"

"You sort of did that yourself," I said.

"Taking colors off a made member is worse," she said. "And what's with giving one of them your business card? You trying to get your business burned down?"

"All part of my cunning plan," I said.

"And the next step of that is...?"

"I'll let you know when I do," I said as the first Sheriff's cruiser screamed into the driveway.

Chapter 26

The first responding officer was Deputy Terrence Stone. He stepped out of his car and took in Mattie's still-smoking rifle, the scattering of shell-casings and the smashed pieces of motorcycle engine in one long glance.

"Marian," he said, "you causing trouble again?"

Mattie smiled at him around her cigarette, innocent as a lamb.

"Why Deputy Stone," she said, "whatever do you mean?"

"We stopped five very unhappy bikers on the way here," he said with stern frown, "pushing their shot-up hogs just as fast as their legs could move. Other officers are questioning them and they aren't saying boo. Before that half the goddamn island called 911, babbling about how World War Three's kicked off at the Fawkes residence. I'm guessing there's quite a story to be told, and I want to hear it."

Mattie pointed at the three cans of gasoline the bikers had left behind. "Bastards were planning to burn us out," she said. "I politely told them that wasn't acceptable."

Stone glanced at the wreckage again. "Politely?"

Mattie snorted. "They're still breathing, aren't they?"

"Marian," Stone said, "there will be consequences this time."

"I know," she said.

"I'll have that rifle," he said.

She passed it over without a fuss, along with her revolver. "You going to cuff me, throw me in the back of your car?"

"Hadn't planned on it," he said.

"Pity," she said, batting her lashes at him like a teenager. "From what I hear that's how you hooked up with Genny."

Between Stone's dark skin and the low light I could not tell if he blushed, but awkward embarrassment was written in every gesture as he opened the back of his car. "Get in, Marian. We'll...talk about this down at the station."

"I'm looking forward to it," she said with a wink.

Stone shut the door on her and slowly shook his head. "Ma'am, if this is your definition of 'quiet' I'm not sure I want to know how you do 'loud'."

I sighed. "Deputy, Again I'm forced to say 'I'm sorry' on somebody's behalf. None of this was my idea." I gave the shell case and engine parts wreckage pile a glance and sighed. "Mattie's, well...Mattie."

"So she is," he said. He opened the trunk of his car and put her rifle and pistol in it. "What she just did breaks a few laws."

"She's a grown woman who made her own choices," I said. "You'll do what you need to and Mattie understands that. What I'm more curious about is what it'll take to have you let the bikers go."

"An act of God," Stone said. "One of them is already in cuffs over an outstanding warrant."

"Forget him then," I said. "What about the rest?"

Stone was silent, face thoughtful. "One of those men was missing his patch," he said.

"Must have left it at the cleaners," I said.

"You've got an angle," he said.

"One more leap of faith, Deputy," I said. "Please. I promise I'll make it worth your while."

"We'll see," he said as more emergency response vehicles pulled up in a cluster of noise and lights.

Whidbey was by and large a sleepy community, and Mattie's aggressive discharging of over twenty rounds meant everybody who drove something with four wheels and a siren wanted in on the action. Stone forced order out of chaos like a tornado in reverse, keeping the various agencies from stepping on each other with a firm voice and crisp directions. It was an impressive display and I found myself taking mental notes. When it comes to crisis management, instruction is where you find it.

When the cops got to me I was polite and respectful and only answered what I was asked, picking my way around each question like a soldier in a minefield. I was pleased to see that Shelle did the same, though her voice was shaky and her eyes wet. I could understand why; she'd started the day being on the receiving end of gunfire and ended it with outlaw bikers and attempted arson.

It was four full hours before the parade of uniforms finally filed out of Mattie's driveway. Neither Shelle nor I ended up having to go with them; the biker Shelle had clocked wasn't pressing charges from his jail cell, and we'd both been rather vague on the progression of the evening's events. When I had a free moment I pulled out my phone and sent Izzy a text.

You and Julian work from home tomorrow, I sent and gave a brief explanation as to why. **Set up the Skype extension for our work line and check the windows like I taught you. If you see ANYTHING that even REMOTELY looks suspicious, call the cops. Don't mention what's going on up here. And**

tomorrow, give me everything you can quickly find on the Tacoma chapter of the Freak Patrol Motorcycle Club. I'll be in touch.

Stone was the last to leave. Before he did he waved me over. "The other four bikers are being let go," he said. "They don't feel like pressing charges and since Mattie isn't going to either, I don't have a reason to hold them. Technically."

"Thank you," I said.

"You thank me," he said, "by seeing to it all this trouble has a happy ending."

I got a flutter in my stomach. I was in deep, no question, but I dug up a confident look and put it on anyway. "I will."

"Mattie ought to be out by tomorrow," he said. "So long."

"Have a good night, Deputy."

He tipped his Stetson to me, climbed in his car and left. I took a deep breath and let it out slowly.

"That was bracing," I said to Shelle.

"You said you had a theory."

"It's being revised," I said. "Let's go back inside and we'll discuss it."

Ten minutes later we sat at Mattie's kitchen table with the bottle of blackberry moonshine between us. I had a glass, and so did Shelle. The bikers were unlikely to try anything on the same night, and both our nerves were as shot to hell as the bikes had gotten.

"Talk to me," Shelle said after a sip.

"Understand that this is a theory which fits the facts, nothing more."

She nodded. "Go on."

I took a sip of my own and winced. "Long story short, I'm guessing your wife sat down at a game that was above her head," I said. "While she was living in the drug world she overheard somebody talking about a big deal that was about to go down. She winkled that somebody's number out of her ex and tried to run some kind of blackmail scheme on him. It didn't work, and she got herself murdered instead."

Shelle slowly shook her head. "But why?"

"Good question, but I don't think her death was completely intentional."

"Huh?"

"Whoever is doing this," I said, "is operating just as much on limited information as we are. When Lanie died she was loaded on heroin, quite likely not fully conscious. I think whoever kidnapped her from your apartment showed up, shoved a gun in her face when she answered the door and then shot her full of junk so she'd stay quiet - the doc found evidence of a clumsy injection on her arm. My guess is they wanted to interrogate her, make sure she hadn't told you or anyone else about the deal they're running. Except something went wrong."

Shelle's fingers tightened around her glass. "Somebody raped and strangled her," she said in a dark tone.

I nodded. "And then there's this morning to consider. Somebody takes a shot at us, then the very same evening a bunch of bikers show up to burn us out. I'm thinking two different groups who aren't keeping tabs on each other very well are after us."

"How does that work?"

"Simple," I said. "If the guy taking the shots and the bikers burning us out are working together, why weren't the bikers more prepared? I mean, come on...we had it easy tonight. Those men were looking to burn down the house of some people expecting a nice, normal Friday night. That isn't likely if the person taking shots at us this morning was talking to them."

"Okay," she said. "Why are the bikers involved at all? What's their deal?"

"The Freak Patrol MC has chapters from Anchorage to San Diego," I said, "and Lanie's killers are in all likelihood moving Afghan heroin into Washington by the literal ton. All that dope needs a big distribution network...something an outlaw motorcycle club could easily provide."

"So drugs," Shelle said.

"Yeah."

Shelle sat back, staring into her glass. "When we first got together, Lanie was happy," she said. "She had plans. She wanted to go to school...she was talking about becoming a veterinarian for God's sake."

"I'm sorry," I said.

"What made her go back, Amber?"

"I don't know," I said. "Only Lanie did, and I can't ask her."

She held the gold cross around her neck between two fingers. "I plan to," she said, "when I see her again."

"You do that," I said.

Chapter 27

I got up early the next morning, but Murphy got up even earlier.

It was the day of Lanie's funeral service. Shelle and I skipped our morning exercise routines to prepare for it, as both of us needed extra time with our grooming. She was silent over breakfast and coffee and I let her be alone with her thoughts; I'd never buried a lover and anything I said would be pretty meaningless given the context.

I let Shelle have the outer bathroom and borrowed the smaller one off Mattie's room. I had offered to let Shelle have the day to herself but she'd insisted I attend the service. Fortunately I had packed clothes nice enough for it, plus my black trench coat which would help to keep my automatic from printing through my clothing.

The trouble started when my phone rang; I grabbed it as I put the finishing touches on my appearance. "Amber Eckart," I said.

"Bad news," Deputy Stone said. "Looks like Mattie's being charged after all."

My eyes narrowed. "With what? I thought you said the bikers refused to testify."

"The department is slapping her with reckless discharge of a firearm," Stone said.

"And by the department, you mean Sergeant Strandell."

A short silence. "How'd you guess?"

I capped my lipstick and set it down carefully. I wanted to slam it on the counter. "This is pure meanness," I said. "He's only throwing the book at Mattie because she's my friend."

"Of course he is," Stone said. "The charges probably won't stick, but that means Mattie's in jail until at least Monday."

I nodded, understanding the tactic being used. The court system didn't operate on the weekends, and Strandell wouldn't have been the first police officer to use bureaucracy instead of due process to hold someone. "Well, there's nothing to be done about it right now," I said. "But I tell you, I'm not going to forget this."

"Understood, Ms. Eckart."

I signed off, closed my eyes and took several deep breaths. When I opened them a calm-faced woman with icy eyes stared back at me. "Joo wanna fuck wit' me, Ricky boy? Hokay," I said to my reflection in a cheesy Cuban accent. "Joo wanna play rough?

Hokay."

I picked up my cell phone, punched up Kevin Andersen's home number. It was several rings before I got an answer, and when I did Andersen's friendly voice was muffled from sleep.

"Amber, do you ever stop working?"

"Not as long as I'm getting paid," I said. "Anyway, there's been some developments."

"Lay them on me," he said, coming further awake.

I explained for several minutes about the bikers, Stone's help, and Strandell's oafish intransigence. While I talked I could hear a woman's voice murmuring in the background, sleepy but sultry.

"Wow," Andersen said. "This got dangerous in a hurry."

"Yep," I said.

"It's been a while since I've enjoyed the idea of going after a police department," said Andersen.

"I've got a better idea," I said.

"Oh?"

"Don't make your suit against the Sheriff's department," I said. "If you do that you and Rachelle will look like money-grubbing jerks fleecing the taxpayer over a grudge. Besides, parts of the department have been cooperative and interested in finding out the truth behind Lanie Hooper's death and it isn't good policy to slap help in the face. Go after Rick Strandell in person instead...he's the officer who did all the damage. That way you look like a crusading attorney saving the maligned black lesbian and her poor dead wife from a bigot with a badge."

Andersen thought a moment. On the other end the woman's voice grew louder. She was whispering in his other ear. "That plays," he said. "Considering the media problems and all. Now, what do you get out of it?"

"Orgasmic levels of personal satisfaction," I said.

"I'm guessing you're willing to testify against him on the stand," he said.

I laughed, slipping into my shoulder holster. "Andersen, you can subpoena me, depose me...hell, you can drag a stripper pole into the courtroom and I'll work it like Gypsy Rose Lee if you think it'd help."

Andersen laughed. "What did this Strandell guy do?"

"He pissed me off," I said.

"I hope I never do that," he said. I heard sultry whispering, the sound of lips on flesh. "Ah...Amber, can I call you back? Something's come up."

"Sounds like it," I said. "Think it over when your lady friend lets you have your brain back."

"Sure," he said, and hung up.

I stared at my phone. He'd go for it, I knew he would. It gave him both a chance at money and the social street cred he wanted without alienating the police along the way.

"Say 'allo to my li'l friend, Ricky boy," I said with a smile.

I spent a few more minutes at my grooming, mostly making certain my shoulder holster wouldn't show under my jacket. When I walked out to the front room I found Shelle waiting; she was dressed very similar to me, in a black skirt, blouse and jacket, except her legs didn't need the assistance of hose. Gloves sheathed her hands. She wore her cross outside her shirt and it gleamed against the black fabric. She hadn't done much in the way of makeup and I knew why; no cosmetic ever manufactured could stand up to a funeral's tears.

"I heard you on the phone," she said. "What happened?"

"Mattie's being charged," I said, and explained for a few minutes.

"I guess capping off twenty-odd rounds *is* pretty reckless," she said.

"Mattie shoots out here all the time," I said. "Strandell just wants to inconvenience me by holding her. I've already made sure he'll regret that decision."

"Okay." Shelle nodded and glanced around the room before returning her gaze to me. "You ready to go?"

I picked up my trench coat and slid into it. "Are you?"

She drew herself up. "Yes," she said.

We took Shelle's car rather than mine. Her Miata was nicer than my Golf and I wanted the ability to watch for tails one hundred percent of the time. Shelle drove in silence, and I let her.

Shahiristani's funeral home was as clean and orderly as it had been the last time I'd visited; a sign set out by the entrance announced the viewing services for Elaine. There were no other cars in the parking lot, but we were early. I stepped out of the car first and gave the surroundings a scan, looking for suspicious cars or people. There were none, but I kept my head on a swivel all the way to the door, staying between Shelle and the road while I did. If Shelle noticed my actions she gave no sign.

Doctor Shahiristani met Shelle at the front entrance in a freshly pressed suit, greeting her with a handshake that combined warmth and gravity. I stood aside while they discussed matters relating to the service, but when Shahiristani looked up I gave him an *I-need-to-talk-to-you* glance and indicated a nearby alcove with my chin. He nodded slightly and continued speaking with Shelle as I stepped into the alcove.

Several minutes later he joined me. "Rachelle is viewing her wife's remains," he said. "I have a few minutes, can I help you?"

I pointed at the sign on the door barring concealed weapons, then opened my jacket to show him my H & K. One silver eyebrow climbed up his forehead. "Oh," he said.

"I'm sorry to put you in this position," I said, "but there have been two attempts on Rachelle's life recently." I pulled my state CPL out of my purse and showed it to him. "I'm legal, licensed and asking for you to make a discrete exception."

He took my license and examined it before handing it back. "Under the circumstances, I will allow this," he said. "Just be certain no one sees your weapon. I've no wish for anyone to be disturbed."

"The only time people will see it," I said, "is if events have become disturbing on their own." I smiled at him. "Thank you, doctor."

"Thank you for asking," he said. "Is there anything else I should do?"

I nodded. "If you see anybody acting suspicious or out of place, don't try and confront them on your own. Get my attention and we'll confront them together. I don't want the ceremony disrupted any more than you do."

"Good to know," he said. "I will do as you instruct."

We shook hands and I let him return to the business of setting up a funeral service. I prowled around the public parts of the funeral parlor for a few minutes, checking this and that, before realizing I was putting off rejoining Shelle. With a sigh I went and found her.

The space was set up almost but not quite in the fashion of a church; high narrow windows, rows of benches and a podium for people to speak from. Lanie's body sat in a coffin on a low table, along with a photo of her in life. I recognized it; Shelle and Lanie's wedding picture.

Shelle stood in front of the coffin, tall and regal in her grief, one hand resting gently on the coffin's edge. I came up to stand beside her. Thanks to Shahiristani's mortuary work Lanie's body no longer repelled or disturbed. She wore a white silk dress, a high collar and long gloves concealing her scars and the ruin the rope had made of her throat. Still and pale and surrounded by flowers Elaine Laurel Hooper could have been a fairy-tale princess, sleeping peacefully and waiting for a prince to wake her.

But she wasn't.

A lump came into my throat just then, but I couldn't have said why. I'd never liked funerals and I had my reasons, but Shelle needed somebody to help her through this; though I was only recently a friend I had drawn the duty.

I glanced around. "No pastor?"

Shelle shook her head. "Lanie wouldn't have wanted a preacher saying words over her," she said.

"Who'll speak?"

Shelle looked up. "I will," she said softly.

"You have the words picked out?"

"Well as I can," she said. She reached down and squeezed Lanie's hand.

I glanced up and saw Shahiristani in the doorway with the same *come-talk-to-me* look I'd given him. I walked over.

"There is a gentleman pacing about the parking lot," he said quietly. "He has not announced himself and appears rather agitated. An older man, African-American. "

A moment's thought netted me a theory. "He dressed for the occasion?"

"More or less," Shahiristani said.

"I'll go talk to him," I said. "You watch from the door. If it becomes anything more than a polite conversation, call the cops."

He nodded. I collected my trench coat and headed for the door, loosening my automatic along the way. When I reached the door I could see the person in question. He was a dark-skinned male in his fifties, dressed in tan slacks and a blue blazer cut in a style two decades out of fashion. His hair was a receding shock of cloudy white, his posture the slight stoop of a lifelong laborer. He smoked a cigarette and paced back and forth, stopping on occasion to give the funeral home a look.

I glanced back at Shahiristani. "I think I know who that is," I said.

It was a fifteen foot walk from the door to the parking lot and the man noticed me before I'd gone half the distance; suspicion slid over his face like shutters. Creased skin moved in a frown as he eyed me, not as a man eyes a woman, but as a soldier eyes another soldier in a different uniform looking for threats.

"Miss, if I'm botherin' people," he said, "I'll be on my way."

I closed the distance between us and kept my hands where he could see them. "Are you here for the Hooper funeral?"

He drew on his cigarette. "I'm not rightly sure."

"You're Rachelle's father," I said.

"Elias Hooper," he said. "And you are?"

"Amber Eckart," I said. "I've been working for your daughter as an investigator."

"Bodyguard too," he said, pointing with his cigarette to where my pistol rode.

I nodded. "The situation is complicated, Mister Hooper."

"I know," he said. "A buddy of mine told me. Said Shellie's wife was murdered. Said somebody tried to kill her too."

"If you'd like to sit in on the service, I can go ask her."

He tossed his cigarette on the pavement and ground it out with his foot, a grimace on his face. "I'm not invited," he said. "Just tell her I was by." He turned towards a battered white Buick.

"Dad?"

Rachelle stood just up the path from us, hands trembling, eyes wide and round. Elias Hooper all but staggered when he saw her.

"Shellie," he said.

"What are you doing here?" Her voice was a question, not an accusation.

"Like to pay my respects, if I can," he said.

"But you hated Lanie," Shelle said. "You said she was bad for me." *You said a lot of other things,* I heard in her tone, *and I'm still hurting over them.*

The dignity Elias Hooper summoned was as awkward and frayed as the suit he wore, but he donned it all the same. "She was still your wife," the elder Hooper said. "That makes her family. You pay your respects when family passes."

"Go ahead," said Shelle.

"Won't be long," he said, and strode up the path to

the door. Shelle watched him go. There was a pregnant silence as Elias Hooper walked into the funeral home and disappeared. The lump in my throat grew fangs. I took a deep breath and made a difficult decision.

"Shelle, do you mind a piece of advice?"

She turned to me. "Let me guess...forgive and forget."

"That'd be bad advice, considering I've no idea what this is about," I said. "Ask him, though. Hear him out. He's here to talk."

She blinked, a tear sliding down her cheek. "Why should I?"

I swallowed to push the lump away. It didn't work. "You'll regret it if you don't," I said.

She shook her head. "How do you know?"

Another deep breath. "Once upon a time I didn't," I said, "and not a day goes by where I don't wish I had."

Rachelle looked from my face to the white bulk of the funeral home. "I'll be back," she said, and walked up the steps.

It was several deep breaths before the lump stopped gnawing at my heart, several more before I stopped worrying about bursting into tears. I patted my pockets for some of Mattie's cigarettes, tapped one out and lit it with a match. Smoking was as good an excuse as any to stay outside.

My pocket buzzed; I'd set my phone on silent so its ringing wouldn't disturb the ceremony but I could not afford to shut it off. I fished it out and saw the number wasn't one I recognized. I accepted the call and pressed the phone to my ear. "Amber Eckart," I said.

"Good," a gritty male voice said, with a tone to it that made my breathing skip a cycle.

"Can I help you?"

"You sure can," he said. "You've got some things that belong to me, and I want 'em back."

My heart went on strike as I reached for another cigarette. "Irish Bob," I said.

"Got it in one," he said.

"I'm prepared to negotiate for the return of your property," I said.

"Give me one good reason why I shouldn't drive up there, slit your fucking throat and shove my dick in the wound 'till I come twice," he snarled.

I lit up with a shaking hand. "I'll give you several," I

said, "but only in person."

"What?"

I drew on my cigarette. My hand shook.

"I name the time and the place," I said. "You show up. We talk."

He laughed, a sound that made my skin want to crawl away and hide. "You serious?"

"Always," I said.

"What makes you think I'll go along with that?"

I grinned around my cigarette. "Curiosity," I said.

Chapter 28

After finishing my call with Irish Bob I walked back into the service and sat down. Other people had shown up. Rachelle's co-workers and a few family friends made for a thinly attended service. I noticed two of the teenagers from the apartment sitting across from me in the same back row, awkwardly garbed in black and staring at Lanie's corpse with the wide eyes of people who had never contemplated death before. I found it hard to pay attention.

I had a good deal to think about.

Irish Bob and I had a meeting for tomorrow at noon, at a sports bar on Aurora Avenue; it was the first location which popped into my frightened head during the conversation and since I blurted it out I had to stick with it. Always talk faster than the other person can think, but never go back on what you've already said no matter how ill-advised it was. Getting it done is better than getting it perfect. As long as you live.

Rachelle took the podium and spoke about Lanie; the words rebounded off my ears. I felt guilty about not hearing her speech, but my thoughts instead kept returning to the man I would be meeting tomorrow.

Robert Killian "Irish Bob" Brodie; often charged, never convicted. A man who had been in court on almost a dozen occasions in connection with serious felonies but had always walked away free. A man who by the system's count was just a part-time auto mechanic and chapter president of a motorcycle club, somebody who'd only done time for a few penny-ante bar fights and drunken hijinks. Yet the heavy charges kept happening, and Irish Bob kept walking away.

Tomorrow, I would be meeting with him.

I pulled out my phone and texted Izzy, careful to keep the screen shielded with my trench coat. **I know its the weekend and I'm sorry for that. You'll get overtime for this plus a bonus. I need a rundown on a man named Irish Bob, he's the President of the Tacoma chapter of the Freak Patrol MC I told you to look at before.**

One of the teenagers glared at me in disapproval as I sat, phone in hand. I gave them an *I'm sorry* glance and returned to my work.

It wasn't long before my phone vibrated with a reply. **Boss I've already got a few things. Irish Bob's a bad guy; he's been in court a bunch of times over murder and conspiracy charges, but**

he's never been convicted. According to some blog posts I've read, he's suspected in about 18 homicides - either people think he ordered them or he did the deed himself.

Thanks, I typed, **but I already knew all of that. I need more. Something I can use.**

Why? Use how?

I took a deep breath. **Tomorrow I meet with him.**

Jesus Boss O.O

I know. Consider that motivation to get more info.

okay was all I got in return. As I put away my phone people began getting to their feet. Rachelle approached me, eyes glistening. "How'd I do?"

"You did great," I said.

"You spent the whole service on your phone," she said.

"I know. I'm sorry, but something came up. I'll tell you about it in the car."

She hesitated. "Actually...Dad and I are going to go for coffee."

"Glad to hear it," I said.

"I was wondering if you'd be willing to take my car back to Mattie's. My dad will drop me off when we're done."

"Sure," I said. "I have work to do anyway."

She passed me her keys and I hugged her, as one does during traumatic events. As our cheeks touched she whispered "what's going on?"

"The bikers called me," I whispered back. "I have a meeting tomorrow with their leader, Irish Bob. I'm nervous."

"Stay in touch," she said as I released her.

"I will."

I left the service and drove back to Mattie's in Shelle's Miata, checking the mirrors the whole way - and while doing that suddenly had a thought.

"Okay, bad guys," I said to my reflection, "how *did* you find me?"

Sure, Mattie wasn't as hidden as she liked to think; she still had a public identity as a journalist and blogger, and I was more familiar than most with how easy it was for people to be tracked down in today's world. But how did they know I would be there?

My pace back to Mattie's slowed to the low end of the speed limit as I considered the problem. Certainly I had not been quiet about my investigation; as soon as the viral-outrage storm had hit and the conspirators had been notified of my existence, confirming it would've been as simple as asking around. But my location at Mattie's would have been harder for them to figure out, especially because I'd been diligent about checking my trail.

Or had I?

My situational-awareness training had assumed the presence of two things; traffic and the straight roads inherent in any urban area, neither of which were present here on Whidbey. I sped back up and performed an experiment, checking my mirrors every fifteen seconds and seeing how much I was actually able to observe due to the winding nature of the roads. The answer I got was 'not nearly enough'. Also, I'd been giving a lot of leeway to cars staying behind me as long as they weren't too close, due to the lack of driveways and side streets. Thanks to all that, a pair of someones could have easily tag-teamed me with a tail and I would've missed it completely. Which I apparently had. I bit back curses.

"Adapt your technique to your environment, dumbass," I muttered to myself as I found Mattie's driveway and pulled down it.

Mattie's house was still standing when I arrived, the security system still armed and running. I poked about the yard anyway and was glad I did. In the gravel of the driveway in front of the house there were three narrow ruts that had come from motorcycles, and recently. There were boot prints on the steps from male-sized shoes. And the deadbolt had a series of scratches in the face place that could only have come from an attempt to pick it.

Upon that discovery I sat back with a grim smile. The deadbolt was a distraction, nothing more. The real lock was elsewhere, hidden behind a false panel in the door, and upon inspection it proved to be undamaged. The bikers had likely pulled up, tried to break in, discovered the alarm system and left. I still prowled around looking for left-behind surprises like a bomb before entering, and checked all the rooms in the cabin with my pistol in my hand. No surprises or murderers awaited me. After that I set Mattie's castle latch and breathed a sigh of faint relief.

"This is getting out of hand," I said to the empty room. On a whim I checked the security camera feeds, still running since Mattie had turned them on.

Sure enough, the bikers had showed up. On the feed they prowled around the property, careful not to touch or disturb anything. I recognized Beard from the previous night as one of them, the other two a pair of rough-looking specimens I hadn't seen yet. Their vests and tattoos were more elaborate, higher-ranking members most likely. I noted that they all wore gloves. After several minutes of checking around Beard came to the door; the wide-angle lens meant that his attempt to pick Mattie's front door was captured for posterity. I grinned.

"Gotcha," I said.

I saved a good-quality still of each biker's face and printed two copies of each, along with stills from the night of the attempted arson. One set of stills went into an envelope and got stuck to Mattie's fridge with a magnet. The other went into a file folder. After that I lit one of Mattie's cigarettes and paced. I'd never been able to think while sitting still.

Irish Bob had learned a few things about me so far, but his actions told me something of him, as well. He had taken the time to do his homework; finding out that the funeral was today would have been an easy matter of a Google search but small-time criminals wouldn't have thought to do it. Furthermore, he could have burned down Mattie's house as a message, but he hadn't. Instead he had sent his men here, probably to try and recover his property but likely also with orders to gather intelligence. That told me he was canny enough to take the situation seriously and intelligent enough to realize the value of action based on facts. I puffed on the cigarette and worried some more. Vicious plus canny equaled out to very, very dangerous.

I sighed, reminding myself to stay positive. Bob demonstrating intelligence helped me more than it hurt; it also likely meant he'd be amenable to negotiation and see the value of compromise. I just had to see things his way and make killing all of us the least attractive option available. If I could pull that off, he'd go for it.

"Yeah," I said to the empty room, "now...how on earth do I do that?"

A few hours of pacing and smoking and thinking along with Googling and catching up on some busywork didn't yield any solid answers. I'd just have to wing it.

A car pulled up outside. After glancing at the security feed I relaxed; Elias Hooper's old Buick sat between Shelle's Miata and my Golf. I realized how long it had been, but I had expected their conversation to be either incredibly brief or quite long. Shelle climbed out of the passenger seat, walked around to the driver's side and leaned through the window to hug her father. I couldn't help but smile slightly.

"Once in a while," I said to myself, "I do a little

good."

Upon being let in Shelle was tired and worn, but a soft smile played at the corners of her mouth. As soon as the door was closed she hugged me. "Thanks, Amber."

"No worries," I said. "Talk went well?"

"Yeah." She shook her head. "I learned a lot today."

I sat down, stubbed out my cigarette and waited; Shelle had the look of somebody who wanted to keep talking and the best thing I could do was stay quiet and wait. Sure enough, she sat at the table across from me.

"Before I was born my dad wasn't all that great a guy," Shelle said. "His words, not mine. He used to drink and do drugs and get in trouble with the law. Then he met my mother and got her pregnant with me. That gave him a reason to clean up his act. He started going to church and found God. I didn't know any of that...as long as I've been alive my dad's always been strict, proper. I mean, he never touched a drink, not even after Mom died."

She paused. "When I came out to him it was hard," she said. "I've known what I was since ninth grade, but I was scared to tell him back then because of what Pastor Mason said about homosexuals. But it was just him and me after Mom passed. I couldn't keep it from him. It just...didn't feel right."

I eyed the pack of cigarettes but didn't light one. Shelle didn't smoke and fumes are annoying when you don't. "How'd he take it?"

"Okay," she said. "It was hard for him, but he did his best to understand. Then I got out of the Guard and met Lanie." Her face tightened around a grimace. "Dad hated her from the moment he saw her."

The pieces fell into place. "...and when you saw he didn't like her, you thought 'wow, its okay if I'm a lesbian, just as long as I never actually date a girl'."

"Yeah," she said. "We fought about it, and what he said...it hurt to hear. I took Lanie home and we never went back. He'd call and leave messages and I wouldn't listen to them. Lanie said that was best. Said the church makes people bigots and they don't ever stop being bigots."

"I bet that hurt to hear too," I said.

She fingered her golden cross. "It did," she said softly.

"But Lanie didn't have that one right," I said. "I'd guess your dad, having been a hellion in his younger days, took one look at Lanie and figured her for the kind of girl who'd break your heart."

Shelle nodded. "Yeah. 'Trouble in a Sunday hat' was

what he called her back then. He was trying to keep me from getting hurt, like any father would. He just didn't know how to say it, and I didn't know how to hear it."

"That happens," I said. "A lot."

"I feel bad," she said. "I feel bad for being angry at him all this time."

"You had your reasons," I said. "I'm guessing he could've been better with his delivery. Besides, you were a grown woman, even back then. Who you date or marry ceased to be his call when you moved out."

"I still feel bad," she said.

"And you will, for a while." I reached across the table and squeezed her hand. "But you two made it right. Sooner or later that'll be more important."

"Thanks for prodding me into it," she said.

"You were the one who decided to," I said. "Congratulations on being smarter than I was."

I could tell she wanted to ask, but she didn't and I knew why. She was a private person and recognized a similar quality in me. Instead she leaned back and stretched. "So, you said the biker guy called."

"Yeah." I stood and paced, trying to avoid another cigarette. "Tomorrow, I go meet with Irish Bob. It isn't going to be fun."

"Do you have a plan?"

I reached for the cigarettes. "Yeah," I said. "Walk soft, talk fast and live through it."

"That's a pretty vague plan," she said.

"Has to be," I said on my way out to the balcony.

I stood under the night sky and smoked three cigarettes, one after the other, while I stared at the low moon and contemplated many frightening things, only some of which had to do with murderous bikers and Lanie's death. When I came back inside, Shelle had gone to bed. I rummaged in the kitchen cabinets until I found Mattie's moonshine bottle, poured myself a shot and drank it down. The sudden slug of liquor made me cough. I poured a second and it didn't burn half so bad; the third I barely felt.

After that I reached for my phone, hesitating over the call list before punching up Drake Albie's number. He'd given it to me four months back, but I'd only called it once.

This is a bad idea, irrational me hissed in its corner. *You don't need an awkward brush-off before tomorrow.*

Shut up, I told my insecurities while I waited for an answer. After five rings the phone picked up.

"Amber?"

"Hi," I said.

"Jesus, I've been meaning to call you," he said in a worried tone. "Your name's all over the Internet...something about a murder?"

"It's true, more or less," I said. "Still, don't believe what you read. Nine tenths of it is BS and the rest is shakier than a cerebral palsy patient." I giggled at my own wit. Probably the moonshine.

"Are you safe?"

"Reasonably," I said. *I'm about to go risk my life.* "I just wanted to let you know I was okay." *I want to tell you a lot more and I have for a while and I can't ever find the fucking words.*

"Glad to hear it," he said.

There was a long silence. "Look, Amber...there's something I've wanted to ask you. I'm just...not sure how to."

I took a deep breath, screwed up my courage and stepped off the cliff in my head.

"I miss you Drake," I said. "I miss you at least once a day and it's been that way since you left. I told you it wasn't over between us when you climbed out my window." I closed my eyes. "That hasn't changed."

The pause between my words and his response could have been measured in seconds or years, depending on if one looked at my brain or a clock.

"You read my mind," he said softly. "I miss you too, you know."

"I didn't," I said, "but I do now."

"Wish I could be there," he said.

"I do too." I flopped down on the couch. "I could really go for one of your patented back rubs right about now."

"My patented -" there was a pause, and across two thousand miles spanned by a thread of radio energy I heard Drake Albie blush. "Oh," he said.

"I care about you," I said. "I miss you and I care and I wish you were here. I'm sorry I didn't tell you before now."

"I believe you," he said.

"I need to go," I said, "but I'll be in touch."

"Here's to us?"

I smiled, lying back on the couch and feeling somewhere between sixteen and fifty. "Yes, Drake.

Here's to us." I signed off and plugged my phone in to charge, wrapping myself in Mattie's big quilt.

Put that in your pipe and smoke it, I hissed at my irrational side. It didn't reply.

Chapter 29

When I prepared for my meeting with Irish Bob I went heavy. My situation called for it.

Though my plan was to negotiate there was a chance of things going south and I needed to be ready for everything I had the ability to prepare for.

I started with the most functional clothes I had, what I'd termed my "trouble outfit"; a black turtleneck, steel-toed combat boots and loose jeans I could move in, along with a cowboy-style belt sporting a Celtic cross buckle. I did not put on any makeup and slicked my hair down into a tight French braid, blessing my straight locks for being so easy to keep out of the way. My H &K got clipped to the belt, so I could un-clip it when I got to my location. Carrying a firearm into a bar in Washington is a big time no-no, and using one is even worse. Whether Bob and whatever entourage he brought with him would be foolish enough to go strapped was something I couldn't plan for, but if guns entered the equation I was likely screwed anyhow. Still, there was no sense in trusting a bunch of hard-core bikers to play nice in a fight.

An ASP expandable baton went under my right arm in a homemade shoulder rig that also held a pepper spray container under my left. My four-inch Benchmade folding knife I strapped to my right forearm in a similarly homemade sheath. Ordinarily such exotic holsters weren't great an idea, but belt carry would be useless if I was attacked while sitting and that was the likely tactical situation.

From my trunk came another part of my outfit, a thing I referred to as my "shank coat"; an old military-style bush jacket which I'd added large pockets inside the liner around my lower back and sides. Those were filled with sections from a telephone book. Each pocket had an eighth-inch carbon fiber panel stitched behind it, not quite a trauma plate but together they could stop a knife and slow down a small-caliber bullet.

I walked out into the main room to discover Shelle had been nice enough to make me breakfast. She was dressed similarly to me, in sturdy clothes that could be moved in. "Thanks for the food," I said as I sat down.

"I still say I should be going with you," she said.

"Not a good idea, for three reasons." I tucked into the eggs and bacon. They were bad for my waistline but good for the soul. "One, I set up the meeting with Irish Bob, and that means he's only there to talk to me. You'd be fair game if trouble broke out. Which leads to two...if the Freak Patrol and our drug smugglers are in fact working together that means the drug dealers might still want you dead."

"All the better reason for us to stick together," she said.

"No, all the better reason for you to stay here where there's a security system, a phone line and a closet full of guns," I said. "Thanks to the bikers attempting arson out here any call you make to the police will get taken very, very seriously. I'm pretty sure the bad guys know that."

Shelle digested all that. I could tell she didn't much like it but was prepared to go along. "And three?"

I grinned. "Somebody needs to feed Mattie's chickens."

Shelle nodded. "Okay, Amber. Just...stay in touch, will you? I don't like the sound of this Irish Bob guy."

"There's a reason," I said. "Don't worry, I've dealt with his kind before. I can handle myself."

We traded grips, and I left for the meeting.

It was a fair drive from Mattie's house to the Gridiron Tavern, long enough for me to have and get over a serious case of nerves. I went over the various facts of the case and what I knew of outlaw bikers in my head while I drove, remembering to *properly* check for tails as I got off Whidbey and into Seattle proper. I made one stop along the way for my last bit of preparation; renting a locker at the transit station. The kutte got stuck in there in a plastic grocery bag. I pocketed the key and continued on my way.

Pulling up across the street from the Gridiron gave me a massive case of *deja vu* and I wondered what mad urge had led me to ask for it as the meeting place. Still, there was some advantages to be had; I knew the layout, and hopefully at least one of the employees. I kept my head on a swivel as I crossed the street, scanning for bikes and bikers. I saw neither as I negotiated the crowd of smokers hanging out on the sidewalk and pushed through the front door.

A bar at noon always feels like a sad, sad zoo, and the Gridiron Tavern was no exception. It was all but empty save for a few denim-and-Carhartt clad regulars quietly drinking beer and playing pull-tabs on one side of the L-shaped bar and a group of college kids watching the television from a table crowded with empty plates and beer bottles. A bored-looking bartender looked up when I came in, then looked away. An even more sullen young waitress couldn't be bothered to do that much.

The feelings of *deja vu* intensified when I saw who

manned the security podium. He'd already recognized me. "Well look who's here," he drawled in a voice I remembered well, pale eyes alert and calm.

I smiled. "Kasey, you don't do that corn-fed accent any better than you used to."

"Oughta hear me whistle Dixie," Charles Kasey said. He was a lean, poker-faced man with wiry forearms and thinning stubble for hair. "We gonna have trouble in here?"

"Why would you?"

"I know who you're meeting," he said, "and I know how you like to operate."

I nodded, covering a wince. I should have figured on Kasey and Irish Bob knowing each other. For one thing, they both liked cars and bars. For another, Kasey was a professional leg-breaker in addition to being a bouncer; the population of the truly violent was small and close-knit. "Don't worry, I plan on behaving myself." I glanced around. "Any chance you could disarm them? I know bikers love their knives."

He rubbed a bump on his nose, one I had created the last time we'd talked. "We ain't friends, Amber," he said with a nasty grin. "You said so yourself, remember?"

I handed him my driver's license; under it was a hundred-dollar bill. "Pretty please," I said.

The hundred vanished as if it had never been. "Only to avoid trouble," he said handing me back my license. "You strapped?"

I shook my head. "I'm legal, remember? Guns and bars don't mix."

He nodded. "I'll point you out when they arrive."

"Thanks," I said.

Kasey put his hand on a six-inch steel rod sitting on his podium. "Trouble breaks out, I'll go for you first. Remember that."

I smiled at him and picked out one of the corner booth after a quick scan; due to the layout of the Gridiron, neither party sitting in the booth had to put their back to the door. I hoped Bob would appreciate the gesture. When the waitress approached me, I ordered a Coke and kept my eyes on the door, resisting the urge to fidget and pace. I really wished I could still smoke in a damn bar, but that wasn't doable and I wanted to be at the table when they arrived, so I sat and stewed. The butterflies in my stomach made even sipping the Coke a chore.

The stuttering roar of Harley engines came from

outside, three of them from the sound. I took the locker key out of my pocket and set it under my napkin, the security stills on the table next to me; I did not want to stick a hand out of sight during the meeting and trigger a bloodbath.

Several minutes later three rough men in Freak Patrol kuttes ambled in. I aimed my perception at the man walking front and center as they stopped at the security podium. I watched him surrender his knife to Kasey, and my heart did a little misfire as Kasey pointed me out. The three approached me with a bowl-legged swagger.

Irish Bob Brodie stood two inches shorter than me but at least six broader, belly distorted by a beer gut but the rest of him dense as a fireplug. His dark shoulder-length hair and beard were threaded with silver, his grin a patchwork of dentist's gold and tobacco stains. Most would have had difficulty believing a man barely tall enough to ride a ferris wheel could lead a chapter of outlaw bikers.

I had no trouble with it at all.

The evidence of Irish Bob's nature clung to him like old smoke; I saw it in the pugilist's hands, swinging gnarled and hook-fingered at his sides. I saw it in the way he eyeballed every person in the room, sizing them up one by one and ordering them like an accountant with a ledger. I saw it in the way the two other men, both taller and larger and fitter, walked behind him as subordinates without a trace of resentment.

The world was full of men who would threaten to cut a woman's throat and rape the wound; what sat down across the table from me with a cold little smile was a man who would *do* it. Survival means recognizing the difference before it closes to striking distance and behaving accordingly. My pulse quickened but I kept my face calm and pleasant, left hand sitting three inches from the knife in my right sleeve.

"Irish Bob," I said.

He applied his accountant's stare to me, flinty gray eyes flicking over my every visible inch. I could tell he was aware of my weapons.

"Grab a beer at the bar, brothers," he said in the raspy growl I remembered from the phone. They did without comment. I knew they weren't only here to impress me, but also to guard against other threats. In the life of a man like Irish Bob, violence wasn't a shift gig.

"So," he said to me, "you're the chick who shoots up five bikes, knocks one of my boys out, jacks his kutte, sets a meeting...and then actually fuckin' shows up for it."

"That's me," I said. "The bikes weren't my doing though."

"I know," he said. "Some crazy old bat with a rifle, way I hear it." He leaned back in the booth. "So again I say...give me a reason."

"I'll give you several," I said. I passed over the stills from the security camera. "These are pictures taken by the crazy old bat's security system," I said. "They show members of your MC engaging in several criminal acts. The FBI's been looking for a reason to put the Freak Patrol on their gang list for a while now. Arson, burglary, trespassing...all while wearing colors."

Irish Bob glanced through the photos with a dark expression. "This ain't helping your case," he said.

"The cops don't know about these," I said. "They don't have your boys' guns or the gas cans. Notice also how nobody's pressed any charges yet, and that was on my say-so."

"Really," he said.

"Yeah," I said. "Of course, that could change."

He cocked a bushy eyebrow at me. "You threatenin' me?"

"No," I said. "I'm just laying out my position."

"Which is?"

"Killing me won't get you what you want," I said. "Dealing with me just might."

Irish Bob stroked his beard. "I'm listening," he said.

"There's only one thing I really want out of this from you," I said, "and that's to make sure there's no beef between you and me...or you and Mattie. Your men came looking for trouble and found it. Now we both agree to walk away."

Bob snorted. "Like hell," he said.

"Do you know who Sonny Parnell is?"

He cocked his head, eyebrows coming together in thought. "Militia leader, white-supremacist type, got himself collared in ninety-eight for gunrunning and treason. He's doing sixty-some years at Marion. What's he got to do with anything?"

"Mattie's the one who got him collared," I said. "Parnell put a forty-grand bounty on her head. So far five people have tried to collect." I took a sip of Coke. "Four of the five are in prison cells along with him. One's in a wheelchair, another can't use his right arm anymore."

"And the fifth?"

"Nourishing the cemetery grass at a potter's field in

Seattle," I said, meeting his eyes. "Mattie gave him two in the chest when he climbed through her kitchen window."

"Well I'll be," he said.

"If your boys go up to her house again it won't be bikes getting holes put in them," I said. "Mattie's shot people in self-defense before. She'll do it again if she's pushed."

"Still leaves the books unbalanced," he said.

"Allow me to balance them," I said.

"How?"

I waved to the waitress. "Well for starters...how about a pitcher?"

He blinked and I grinned.

"You pick, I pay," I said. "I did make the date."

The waitress walked up, a pretty blond thing with an apple face. Irish Bob glanced over to her. "Pitcher of Mack & Jacks," he said.

She nodded and scurried off. After she did I took the locker key from under my napkin and slid it across the table.

"The kutte's in a locker at the Seattle Metro station," I said. "Number's on the key. I only took it to get your attention. Whatever we agree or don't agree to, it belongs to you and yours."

Bob stuck the key in a pocket of his vest. "I got a question," he said. "What are you in this for anyway?"

I made sure to keep my voice low. "The people you're running Afghan heroin for killed a girl," I said. "I'm trying to prove it."

"Got no idea what you're talking about," he said, "in either case." The look he gave me all but left a hole in my forehead.

Our pitcher showed up and I let him pour one before helping myself, staying silent until the waitress was out of earshot.

"I'm not trying to get in your hair," I said. "In point of fact I want out of it as quickly as possible. Everything I've showed you, I'm willing to make disappear in exchange for you and I and Mattie agreeing to live and let live."

He took a sip of beer. "The dead girl," he said. "She the one everybody on the internet's all up in arms over?"

I nodded, wondering where he was going with that.

"Figures," he said. "Some hophead white girl gets her neck wrung and everyone loses their shit."

"Wars have been started over less," I said.

"I saw the pictures," he said. "Not surprised somebody dicked her first. Real fuckable, that one."

"Not anymore," I said.

He leered. "Hell, all that means is less dealin' and squealin'."

"To each their own," I said. "I prefer participation."

His leer deepened. "Yeah, I bet you like it on your hands and knees."

I shook my head. "Reverse cowgirl."

"Ha!" Irish Bob guffawed, slapping his thigh and shaking his head in mirth. A couple of people looked over while he laughed long and loud, but nobody stared too much. Irish Bob stroked his beard again, and I did my best not to wilt under his calculating stare. Instead I sipped beer and waited.

"You really willin' to make everything go away if I leave you and the old lady alone?"

I nodded. "The guns and gas cans I keep until I'm done with my case," I said. "If your boys don't hassle me or mine I'll get them back to you. And to sweeten the deal, I'll throw in a freebie." I set my pint aside. "That thing you and your boys aren't into...well, it's good that you aren't. Because if you were it'd be a disaster waiting to happen. The men running that deal are total fucking amateurs and they're about to get busted. Staying away from them, well...that's really smart, Brodie."

"Were I involved," he said, "that'd be a lot of money to walk away from."

"Would it be the kind that spends in prison?"

"A man's got to maintain his loyalties," he said, "and you're still sorta the enemy."

"Yesterday you threatened to rape my esophagus," I said. "Today we're splitting a pitcher and joking about our sex lives. Imagine where we'll all be tomorrow."

He laughed again, harder.

"I don't know what I was expecting," he said after he was done, "but whatever it was, you sure ain't it."

"I left my pearls at home," I said. "Makes it hard for me to clutch at them."

He drained his glass and poured another. "I asked around about you, Eckart. Kasey over there says he knows you. He said you're a ball-busting cunt."

"Aww, I'm touched," I said.

Irish Bob quaffed half his new pint. I took a drink from mine. "But he also said you're a ball-busting cunt who keeps her word even when it's hard to."

"So, we cool?"

He drained the rest of his glass and stood. You've got a deal, Eckart. Thanks for the beer."

"Welcome," I said.

"See you around."

Irish Bob Brodie hitched up his jeans, gathered his two bodyguards in by eye and ambled out the door, collecting his knife from Kasey on the way by. I stayed at the table for thirty seconds in silence, sipping beer and letting my white-hot knot of tension ease.

"I hope I don't, Bob," I said. "I really, really fucking *really* hope I don't."

Chapter 30

There was a Sheriff's cruiser parked in Mattie's driveway when I returned; my heart leapt into my mouth and I jumped out of my car, only to notice Shelle and Deputy Stone sitting on the front porch, a pitcher of lemonade between them. I sighed in relief and walked up onto the porch to join them.

"Afternoon," Stone said. He took in my outfit and raised an eyebrow. "That's a new look for you."

"In some circles this counts as business casual," I said.

He laughed. "I've got some information on that shooting incident."

He opened a zippered pouch next to his arm and took out a plastic bag. In it were two shell casings.

"Found these about a hundred yards from the road," he said.

I bent over and examined them. The casings were substantial, nearly two-thirds the length of my hand, .338 LAPUA MAG stamped on the rear end.

"Never heard of it," I said. "Wildcat cartridge?"

"Military," Stone said. "Limited issue. Snipers use them for special work. They'll hit a target over a mile away and do it harder than a thrown brick."

"You say you found them at a hundred yards?"

"Give or take," said Stone.

"Way too much gun for the range," I said. I bounced the bag in my hand. "Also one hell of an eyebrow-raising signature to leave behind at a crime scene." I shook my head. "No trained sniper would have used these. Your garden-variety deer rifle would've been a better choice."

"Like I told Stone already, somebody wanted to play with their toys," Shelle said. "Military groupies are a dime a dozen."

"We have ourselves a wanna-be," said Stone.

"It fits," I said, hefting the cartridge casings again as my brain gnawed on the facts. "How much is a rifle for these?"

"More than the average armchair soldier can afford," Stone said. "They start at five grand and go up from there. Ammunition's over ten bucks a round."

"There can't be too many rifles like that in the area, and a poseur would be looking to show it off." I looked at Stone. "Canvass the gun ranges?"

Stone grimaced. "It's worth a try and I already

planned to, but gun guys, well...they're insular folk, especially the nutters. They look after each other and don't like giving cops the time of day."

I smiled as current need connected with past encounters. "I've got a place you can start," I said, digging out my pad and pen. I flipped to a fresh sheet and scribbled.

Kurt -

The cop who has this is working with me. He's looking for somebody who tried to kill me and another woman, and may be connected to the bastards who murdered Elaine Hooper (nice girl w/ the old .38 Smith). He's looking for a shooter with a .338 Lapua Magnum semi-automatic. The guy is probably a rich mall-ninja type and might have some Army-looking sorts with him. If you help this cop, it'll help me get the sons of bitches who killed Elaine.

Signed, - Amber Eckart (fellow southpaw, H & K P7 9mm, remembers to use jacketed ammo)

I folded the note and passed it to Stone, along with McConnell's business card. "Give this to Kurt McConnell over at the Firing Line," I said. "It might provoke cooperation."

Stone tucked the note in his pocket without reading it. "Let's hope," he said. "Anyway, I need to get back to work." He finished off his lemonade, tipped his

Stetson and walked down the porch to climb into his cruiser.

As he pulled down the driveway Shelle glanced at me. "You didn't tell him about the meeting with Irish Bob," she said.

"Of course not," I said.

"Why?"

"Stone is the right hand," I said. "Irish Bob is the left. It's best for everyone if neither knows the other is being shook."

Shelle sat and digested that. I could tell she didn't like it but I could also tell she understood it. "How'd the meeting go?"

"We're off the hook," I said, and explained for several minutes.

She gave me a disbelieving glance. "You're helping them? Why?"

"I have to," I said. "If I didn't, the Freak Patrol would still be looking to balance the scales their way and we'd spend the rest of our lives glancing over our shoulders. This way they leave us alone."

"But what if they're the ones who killed Lanie?"

I sat down and poured some lemonade into Stone's empty glass. "I highly doubt they were," I said.

"Irish Bob's a vicious bastard. You said so yourself."

"He's a vicious bastard who knows how to kill people and get away with it," I said. "He's been indicted on numerous murder and conspiracy charges and walked each time. If Irish Bob had wanted Lanie dead, she'd be a missing person right now."

"You sure?"

I sipped some lemonade. "It's hard to solve a murder without a body," I told her. "Irish Bob would have gone for the safe, direct approach. The half-baked suicide cover-up we've got now, that was somebody panicking over an unforeseen occurrence."

My phone buzzed. I took it out and looked at it; a text from Izzy. **BOSS CHECK YOUR EMAIL I FOUND STUFF** I raised my eyebrows and stood, heading for the front door.

Shelle stood likewise. "What is it?"

I held up my phone. "My researcher doesn't cap-smash," I said, and walked inside. I'd left my laptop in sleep mode and a nudge of the mouse roused it up; sure enough, an email from Izzy sat in my inbox. I opened the message.

Boss,

You told me to look into that Brodie guy. At first I didn't find anything more than what we already know, that he's a bad guy and all that. But then I started looking into his gang. I pulled this photo off a biker's forum some Freak Patrol club members frequent. This guy look familiar?

Below it was a picture of five men, standing around motorcycles and wearing biker gear. They were all sporting large black rifles and open beers, posing in various Rambo-style fashions. Three were the genuine article; rough men with dirty clothes who had deferred shaving to various degrees. The fourth Izzy had circled; it was a bald-headed muscle case in a creaky-new leather jacket. I had seen him before.

It was Billy Calloway.

The men were all facing the camera so I couldn't see if they were wearing Freak Patrol colors, but it didn't matter. I recognized Beard, as well as one of the men who'd accompanied Irish Bob to our meeting. In the background was a rambling old beach house, walls the gray of wood that weathers without protection.

The fifth figure caught my interest, mostly because his riding gear wasn't the leather-and-denim kind...but also because he was the only person sporting neither firearm nor beer can. He stood almost out of frame, a square-faced man in his late twenties on the wiry side of average, looking off to his left. His hair was cropped short, army-style.

That picture was taken at a house out on Blakely Island. Calloway's family owns it but doesn't use it for anything. Apparently Billy likes to take his friends up there for beer and shooting. Dumbasses...aren't you always telling me booze and guns don't mix? :P

Anyway, I can't be sure but I think the fifth guy is Peter Weiss...you know, Calloway's high school buddy who's actually IN the army? I found his graduation photo...similar, but it's hard to tell. Photo's in with the other attachments. Tracking Weiss online was a dead end...weird to run up against someone who actually DOES know how to cover their tracks. I couldn't get any further without breaking laws. Sorry. :(

I tracked Billy Calloway's online activity instead, found some shooting forums he's been a member on...he likes to brag and gets banned a lot because of it. And boss, he's a MASSIVE gun freak. The ones in the first picture are all his, and that's just a small sample. I totaled up everything he ever claimed to own or I found pictures of him holding. Here's the list, its crazy-pants.

A series of pictures followed, with a link to the manufacturer and the forum post it had come from. I could name maybe a third of what I saw, but I knew one thing; all of it was military or military-inspired and all of it was expensive.

"Jesus," I muttered.

Shelle leaned over and gave the list a scan. "Glock, Bushmaster, Fianchi, SIG, Accuracy International..." she glanced over at me and smirked. "A gun-bunny with a wallet and a serious inferiority complex."

"Calloway's basically sponging off his mother." I said. "She'd never pay for all this...hell, she *couldn't* pay for all this. You could buy a fucking house for what I'm seeing here." I scanned the list of guns again, stopping near the bottom. "And, check this out."

I brought up a picture; BARRETT 1137 M98 .338 LAPUA was stamped underneath an angular rifle with a skeletonized stock. "Purchased three weeks before Lanie died," I said.

"He'd be itching to try it," Shelle said.

"Yeah." I scrolled further through the message.

The rest of the attachments are how I got to where I got, but here's the basics; Calloway brings Freak Patrol guys out to his cabin for parties and lets them shoot his guns. If he's part of the drug crew that murdered Lanie, it would explain where the money came from to pay for his collection and why he's still part of the ring despite being a big-time dumbass. I'll keep on this, but I think anything else will have to be you.

Keep you posted,

~Izzy

PS: Boss, stay AWAY from this Calloway guy. I saw his posts and ICK.

I sat back. Something nagged at my back brain, a connection I'd failed to make, or something I'd failed to do. I scanned through the pictures again, thinking maybe the clue was there, but nothing jumped out at me. Izzy's post-script was disturbing enough on its own; she was a denizen of the Internet back alley. Nothing bothered her, at least nothing on a screen.

Shelle sat down next to me. "So what now?"

"I don't know," I said. "Now we have a solid tie from the Freak Patrol MC to Billy Calloway, and a tenuous one to Peter Weiss, but it isn't enough. Everything else I've got rests with a small-time drug dealer who likes teenage girls." I sighed. And I'm feeling like I've missed something. I hate that feeling."

"Well, somebody needs to go feed the chickens," Shelle said, pulling a bandanna out of her jacket and tying it over her cornrows. "Care to help?"

"Be out in a sec," I said. "Need to give my researcher some instructions."

She nodded. "See you out there." She got her shoes and headed out the door while I composed a response to Izzy.

Great work, I typed. *I wish we had something more...wish we could get call records for go-phones but*

-I stopped typing.

"Phones," I said aloud, taking my hands off the keyboard as my brain's nagging turned into screaming. "Phones," I said again. "This whole thing started with phones."

I stood up and paced, email forgotten, lighting up a cigarette as my brain did its thing.

Lanie's attempt at blackmail had started with her getting Calloway's number from Harkness because she remembered Calloway's bold talk about a big drug deal. *Whoever bought it took more than the usual set of precautions to prevent being made* was what she had told me about that number.

"Calloway isn't smart enough for that," I said to the empty room.

I turned back and read Izzy's email again. *Tracking Weiss online was a dead end...weird to run up against someone who actually DOES know how to cover their tracks.* I remembered a similar experience when I'd tried to build a profile on him.

"Phones," I muttered.

Calloway wasn't smart enough to take precautions with a disposable cell...but Weiss certainly was.

Flying on impulse, I fumbled for my cell and punched up Harkness' number. It was answered after two rings. "Yeah?" Harkness' voice was a dead husk. I flinched at his tone, but only for a second.

"Harkness, its Amber Eckart. What number did you give Lanie when she asked?"

"I told you, Calloway's," he said.

"Yes I know, but what was the actual *number* and where did it go?"

"His condo," he said. "Dumbass gave drug dealers his home number. Look what is this -"

"Give it to me, please. It's important."

He rattled off the digits and I scribbled them down. "Thanks," I said.

"What's this about?"

"Phones," I said, and hung up.

With all the emotions flying around Xander Harkness' hospital room I'd forgotten to ask him for the actual *number* he'd given to Lanie, so I could compare it to the one in her second cell. I'd taken it on faith that they were the same because it made sense that they would be. Just to be sure I dug out Lanie's disposable cell and compared the call record to the number I'd just scribbled down. They didn't match. I cursed and resumed pacing.

"So okay, she has Calloway's number but she doesn't use it? That doesn't make sense, how'd she get the other -"

I smacked my forehead as I realized the other thing I'd forgotten to check.

"Oh, you dumbass," I muttered.

The other thing was the call record on Lanie's *regular* cell, so distracted had I been from the discovery of her sad, sad video farewell to her loving wife. I dug out Lanie's regular phone and hastily scrolled through the call history.

Sure enough, there it was; Calloway's condo number. I did a quick Google search and confirmed that, too.

"You clumsy impulsive *twit,*" I snarled at myself. "You need to go back to school. No, you need to go back to slinging drinks at that fucking trucker bar, getting your butt pinched and your cleavage ogled. And stay there. For the next twenty years." I smacked my forehead again, harder. "Seriously, how could you *miss* that?"

I sucked down more of the cigarette and went back to pacing, doing circuits of Mattie's living room and blowing smoke while I ranted to the four walls and put it all together.

"Okay," I said. "Okay. Lanie falls off the wagon and has a fight with Shelle, who's struggling to keep their heads above water on one income and a mountain of debt. Lanie wants to make things right, she said so in her video. Only she's a junkie with a record and no marketable skills who's never held a job for longer than two months in her life."

More cigarette, more pacing, more ranting, more facts.

"In a fit of desperation, she remembers this steroid-pumped asshole who talked a big game about a drug deal he wanted to set up, back when she was living with Harkness."

"Billy Calloway is a dumb shit-talker with an inferiority streak a mile wide, and Lanie's hot, high and probably dressed skimpy on top of it, looks like a whore but isn't. He talks up who he is, but she isn't interested in blowing him or whatever. He gives up and forgets about the whole thing, but she doesn't. A year later, she needs money to help her wife and figures if he's as dumb as he acted that night his balls ought to easily fit in a vise for a nice steady stream of payoff cash."

I stubbed out the cigarette and lit another.

"But he wasn't as far up the food chain as he was claiming, oh no. Lanie, she calls him and he goes running to his boss, who gives her another number and some instructions through Calloway. Lanie realizes how deep she's gotten, collects Shelle's gun, buys a go-phone, tries to play it smart."

My smoke cloud had grown impressive as I paced back and forth in it.

"Only she'd already made the call to Calloway on her regular phone, and that, well shit that's what really sealed her fate. Calloway's boss gets his condo's phone records, and the boss, who knows how to find people, runs down Lanie's cell, and that has her home address linked to it..."

"Then the bad guys grab her with the intent of working her over, maybe paying her off once and letting her go which is why they kidnapped her instead of making her OD. Yeah, that *was* their plan."

I stopped pacing as the last piece fell into place.

"But Lanie, she'd gone and made Calloway look stupid," I said, voice brittle. "Calloway really *really* doesn't like women already... and there's Lanie, all alone and out of it on dope, and he wants revenge on her."

I drew on the cigarette with a shaking hand.

"So he took it," I said into the silence and smoke. "He took it, he went too far and everybody panicked."

I grabbed for pen and paper to write it all down before it left me.

"Amber," I heard Shelle's voice from outside. "I need a hand. One of the chickens got out."

"Damn," I muttered. Mattie's chickens weren't usually escape artists, but Shelle wasn't a farm girl. I grabbed my coat and took the door at high speed.

"They aren't hard to catch," I called, "and after we're done I've got a -"

BAM.

Something struck me in the chest and a buzzing hum filled my ears. Every muscle in my body exploded in blinding pain. It hurt worse than the sudden uncontrolled spill I took off Mattie's porch and into the hard-packed grass of her lawn. I groaned through gritted teeth, tasting blood as hot lightning coursed through my body.

The buzzing ceased along with the pain. Hands rolled me over onto my back. I couldn't move and could barely breathe but I could see the silhouettes of men standing over me, painted against the clouds in the afternoon sky.

"I agree," I heard a smooth male voice say, as one of the silhouettes leaned down and a bag was slid over my head. "You should have stayed a waitress."

Chapter 31

Like a lot of people in my profession I'd seen videos of big tough men taking a zap from a Taser and cringed while watching. That it hurt had been obvious from the footage. What I hadn't known was that you stay totally conscious while fifty thousand low-amp volts throw a donkey punch at your central nervous system. I was left helpless and pain-wracked and acutely aware of both problems.

Hands patted me down and took my weapons away; baton, pepper spray, knife and pistol, they all were plucked off my person one by one. They took my keys and my phone as well, patting me down to make sure I didn't have anything else. They rolled me back over and stripped me out of my shank coat. All of this happened while my fingers twitched and the hot dampness in my jeans turned cold and clammy.

I hadn't expected a Taser shot to make me pee my pants either. That was almost worse than the pain.

Fuck you all, I tried to snarl. A groan bubbled out of my mouth along with drool. *Okay, never mind, shoot me please.* I was absurdly grateful for the bag over my head. I didn't know how many people were observing me and I didn't want to.

"Amber?" Shelle's voice, tightly controlled. "Amber can you hear me?"

"She'll be fine," the smooth-voiced man said.

"I better check her," a younger man said. "She hit pretty hard."

"Nghhmrrrrg," I said as somebody felt my neck for a pulse, then probed about my head for injuries. My eyes squinted as the bag was lifted and a light was shone in them.

"She's okay," the younger man said, pulling the bag back down over my face.

"I'm sorry Amber," Shelle called out. "They got me from behind."

"Shut up," the smooth voice again. "You two, restrain her before she comes around."

My wrists got crossed behind my back and a hard narrow band was closed around them with a sound like a zipper; cable ties, the heavy-duty kind that come from an office-supply store. We'd done our own wiring at the office and I was familiar with them. A second tie fastened my wrists to my belt loop.

"Still can't believe Billy don't have any rope." A fresh voice, heavy with scorn. "Big-time tactical-minded dude with a motherfucking *boat* and he ain't got any spare rope."

"Deal with it Sammy," another man said. "Let's just get this done."

"Indeed," Smooth said. "Give me a quick search of the house. Get the phones, this woman's laptop and any papers you find. Make sure all the doors are closed and the security system is reset. Be quick."

I sighed. In a few short minutes the bad guys would have all the evidence I'd spent a week building up, in some cases risking my life to do it. I'd still have all the internet trails and some of the paper but neither would be all that great in a courtroom. Without Lanie's phones in particular I'd have a hell of a time. Assuming I lived long enough to get to court.

Arms looped under my elbows and hoisted me to my feet. Control of my body had returned, but I had a bad case of vertigo and couldn't stand right. I stumbled into somebody, and he cursed.

"Jesus, she pissed herself," Sammy said. Inside the hood my face flushed hot with embarrassment.

Stairs came next, along with a chorus of boots on wood. I could negotiate the staircase with difficulty and a little help from my captors, who kept me from tumbling over the railing as we went down the switchback stair. Mattie's property had a dock, I remembered. A big dock, big enough for most private boats.

My heart pounded. *Focus,* I told myself.

Conversation swirled around me as we descended the stair; I couldn't see faces thanks to the hood, but I could do a head count, hear voices and names, match them up. Sammy was a tenor with a California accent who swore a lot. Steve had a deep voice and didn't like Billy. Luke, the one who had medical skill, was young and ill-at-ease. Then there was the erudite one all the rest called Sir, who gave the orders. Peter Weiss at a guess, though there was no way for me to be sure.

Shelle didn't speak again but from a count of footsteps I knew she was in the same group I was. I breathed a sigh of relief; while we were together we could work together if we got an opportunity. It wasn't our moment right then, bound and hooded and watched by many as we were. Placidity was my friend; it stood a chance of making my captors drop their guard. I kept my steps wobbly and made them help me more than I actually needed. I even threw in the occasional whimper; the more the bad guys thought I was weak, the likelier they were to underestimate me later.

Mattie's dock was the floating variety, and I knew we'd stepped onto it when the ground moved this way and that beneath my feet. Ten more steps and I was picked up and frog-carried into a boat like cargo. I went limp and made them work harder out of sheer spite.

"You get 'em?" Another voice, higher-pitched than the rest.

"Yeah," one of my carriers - Luke - muttered. "Taser really put her out."

"That's bitches for you," the first said. "Act all tough until something really happens to 'em."

My mouth went off before my brain could stop it. "You'd know," I called out. Heavy footsteps sounded in my ears, drawing close.

"The fuck did you just say?" The voice was right in front of me.

"Leave it alone, Billy," Luke said.

"No way." Someone grabbed a handful of my hair through the bag and wrenched my head around. "Bitch I wanna know what you just said."

"You heard me the first time," I muttered.

"Hey I got an idea," Billy said as if it had just occurred to him. "Why don't we strip-search this one? I mean, make sure she ain't hiding anything."

My stomach clenched in terror but my mouth

wouldn't stop. "You're single, right?"

Pow. My world flashed red and orange as a shovel-sized hand struck my face.

"Jesus Billy, cut it out." Luke again, angry.

"I say we strip her down," Billy said. There came the rasp of a drawn knife.

"No, Billy." The voice rang with command; Smooth again. "Let her go and take the wheel."

Billy shook my head once and then dropped it. "She's gonna regret that shit," he said as he stomped away.

My ears rang and blood dripped over my lips from my nose, but I was otherwise functional. Luke and my other carrier sighed and walked me to another part of the boat.

"Watch your mouth around him," Luke said. "He'll hurt you."

"I hate to ruin his fun but this isn't the first time I've been black-bagged," I said.

"Then you ought to know better," Luke said as I was put down. The deck was hard and wet, smelling of fish and engine oil. A warm weight was set down against me; Shelle, from the shape.

Sammy spoke next, rough and loud. "Okay, you

girls know what this is?" I heard a familiar ratcheting sound.

"A baton," Shelle said before I could make an off-color remark.

"Good," Sammy said. "You try and stand up or crawl anywhere and I'll break both your legs with it. Understand?"

I nodded and guessed Shelle did likewise for the footsteps retreated without any more tough-guy talk. I wriggled around until I was in a sitting position. Conversations happened off to my left, too far away for me to make out over the slosh and crash of the surf.

"Shelle, you okay?" I kept my voice low.

"I should be asking you," she said, quietly.

"Other than a headache and a rather noxious hit to my dignity I'm fine," I muttered. "What happened?"

"They just came out of nowhere and got a gun to my head. I didn't get Tased." From her tone she was about as embarrassed as I felt. "How the hell did they get in the barn like that?"

"Dunno," I said, "but I feel like an idiot all the same. We should've moved after the first attack." Between my lack of a coat, the chill breeze and sitting on a damp deck the body heat leached out of me. I shivered.

Shelle wriggled about until we were sitting against each other. I was grateful for her body warmth. "What do we do now?"

"What they tell us, for now," I said. "We're bound, blind and outnumbered. Resistance will just get us hurt more."

"Plan on taking that advice?" Faint humor crept into her tone.

"Sorry." I shrugged as much as being bound would let me. "I get snarky when my life is threatened. It's going to get me into trouble one of these days."

"I bet." She wriggled, and so did I. Cable ties weren't the most comfortable of bracelets. "Where are they taking us?"

"Simple," I said, as the boat's engine roared and I felt the sensation of movement. "They're taking us to where we can be disappeared." Spray whipped across my face as hope grew fainter and fainter. "They're taking us to Calloway's Blakely Island cabin."

Chapter 32

The boat ride would have been pure misery even without the threat of death hanging over my head. Within twenty minutes I was soaked and half-frozen with numb hands and a terrible crick in my shoulder from being bound. The bounce of the hull against the waves sent shocks up my spine every five seconds. It didn't take long for my back to knot up in rebellion. Shelle had it just as bad as I did and she didn't complain, so I kept my discomfort to myself.

Five minutes into the voyage Luke came to stand guard over us. I guessed it was him from the lightness of his step and the awkward noises he made when settling in across from me. That precluded any plotting between Shelle and me. I took a deep breath and tried a different tack.

"So Luke," I said, "what's a nice guy like you doing in a place like this?" I made my voice loud enough to be heard by him over the ocean and the motor, but hopefully not loud enough to be heard by anyone else.

"How do you know my name?"

"That's what everyone's been calling you," I said.

"You better stay quiet now," he said.

"They're going to kill us, Luke," I said. "Not much motivation for me to stay quiet."

"Nobody's killing anybody," Luke said, voice heavy with unease. He wanted his words to be true but he knew they weren't. I heard as much in his tone. "W - my boss just needs you out of the way for a while is all."

He'd almost said 'Weiss', which was more information I hadn't possessed before talking. I swiveled my head to where I thought he sat.

"I don't think you believe that, Luke," I said, keeping my tone soft, level and gentle. "Were you there when Elaine died?"

"That was an acci-" He cut himself off. "Lady, just keep quiet okay?"

"Did they tell you the same thing about Elaine, Luke? That she'd be okay as long as she was good?"

A hand seized the front of my shirt and jerked me partially upright. "Listen lady," he said, "I don't want to rough you up but I will if you don't shut it." His words were harsh but his tone didn't match. Underneath his bravado his voice shook like a leaf.

"I believe you, Luke," I said softly. "I believe you don't want to hurt anyone. You know first aid...are you a medic?"

He dropped me and leaned back. "Quit fucking with me," he said.

"There a problem?"

"No sir," said Luke.

"Then I don't see a need to speak with the prisoners," Weiss said.

"Aye sir." Footsteps receded in my hearing; Luke, moving out of earshot. It was half a victory. I leaned closer to Shelle so we could speak.

"That worked better than I thought," I whispered.

"What did?" She kept her voice as quiet as mine and just as close. "I heard you...you sounded like a counselor or something."

"That was what they call social engineering, and it's more effective than people realize," I said. "Luke's their weak link. He's one of our hopes of getting out of this in one piece. I don't think him being here is entirely voluntary."

"You're trying to con him into helping us?" She made a disgusted noise. "That only works in the movies."

"Second rule," I said. "Play every card you're dealt. Besides, you see a better option?"

The engine noise diminished and the boat slowed;

there was a chorus of jargon and the creak of footsteps on fiberglass. We arrived at the dock with a loud *thump* and a tooth-rattling shake.

"Came in too fast," Shelle whispered. "Dumbass can't even drive a boat worth a damn."

I smothered a chuckle as we were hoisted to our feet. There followed the same frog-carrying ritual that had gotten us onto the boat, only in reverse and with one wrinkle; a hand gave one of my breasts a squeeze as I was transferred from boat to dock. It wasn't Calloway's, and that told me volumes about the sort of men I'd been caught by. I bit my lip hard enough to taste blood and kept quiet.

A gun barrel prodded me down the dock and along a gravel path; I guessed a twelve-gauge shotgun from the size of the circle in my back. Around me wind rustled trees and whipped surf to a low crashing, punctuated by the cawing of seagulls. In other circumstances the sounds would have been peaceful, just another day at the beach. A door creaked and I was shoved forward. I stumbled over a lintel and the nature sounds quieted but did not disappear. A hand pushed me to my knees and someone hit the ground next to me; Shelle, from the familiar fabric against my arm. Five seconds later the hood was yanked off my head. I blinked and looked around.

I was in a dirt-floor shed made from old rough boards, bare except for a ramshackle table in one corner. Wind whistled through knotholes in the wall and made cold patches on my wet clothing. The only illumination came from a flashlight held by somebody off to my left. I glanced that way and it netted me a vague shape, a bad case of flash blindness. I blinked and looked away.

Standing across from me was a man of medium height in jeans and a foul-weather jacket, black balaclava hiding his features. He had a Beretta automatic in his right hand, finger off the trigger. Spare magazines and a holster adorned the web belt around his waist. The gun wasn't pointed at me, but from the sure way he held it I could tell that'd change in a fraction of a second if I made it necessary. I stayed still.

"Ladies," he said, "let me explain the reality of your situation. We are detaining you against your will for our own purposes...something I'm sorry to say you made us do by continually poking your nose into our activities. We have no intent of harming you, at least any more than you make necessary."

"Bet you said the same thing to Lanie," Shelle spat. "Think I'm stupid enough buy that shit?"

"Hmm." Weiss tapped his chin with a fingertip, and I did not like the way his hazel eyes flicked from me to Shelle. "Billy," he said, "come in here, if you would."

A bomb went off in my stomach as the man with the light came into view. William Calloway was huge, his form so buried under a superstructure of bulging muscle he scarcely looked human. He wore black fatigue pants and a sleeveless exercise top; the top showed off tanned rippling arms with a bad case of acne. Like Weiss, his head and face were covered by a black balaclava. An angular automatic was holstered at his right hip, a large survival knife and spare magazines at his left. My pulse pounded in my ears as he looked Shelle and I over like a pair of competing products.

"Tell me," Weiss said. "Which one do you prefer?"

"The black one," Calloway's voice came from behind the light. "I don't like chunky bitches."

"Feeling's mutual," I said without thinking.

Calloway took two steps forward and backhanded me into the dirt. Tied up I could do nothing except roll with it slightly, and doing so didn't help much. I hit the ground hard, left side of my face on fire from where he'd struck me. I struggled into a crouch. By the time I had Calloway stood in front of Shelle.

"Get up," he said to her, staring. The look in his eyes all but left a grease spot behind. She didn't move.

He kicked her leg.

"Get up, I said."

I got my weight over the balls of my feet and prepared to fight as the specter of an ugly nightmare settled into the room. I couldn't do much, but there was no way I would sit there and do nothing at all.

Click. A safety catch was released behind me and a cold metal circle nudged me in the skull. I froze, bile at the back of my throat.

"Watch," he said, "and stay still." There was a pause.

"Billy, as we discussed."

With one hand Calloway seized Shelle by the face and dragged her upright. She grunted but didn't scream. The muscles on his forearm rippled as he lifted her until they were eye to eye. Her feet dangled at his ankles. Slowly he squeezed her cheeks until her lips parted and leaned forward until their noses almost touched. Shelle twitched and writhed, eyes wide with terror and outrage.

Calloway spat in her mouth.

Shelle's body twitched, but she didn't move otherwise. With lazy deliberation Calloway set her down and stepped back. She stood rigid but did not move or gag or shift her gaze from her tormentor.

"Oops," said Calloway.

Shelle stayed stock still. The anger in her eyes could have boiled a pound of lead.

"If you both behave," Weiss said, "in a few hours you will be released. If in any way you do not I will let my friend in here, shut the door and ignore all the sounds I hear. He'll be allowed to do anything that strikes his fancy and after that, whatever is left of you two will be sunk out in Puget Sound. Is that clear?"

I was silent. Weiss prodded me with the Beretta. "Say it."

"Crystal," I said.

"Good. Billy, with me."

Calloway hitched up his gunbelt and leered at Shelle before walking out of the shed with a chuckle. Weiss followed him out, shut the door and latched it, leaving us in darkness. I listened for any further sounds but heard none. Their footsteps diminished on the path until all I could hear was the whistle of wind through the boards.

Only then did Shelle sink to her knees, gagging and hacking. I didn't say anything. I couldn't think of anything to say.

"So," Shelle muttered at the dirt, "that's the guy."

"Yeah." I wriggled closer to her. "I'm sorry," I said. "At least half of that was my fault."

"He'd have done it anyway," Shelle said.

"I'm still sorry."

"He's going to be sorrier," she said. I didn't doubt it.

"We need to get out of here," I said. "Weiss is full of it. There's no way they plan on letting us go."

"No kidding," she said. "Question...how?"

"I'm working on it," I said. We had a small measure of luck; according to my ears no one had padlocked the door and they hadn't left a guard, two facts that told me something big had distracted our captors into making mistakes. It was our time to act, if only I could think of a way to. I shifted my weight from side to side, trying to get comfortable as an irritant kept distracting me with its poking. I stopped wriggling as annoyance became a bolt of inspiration.

"Oh, you beautiful little irony," I said with a grin nobody could see.

Shelle looked over. "Got a plan?"

I pushed myself closer to her. "Yep."

"Lay it on me."

"Cable ties," I said, "can be shimmed open. I do it all the time at work when we have to replace network wiring. It saves on buying new ties all the time. Opening them is easy, you can do it with a screwdriver."

"Sorry," she said with grim humor, "I don't have one on me."

"No worries," I said, grin widening. "I'm carrying a substitute, but you'll have to get at it."

Shelle's voice flickered with excitement. "Okay, how?"

"By tearing open my bra with your teeth," I said.

"What?"

Chapter 33

Attempts at escape from captivity always involve a fair amount of discomfort and ours was no exception. The loose underwire that had been nothing but an annoyance all week had been transformed by events into a crucial tool.

I couldn't get at it, but Shelle could.

It had taken me a few moments to explain what I was talking about; I was a 38D and bras with underwires were required equipment, but being slender Shelle hadn't worn anything with one in her life. I stood braced against the wall. Shelle knelt in front of me, face level with my stomach. For a few seconds she hesitated.

"Just like we talked about," I said.

"Can't believe *this* is how we're escaping."

"Try not to think about it," I said.

By her own admission Shelle had been intimate with one woman in her life. Mine were only the second pair of breasts she'd been close to and while what was about to happen wouldn't be sexual I could imagine the awkwardness. I compared it to a situation requiring me to unzip a strange man's trousers with my teeth at age sixteen and then fetch a key tied to his dick the same way. No matter how necessary doing it might have been it would've been a mortifying moment; for Shelle, it was the same situation. Jokes wouldn't serve.

Shelle took a deep breath, got my turtleneck between her teeth and slowly stood up, taking my shirt with her as she moved. I shimmied my torso from side to side in an attempt to help the damp fabric over my skin. It caught in a few places but between cotton stretching and Shelle straining we got it over my chest. She pushed the hem of my shirt into my collarbone and I tucked it under my chin.

"Okay," she said, "now where is the thing?"

"Right side, near the bottom where the cups come together," I said. "There should be a bead of plastic sticking out."

"You do realize I can't see, right?"

"Feel around," I said, kicking myself for the accidental innuendo. "Trust me, it's there."

She bent over and stuck her face in my cleavage. The resulting position reminded me of making out with my first boyfriend under the bleachers in high school...a comparison I was sure Shelle could live without hearing.

"Little to the left," I said. She moved that way, and I felt a tugging along the underside of my right cup.

"That it?" Shelle's voice was muffled by a closed teeth and my chest. I tried not to think about what would happen if some of the men came to check on us just then.

"That's it," I said. "Get a good grip and pull."

Slowly she drew her head back; in the semi-darkness of the shed I caught the gleam of metal. A second later the underwire came all the way free.

"Got it," Shelle said through clenched teeth.

"Well played," I said. "Now, we pick some cable ties."

A good deal of clumsy shuffling and wiggling followed as we got into position, as close as possible to a large knothole so we could have as much light as possible. I knelt behind Shelle after getting the underwire into her hands so I could guide her picking attempt. We did have a piece of luck; when they had bound us they had simply wrapped one tie around our wrists then fastened that tie to our belt loops with another. It meant we only had to pick one tie to be free, which was good. The clock was ticking.

"Okay, you're trying to get it inside the square

part...there's a tongue in the tie that sits against the serrations in the strap. If you can push that back, I can pull the tie apart."

"Understood," she said.

It took three false tries. The underwire wasn't the easiest tool in the world, however the curve in it did make Shelle's picking attempts easier than a straight tool. Finally I saw her get it in the slot. "Push," I said, and got a grip on the loop around her wrist with my teeth.

She pushed. I tugged my head back. The tie came free.

"MacGyver ain't got nothing on us," I said, spitting the tie out of my mouth and standing.

It was the work of a few seconds for Shelle to get the tie off my wrists. I worked my arms back and forth and rolled my shoulders, trying to get some of the cricks worked out. Shelle moved to the door, and so did I.

"Second problem," she said.

I gave the door a speculative glance. It was poorly made, with a full quarter-inch of dark sky showing between the frame and the first board on the door. "Pass me the magic tool," I said.

"Think you can pick it?"

"Nobody padlocked it," I said. "It's just one of those bar-latch thingies." I slid the underwire through the crack in the door frame. "You take position over by that knothole and make sure nobody's coming."

She did so as I wriggled the underwire around the corner, endeavoring to hook the bar's handle. I found it, but the resistance overcame my ability to push.

"Never mind being a lookout," I said. "Come over here, get your fingers under the door and lift."

She did so. "What am I trying to do?"

"Hinges are loose," I said. "You're taking tension off the latch."

She nodded and did as I'd instructed. At the same time I pushed the underwire against the latch mechanism. With a soft squeak the latch slid aside and the door drifted open. I caught it before it could go too far and pulled it back mostly closed.

"You beauty," I said to the underwire and kissed it.

"I take it you're not throwing that bra out," Shelle said.

"Are you kidding? When I get home I'll fucking frame it."

I put an eye to the narrow slit of open air and gave

the shed's surroundings a scan. The shed sat at the base of a switchback gravel driveway that time had rendered mostly dirt; above that was an old house I recognized from the photos, with a sharply peaked roof and large windows. The lights were on but the curtains were drawn. A deck jutted out from the house; there was a man standing on it facing the water, identifiable by the orange glow of a cigarette. I sighed. The tactical situation sucked but it could have been worse; the man on the balcony was practically looking right at us, but because of darkness and his night vision ruined by the coal of his smoke we stood a fair-to-middling chance of making it to the dock.

"Shelle, how fast can you start that boat?"

"Depends on if the keys are in the ignition," she said.

"Shit."

We'd been lucky enough already and that would've been tempting fate. "Okay, so we try to slip by the house and find a neighbor, call the cops."

Shelle shook her head. "Amber, we're on an island in the middle of nowhere. I worked these waters back when I was in the Guard...there aren't any cops out here, just one honorary sheriff who isn't given a gun and is probably in bed right now. We'd need a radio, not a phone, and even then it'd be hours before anybody would show. We're on our own."

"Wonderful," I muttered, giving the road a second look. If we hugged one side the man on the deck would have to look straight down to see us. "Stay behind me, and walk soft."

"What's the plan?"

"Take the fight to them," I said.

"That's all but suicide," she said.

"Is there a second choice?"

"I guess not," she said.

Shelle in tow, I crept along the near edge of the road. On impulse, I stuck the underwire in my jeans pocket.

Chapter 34

Halfway up the first switchback I had second thoughts. Serious, fear-driven second thoughts about just how Shelle and I could ever hope to engage Weiss and company and survive. My pace slowed as I contemplated the odds. 'Ridiculous' didn't begin to cover them. I glanced back at the boat.

We should run, said my fear. *You'll be shot,* said my pragmatism.

Behind me Shelle crept silently, mouth a grim line, eyes narrow. I could read the expression; she knew the odds just as well as I did but was willing to try them anyway. I turned and continued up the path, making sure not to step on any twigs. My eyes had adjusted to the darkness; by the light of the moon our surroundings were painted in shades of purple and black, but I could at least see the difference between a dry twig and a blade of grass. I nudged the twigs out of my path with my toe and crept on. My blood roared in my ears like an angry giant.

The slope around the second switchback was dotted with trees, giving us something to dart between as we approached the cabin. Twenty feet off I called a halt; Shelle and I crouched behind a gnarled fir and made our plans.

"Okay," she whispered, "now what?"

"I'm making this up as I go," I whispered back.

She pointed at a second structure that sat perhaps thirty feet from the main cabin. "Check it for weapons?"

"Lead on."

The figure on the balcony kept smoking and watching the water but didn't turn his head; I knew because I kept nervously eying him the whole way across the yard. It was grass, not gravel, and indifferently trimmed. We did the last fifteen feet to the garage in a commando crawl. Our pace slowed as we negotiated the worn gravel around the garage; it was heavy with broken glass and shell casings, evidence of many a drunken shoot-em-up party. Packing crates sat here and there, crowded with empty bottles. Creeping across glass-strewn gravel without making noise is impossible; I cringed at every clink and clatter we made even as my rational side knew nobody in the cabin could've heard us.

The garage smelled of mold and rust and old oil, indifferently lit by moonbeams shining through a yellowed windowpane. In it we found the mummified corpse of a seventies Jeep, a gleaming

Jet Ski, three gallons of gasoline and the remains of various gardening tools, most of which were unsuitable as weapons; despite what Hollywood preaches there's a reason why you don't see soldiers packing a garden hoe. I sighed and we sorted through the jumble as quietly as we could. Shelle found herself an old ax handle. I selected a rusty pipe wrench.

Shelle shook her head. "You realize they've got guns."

"I'm aware," I said. "We need a game-changer."

I gave the garage one more scan, taking in the dusty Jeep, the gleaming Jet-Ski with its engine half taken apart, the gas can, the three bottles of Penzoil sitting next to it -

- And then I grinned. "Oh well why not," I said.

"You got an idea?"

"Hang on." I crept back outside and fetched the largest bottle I could find, an empty Seagram's half-gallon along with a greasy cork. Shelle followed, obviously confused. I grabbed the gas and oil and filled the bottle half-full with them, two parts gas to one part oil. Shelle raised an eyebrow as I put my thumb over the bottle's mouth and shook. "Give me your bandanna," I said.

Shelle shucked her headscarf and passed it over. "Is that what I think it is?"

"Molotov cocktail," I said, dousing the cloth in gasoline and wedging it into the bottle's mouth along with a cork, making sure the cloth protruded into the bottle's neck. "Favorite of oppressed peoples everywhere."

"You sure it'll work?"

I hefted the thing in my hands. "I know the recipe," I said.

Shelle crouched by the garage door and gave the house a slit-eyed survey. "They teach you how to do that in security school?"

"Of course not," I said. "That'd be dangerous and pointless, not to mention against the law."

"So where did you learn?"

"I dated an anarchist in college."

"Was that dangerous?"

"No," I said. I used my sleeve to wipe down the sides of the bottle; any gas left on it would burst into flame and ignite me rather than the target, something I didn't want.

Shelle grinned. "Pointless then?"

"Not really. Where do you think I learned about makeup sex?"

I gave the cabin's layout a scan, looking for open windows and doors, avenues of escape. Most of the windows big enough to allow for human egress opened out on the front deck, but there was a small opening next to a narrow back door which looked a promising target for a firebomb; given what I could see of the place it must have opened up onto the main living area. I turned back to Shelle.

"Okay," I said, "what we need to do here is make sure we know where they're going to come bolting out. I toss this through the open window. That cuts off every escape but the front deck with the big openings - windows and doors and such. You get up close to the deck, then run around the corner and play whack-a-mole with anyone who comes out. I boogie around front to help just as soon as Mister Molotov makes an appearance."

"Let me throw it," Shelle said. "I lettered in girl's softball in high school."

"Really?"

"Easier than explaining to your dad you're a lesbian," she said.

I bit back a laugh; adrenaline had made us both goofy. Digging in my back pocket I found the one thing I'd realized the bad guys hadn't found and confiscated, a pack of paper matches. I passed them to Shelle. "Give me a thirty-count after you see me disappear around the corner of the house."

She nodded, passing me the ax handle and taking the bomb and matches. "I hope this works."

"Me too," I said, handing her the pipe wrench. "If it doesn't..."

Shelle hefted the wrench. "If it doesn't, we do something different."

I grinned. "When we get back, you want a job?"

She smiled back. "No shit?"

"If we live," I said, offering her my hand. "Call this an interview."

She set the wrench aside and gripped my hand, squeezing it hard the way people do when they're about to face death together. "Fair deal."

No more words were exchanged. There wasn't anything else left to say. We picked up our weapons and got to work.

I darted between trees and got up next to the house, ax handle in hand and pulsing lava in my veins, a feeling just to the left of sickness and not quite to the right of arousal. I could feel every nick and grain line on the wood in my hand, every rock and blade of grass on the ground through my shoes, every thread on the clothes against my skin. I was *alive,* in the way skydivers and soldiers and drug users feel when they're on the cusp of their chosen calling. As I circled around to the balcony I heard voices from inside.

"...should've called us by now," Sammy said.

"Perhaps there are problems." Weiss, tense and trying not to be.

"This is bullshit," Sammy said. "We do a dozen shipments for this asshole and then he fucks us over."

"There is no evidence of that," Weiss said. "Still, we pay enough to be informed. Billy, call Mister Brodie."

I took another half-dozen steps. This close I could hear the creak of wood as the man on the balcony shifted his weight. I thought about why Irish Bob might not be returning calls and smiled tightly. In the drug world, distrust bred distrust. I was not at all surprised Brodie had heeded my warning, although the timing gave me a thrill.

"I just called him," Billy said.

"Call him again," Weiss said.

"Hey," Sammy said, "you guys hear that?"

Nobody got a chance to reply. There was the crash of glass and a loud *woof* like somebody blowing in my ear, followed by a chorus of startled shouting and the roar of sudden fire. I abandoned stealth for speed, dashing up onto the balcony with my club at the ready.

A man blundered into me trying to come down the same stairs as I ran up them. I rammed the end of the ax handle into his stomach and he doubled over, cursing in surprise. A follow-up blow to the side of his head made him fall backwards and hit hard, sliding down the steps with a rattling thud. I continued up the staircase and around the corner.

Darkness gave way to bright orange firelight; a group of men stood around Calloway's massive form thrashing on the deck with a burning leg. Everyone crowded around him with makeshift implements to put out the fire, oblivious to their backsides. I stepped up behind the closest man and took a swing at his head. Him bending over at the last minute made him take the blow on his shoulders; wood splintered and my target grunted with the impact, dropping to the deck as half my club broke off and flew into the night.

Yelling erupted around me like a volcano, and the fight was on.

One of the figures whirled and made a fast grab for his belt - Weiss, reacting as his training dictated. I bashed him in the hand just as it slapped on the grip of his Beretta. He screamed and doubled over. Impact, sweaty hands and slimy wood conspired to make me lose my grip; my club tumbled away.

Someone tried to grapple me, hands sinking into the flesh of my arms I got hold of his belt and collar and threw him into Weiss in a desperate variant on an Irish whip. One man struck the other and they both went down in a tangle, cursing. I drove a fist into a nearby body, ducked a blow in return, caught the next in the short ribs and forgot how to breathe.

Out of nowhere I took a hit to the face. With a bright flash and a *crunch* more felt than heard I collapsed to the ground, hot agony exploding from my nose and replacing my vision with whirling stars. Another blow rebounded off my skull and brought me back. A man straddled me on his knees, hammering punches at my head. I leaned forward and sank my teeth into the front of his jeans. My teeth crunched and a piece came off one incisor when it hit a zipper, but something separated between my jaws; my target screeched and recoiled, falling to one side. I rolled over, grabbed his head and bounced it off the wood of the balcony as hard as I could before scrabbling to my feet.

Billy Calloway stepped in front of me, three hundred pounds of blind rage with black steel clenched in one fist, smoke wafting off his burned fatigues. I dodged his clumsy stab and backed off in a crouch, casting about for a weapon.

A beer bottle lay rolling on the deck; I snatched it up and bashed it against the ground and the bottle became a shank. I got a fencer's grip on the neck and slashed at Calloway as he closed. He cursed and leaped backwards, flailing at me with his knife as blood flowed down his forearm. I ducked his blade and bored in to do damage, odds and pragmatism drowned out by primal savagery. There was more blood in his big ugly body and I wanted to *see* it -

BOOM.

The roar of a twelve-gauge is unmistakable and incredibly loud when it happens up close. It hit my senses like a splash of ice water. Everybody ducked and looked for the source of the noise, including me.

Rachelle Hooper stood in the cabin's doorway, backlit by the spreading flames. Cradled in her arms was an angular semiautomatic shotgun. I recognized it; a Fianchi SPAS-12, one of Calloway's many exotic toys.

"Nobody move," she barked.

Nobody did. Weiss, Calloway and a younger man I didn't recognize stood in half-crouches with hands raised.

"Drop that fucking knife," I said to Calloway, voice shaking with rage. He did, blade clattering on the wood of the deck. I wanted to stab him anyway and it was work not to. I wiped blood and spit off my chin as I surveyed the scene; one man lay whimpering and curled in a fetal ball with hands clamped around a blood-drenched crotch, quivering in agony.

I spat out a tooth fragment. *Remember my name, motherfucker.*

The Fianchi shotgun was massive in Shelle's arms, but the barrel sat rock-steady. "All of you take off your web belts. Do it slowly."

They complied. I spied Weiss' Beretta lying on the deck and swapped my shank for it, racking its slide as I scooped it up. A live round flew out of the chamber but I ignored it; better one short than nothing in the chamber. My fingers flexed around the unfamiliar grip as I frantically tried to recall the one time I'd handled a Beretta M9.

Shelle took two slow steps out onto the deck, cabin burning brightly behind her, eyes locked on Calloway's face.

"So," she said, "you're the guy."

Chapter 35

The adrenaline that had been so helpful during the fight drained out of me. I swayed on my feet, my nervous system giving me its delayed report with interest. My nose was several degrees off straight and a swollen lump of agony. One of my front teeth was missing half its mass. My left knee wouldn't bend without complaining. My left arm wasn't responding to commands as it should have; I had to shift the automatic to my right hand. One eye wouldn't open all the way. My guts were hollow, legs wobbly like I'd just run a marathon. I wanted to breathe deep and gulp down air, but every time I tried my ribs twitched and it was work not to double over coughing.

With the ebb of battle fever came the return of sanity and reason, and I didn't care for the transition at all. What I'd done and what I'd tried to do made me faintly sick.

"Oh my *god,*" the man I'd bit moaned, "somebody fuckin' *help!*" The crotch of his jeans was wet with blood. I swallowed back bile.

I stayed on my feet and kept the gun pointed at the bad guys, though. The fight was over but the situation wasn't resolved. It was required of me to keep it together a little longer and so I did. *Focus,* I told my battered self. *Focus and get out of this so you can fall apart later.*

With a wave of my gun barrel and a few muttered commands I ordered the ambulatory survivors to pick up the unconscious ones and get the hell off the soon-to-be-burning porch, having the younger man - Luke, from his voice - collect the semi-conscious individual I'd clobbered on the way up the stairs. He moaned and twitched as Luke picked him up but didn't do anything otherwise. I ordered Luke to strip the man's gun belt and toss it at my feet. I picked it up and slung it over my non-functioning left shoulder. Behind us the burning cabin crunched as part of it collapsed. It would be a total loss; I hoped the fire wouldn't spread to the surrounding forest, but there was little I could hope to do if it did.

Shelle was silent during the move. After we got onto the grass her eyes focused on Calloway. "Get on your knees."

"Shelle," I said, "you can't -"

"Quiet Amber," she said. "It's my turn." She gestured with the shotgun. "Get on your damn knees."

Calloway complied, eyes wide and frightened.

"Look, I -"

"When I want you to talk, I'll ask," Shelle said, barrel trained on his face. "You know who I am, don't you? Nod if you do."

Calloway nodded, eyes moist with tears.

"So you know I've got plenty of reason to want you dead," she said, voice as calm as a person ordering coffee. "Lanie. You hurt her. You raped her. You choked the life out of her."

The banked righteousness in her eyes that had been so striking upon meeting her flared to full life.

"And hey, look where we are," she said. "There's no law for miles. I could shoot you dead, Billy Calloway, and make up any story I like. The courts would let me off if I told it right. Amber would back me up...hell, you did a number on her while she was tied up, and you threatened to do worse, and you would've done it if you'd gotten the chance. She knows that, just as well as I do. She'd have no reason to contradict my story if I blew you away just now. You hearing me, Billy?"

Calloway's eyes leaked tears and his nose ran with snot. "Oh Jesus, oh God -"

Shelle prodded him in the chest with the shotgun. "I told you," she said. "When I want your words I'll ask for them."

Calloway fell silent. She turned to look at Peter Weiss.

"You give the orders here," she said. "I'm going to ask you once...why did you kidnap my wife?"

In the orange firelight Weiss' eye sockets were pits of darkness. "You sure you want me to answer that?"

"I advise against fucking with me," said Shelle.

"As you wish," Weiss said. "Your wife tried to blackmail us, Mrs. Hooper. She had enough knowledge of our operation to worry me." He shrugged. "I acted in self-defense."

Shelle's eyes narrowed. "By having her raped and killed?"

Weiss frowned. "No," he said. "My plan was to pay her once but also put enough fear into her that she wouldn't become a recurring problem."

"You expect me to believe that?"

"Believe the mess her death caused," Weiss said. "Once you've comprehended that you'll understand why murdering her wasn't what I wanted to do."

"How much did she ask for?"

"Five thousand a month," said Weiss. "Until she told us to stop. Her words, not mine."

Shelle's resolved flickered like a candle flame, but it didn't gutter out. "So what happened?"

Weiss shrugged. "Billy happened."

For a long moment Shelle was silent, hands shifting on the shotgun's polymer grips as she assimilated several ugly truths. At length she spoke.

"I get it," she said to Weiss. "I don't like it, but I get it. You'll pay your own tab for what you've done, in time."

Her eyes returned to Calloway; his face glistened with the fluids of fear. "But you...no, I'm not so sure I can live with what you did. Not when you can blubber to the feds about a drug deal and get easy time in exchange. Not when you can run to your rich mommy and beg for a lawyer good enough to cut you that deal."

Shelle shoved the barrel of her gun into the base of Calloway's throat.

"And not," she snarled, "when all I have to do is pull this trigger to send you straight to Hell."

Snot dripped off his chin. "Jesus, I can *explain-"*

"I don't want you to," said Shelle. "I've got no reason

to let you live and there's nothing you can say that will change that. I want to kill you, Billy Calloway. I want to and there's not many around who would blame me for doing it."

I kept my pistol trained on the rest of the men, but it almost wasn't necessary. Like me they were transfixed on the tableau playing out before them. I couldn't stop Shelle from doing whatever it was she planned on...and I didn't have enough kindness to want to. Calloway sobbed, eyes shut tight as he hung his head. Shelle prodded the barrel underneath his chin and lifted, forcing him to meet her eyes.

"Look at me when I talk to you," she said.

There was the soft patter of liquid on cloth, barely audible over the roar of the fire behind us; it was too dark to see the evidence, but I knew what it was from; Calloway had wet himself in terror. There was a *click* as Shelle set the safety, a soft clacking of cloth straps on metal as she stepped back and put the shotgun at port arms.

"I want to kill you," she said, "but I won't."

Calloway looked up, fear forgotten in a childlike moment of confusion.

"Why?"

"Figure it out," said Shelle.

I glanced over from minding the rest of the bad guys. "You done?"

"Not quite."

With a savage motion Shelle slammed the butt of her shotgun into Calloway's face with a sickening crunch. He flew backward off his knees, hitting the ground like a sack of cement. When he moaned, blood and spit and tooth fragments dribbled out from between his mangled lips.

Luke scrabbled forward before I could tell him to stop. He pried open Calloway's mouth and gave the damage a look.

"Jesus," he said to Shelle. "You broke his damn jaw."

"Oops," she said.

Behind us another part of the burning cabin groaned and collapsed. I ignored it as best I could and kept my pistol trained on the bad guys. Luke moved towards the other downed man. I leveled my automatic at him.

"Stay still," I said.

His jaw took on a hard set. "Lady, I'm a qualified medic and I'm treating the wounded. If you're gonna shoot me for that you go right ahead."

I sighed and nodded. "You win," I said, "but keep your movements slow." I gestured at Calloway's groaning bulk. "And that piece of shit can fucking well bleed a while."

"Nothing I can do for him anyway," said Luke.

I glanced at Weiss. "You've got a phone that works out here," I said. "Hand it over."

With his non-broken hand he dug into his jacket pocket and came out with a bulky yellow-and-black device. "Satellite phone," he said, tossing it into the grass at my feet. I picked it up and examined it; there was only half a charge but that would be plenty for one call to the authorities.

"Shelle, you take Weiss over that way," I said. "I'll babysit Luke here while he doctors these two. If your man gives you any trouble at all, blow him away. We'll sort out our story later."

"You got it," she said, flicking the safety off on her shotgun. "All right, walk," she said to Weiss. "And keep your hands behind your head... remember, I've got no reason to care about you."

"I understand my situation," he said, and let himself be prodded out of earshot.

Luke worked first on the man I'd clobbered on the stairs, straightening out his neck and checking his pupils. "He's alive," said Luke, "and likely to remain so. If that matters to you."

"It does," I said, relief loosening my legs. Now that I wasn't fighting for my life I had no wish to kill anyone.

"So again I ask...what are you doing with these people, Luke?"

With sure hands Luke unzipped my other victim's trousers and examined his injury. "What are you doing trying to stop us?"

"Earning a living," I said.

"Well there you go," he said, bitterness in his voice.

"Drugs, bikers, dead girls...that's a hell of a living," I said.

"Says the lady with my friend's blood running down her chin," he said, applying a compress to the injury I'd made with my teeth. Half-delirious, his patient moaned but did not move. "Sammy here will live also, but he ain't gonna be happy about it."

I flinched at the truth but didn't rise to its bait.

"He was on top of me trying to pound my face into hamburger," I said. "I did what I had to do to stop him."

"Means you don't have the right to judge me," Luke

said.

I hefted the automatic in my right hand, making sure I had a firm grip. "I'm not judging, Luke. I'm asking. I *know* why I'm here...I'm asking you why *you're* here."

"Reasons," he said, tying off the bandage with more force than necessary. His patient whimpered and Luke winced.

"They made you deal with Elaine's body," I said. "Didn't they?"

Luke looked away. "Shut up," he whispered.

"You knew what needed to be done, and none of them wanted to touch it, so you had to do it," I said. "Wash her and dress her and hang her up like a piece of meat so when she was discovered it would all look right."

"Shut your fucking face I said!"

"Not this time," I said. "You still see her, don't you?"

"*I didn't hurt her,*" Luke hissed.

"No. No Luke, you didn't. You just helped put her in a place where she could be hurt, left her alone with the person who did hurt her, and covered up how she got hurt so nobody else would find out." Behind me the burning cabin groaned and collapsed some more, the flare of orange light revealing the tears in Luke's eyes.

"That bothers you, doesn't it? You can tell yourself you never touched her, because you didn't," I said. "You have already, I'm sure. You've said it a thousand times since it happened, every time you try and sleep. But it doesn't help, does it? You still see her face."

"They *made* me," Luke said, voice carrying more edges than a sack of broken glass.

"That's not true, Luke. You made choices. That's why you ended up doing what you did." I gestured around at the firelit forest. "Here and now, you've got another choice. You can serve the dead girl who haunts you and help give the men who hurt her what they deserve, or you can stay silent and do time right next to them, knowing its nowhere near enough."

He didn't respond.

I pointed at the man he had bandaged with the pistol in my hand. "This isn't combat," I said. "These aren't soldiers. They're drug dealers and rapists and murderers, Luke. You're helping them."

He looked up at me, eyes shining.

"You're right, Luke. I'm the last person on this earth

who has the right to judge you, and that's because I know a thing or two about making ugly choices from shitty options. But whatever devil you side with, look it in the eye and take its measure. "I smiled sadly. "You'll have to live with it a long, long time."

I flipped open Weiss' satellite phone as Luke sat on his haunches and wrestled with his decision. "You'll have a few hours to think it over," I told him as I dialed.

"Don't need them," he said softly.

I pressed the phone to my ear. After only one ring a familiar deep voice answered. "Deputy Terrence Stone."

"Are you ready to be happy?"

"Jesus Christ, ma'am...where the hell are you?"

"On Blakely Island," I said.

"What're you doing out there?"

Playing fetch," I said.

Chapter 36

It was a welcome thing when the cavalry showed up.

Two Coast Guard patrol boats and one full of cops from three different agencies all swarmed Calloway's property in chorus of flashing lights and jargon. I handed my commandeered pistol to one cop and fell into the arms of another when my legs decided they were done working; he carried me down the docks to a waiting gurney. I thanked him at least eleven times. He had a nice voice and a calm demeanor and if he'd carried me into a chapel I'd have married him without a second thought. He left me in the care of a hatchet-faced lady medic who clucked over my injuries and handed me an ice pack, disappearing to fetch more involved medical equipment.

I bummed a cigarette from a nearby sailor when I saw him light one. He passed it to me with a conspiratorial wink and lit it for me with a wooden match. The tobacco tasted awful but I smoked it anyway, wondering at the sparkles in my vision as my head grew light and fluffy. My medic came back and gave me an indignant snort.

"You shouldn't be smoking that," she said.

"I know," I said, taking a deep draw.

She set down her bags of gear, plucked the cigarette from my mouth and flicked it into the water. I was too tired to stop her, nor to object when she pushed me into the gurney and strapped me to it. "I can see you're going to be one of *those* patients," she said.

"Fair enough," I mumbled. "I can tell you're going to be one of *those* nurses."

Our relationship didn't improve as she examined me. I did, however, get a full list of my injuries and was quite surprised.

The fight had left me with two cracked ribs, one chipped tooth and a badly broken nose, as well as a sprained knee and some breed of serious shoulder injury her dockside probing couldn't sort out. Along with those came the normal bruises and contusions of a knock down drag out brawl - black eye, skinned knuckles, and so on - all of which sang their outrage into my nervous system. I lay there, oozing and throbbing and trying not to think about how much worse it could have been, how lucky I was.

I tried not to think about other things too, but there was nothing to do except lie there and that's where the ugliness found me.

I closed my one good eye and squeezed the blankets in my fist as the reality of what I'd done took hold.

No, the reality of what I'd wanted to do - and then it wasn't the blanket under my fingers any more, but a round piece of greasy glass. I wasn't staring at my eyelids; instead it was Calloway's face as I came at him with a broken bottle in my hand and murder on my mind. I tried to tell myself it was over what he'd done, but it hadn't been. I'd wanted to kill him, and it hadn't been about justice. It hadn't even been about winning.

It had been about *wanting to kill.*

I'd heard plenty in my college years about how humans are animals at heart; there was always some Nietzsche-loving snark running that line. Lying there with tears on my face and horrible guilt staining my heart, I wondered how many of those smug bastards ever ended up finding themselves on the wrong end of the proof. I opened my eyes and stared at the stars. They were cold and distant, twinkling against the blackness, and I counted them as I struggled to reconcile with an ugly truth about myself. It wasn't easy and I knew I'd be at it a while.

"You all right?" A deep male voice, off to my left.

I jumped, encountered the gurney straps, cursed and looked over. Stone stood on the docks near me, wearing a long green poncho. I summoned up a crooked grin, putting my grim ruminations on hold. They'd be there when I had time to get back to them, I was sure.

"You tell me," I said.

"I heard the reports on the radio," he said, taking a few steps closer. "You look better than I thought you would."

I laughed, then coughed on broken ribs and bruises. "No jokes, please."

Stone smiled and tossed a glance back down the dock, to where Luke sat flanked by two Coast Guardsmen. "That medic kid just got done spilling his guts," he said. "We've got the location on their current shipment of drugs, how they've been getting them into the country, how they're being distributed, names, times, dates...hell, he's even offered to go to a buy for us while wearing a wire." He shook his head. "In twenty-two years as a police officer I've never seen anyone flip so hard."

"I was pretty sure he would," I said. "He didn't have the temperament for the trade."

"How'd you parse that out?"

"Woman's intuition," I said. "He ever tell you why he was doing it in the first place?"

"His mother," Stone said. "She's got Alzheimer's, requires constant care. Her insurance ran out and his VA benefits wouldn't pick up the slack."

"So he needed the money," I said.

"According to him it was supposed to be a one-time thing." Stone snorted with grim humor. "Guess he didn't know that once you're in, you're in."

"He does now," I said.

"Yeah. Anyhow, my department has more arrests to make than we have officers to make them. DEA's already come knocking. So have Seattle PD."

"Tell me you get the credit," I said.

"Course I do," Stone said. "Who do you think Luke Brighton spilled his guts to?" He grinned.

"I guess now is where I leave by the back door," I said.

"Sorry, ma'am." He patted me on the shoulder, the one that wasn't all bound up. "You and your client have a lot of testifying to do."

"Shit," I muttered.

"Thanks to you interpreting private investigation as a contact sport," he said, "you have officially gone from working this case to being a part of it."

"Oh come on," I said. "I brought you the bad guys, just like I promised."

"Yes you did...with colorful actions such as Molotov

cocktails, assault rifles, Internet conflagrations and God only knows what else." He grinned again. "The court system would like a word with you."

I lay back on the gurney with a tired sigh. "I should've stayed calm and remembered the damn paperwork."

Stone favored me with a quizzical look.

"Some advice I gave to one of my employees," I said. "He has a bad habit of trying to walk in my footsteps."

Stone chuckled. "Either he needs to grow some common sense or you need to set a better example."

I started to giggle but cracked ribs grated against one another and the attempt ended with a cough and a wince. "You make me laugh one more time and I'll sue for police brutality."

"See you in court," he said with a tip of his Stetson.

"Stone," I said before he could leave. "Let me guess...the DEA, they want to take over the case against the Freak Patrol MC, Am I right?"

Stone turned back and nodded. "They sure do," he said. "Interstate drug action, not much I can do about it."

"Want a piece of advice?"

"Sure," he said.

I grinned. "Let them."

"Why?"

My grin deepened. "Woman's intuition," I said.

He waited for me to elaborate. I didn't. As he walked away Shelle approached, backlit by flashing lights and wrapped in a gray wool blanket. Her face was a blank slate, eyes wide and hollow. I smiled at her, displaying my broken tooth.

"How you holding up?"

She shook her head. "Again, I really ought to be asking you that question."

"My injuries are obvious," I said. "They hurt and they'll heal."

"Same here," she said.

"You sure?"

"I don't know," she murmured.

"Find out more than you wanted to?"

"Yes Amber, I did. I didn't think I would, but I did."

She stared out at the churning water, seeing times and places I couldn't. My body was a place of pain and I wouldn't have traded shoes with Shelle for anything.

"I got into this to find justice for Lanie," she said, "but now I wonder if I should have." A tear rolled down her cheek. "I just keep going back to the last time we fought, that time where I said to her...I said 'Lanie, enough with this drug shit, you need to get a *job,* we need *money,* why are you wasting your life like this?'"

I didn't say anything. Shelle kept talking.

"Now I know she was murdered because she tried to squeeze money out of drug dealers." Shelle's eyes found me, wide and full of uncomprehending hurt. "She knew the risks of screwing around with these people, and she did it anyway. Christ, Amber... *Why?"*

"It was all she knew," I heard myself say, as cops muttered jargon at each other and a rich man's cabin burned down on the hill behind me.

Chapter 37

I'd never liked hospitals, especially when I was the patient; my trip to the one in Oak Harbor did nothing to change my opinion. The staff were friendly and courteous, but the act of being forced to lie in bed wearing a gown that didn't close across my butt while nurses examined me and doctors pronounced my condition was both humiliating and irritating. I kept my temper, mostly by being too exhausted to exert myself.

Shelle stayed with me for the first day; it passed in a haze of pain medication and sleep. On the second day, I was buried deep in my Kindle, doing my best to keep the plot straight on Parker's latest adventure. I blessed the ability to operate an e-reader with one hand, as my left arm was still bound up in a sling. The doctors weren't sure what was wrong with it, but their tone was always ominous when they spoke to me about it. I tried not to worry.

In the early afternoon someone rapped on the door frame. I looked up. It was Mattie, a backpack over one shoulder and a mischievous grin playing about the corners of her mouth. "Hiya kiddo," she said.

"Glad to see you," I said with a smile.

"Glad to be free to be seen," she said.

My smile became a grimace. "I'm sorry about you getting arrested."

She shrugged and pulled up a chair, setting the backpack down at her feet. "Don't be," she said. "That was Rick Strandell being an ass, and I plan to make sure he pays dearly for it."

"I've already arranged something."

Mattie shook her head. "Dearie, you know me. I always settle my own accounts."

"I'm putting a lawyer on his heels," I said. "What'd you have in mind?"

"I convinced Stone to run for Sheriff next election," she said with a wink.

I leaned forward with interest - or tried to. Various bits of medical junk got in the way and I restrained a curse. "I thought you said he didn't stand a chance," I said.

"That was before you dropped the big case in his lap," said Mattie, beaming. "It's all over the papers how Deputy Terrence Stone, acting on his own initiative, managed to bust an international drug ring operating right here in our own backyard, along with closing an ugly homicide case Rick Strandell had prematurely ruled a suicide."

"You gave the *Whidbey Times* the story," I said softly.

"Don't worry, I left you and Shelle out of it," she said. Out of habit she reached for her pack of Camels before staring at it and sighing. "Between the popular credit Stone's earning and your pet lawyer butt-fucking Sully Strandell's son in civil court, Stone just might win a majority vote. With the proper campaign manager, of course."

"Wait," I said. "You?"

Her eyes sparkled behind her glasses. "Dear, you forget. My doctorate is in political science."

I shook my head, remembering a few other facts; Mattie was almost as well-connected as Izzy online thanks to a prolific second career as a blogger, likewise well-respected in traditional journalism for her work on the militia groups, and absolutely relentless once she got something between her teeth.

"Sullivan Strandell," I said, "doesn't stand a freaking chance."

"And neither does his worthless little shit of a son," she said.

I giggled, accepting the twinge of pain from my ribs as the price of doing business.

"Apparently Ricky boy's mother never warned him about Hell and scorned women," I said.

"Or he didn't listen, which would be my guess." She stood. "Anyway, I do have things to get to today. I just wanted to give you the news, as well as bring by a few of your personal effects." She nudged the bag with her foot.

I hooked the backpack with my good arm, set it on my stomach and unzipped it. Inside were the weapons Weiss and company had confiscated, including my H & K automatic and spare magazines. "Oh man," I said. "That's a relief. How'd you get these?"

She shrugged. "The Coast Guard found them amongst the other weapons in Calloway's boat. Stone recognized them and asked me. I said they were yours. Since they weren't really evidence he gave them to me to give to you. I figured hell, you might need them in here."

I reached out and squeezed her hand. "More debt to pay forward?"

With her other hand Mattie patted me on my uninjured shoulder. "I know you will, kiddo. Get well, okay?"

"As soon as possible," I said.

After Mattie walked out I picked up my Kindle again. I had just found my place when I phone buzzed. I sighed and set one device aside for another. It was the office.

"Talk to me," I said.

"Boss, it's me," Julian said, voice bright with excitement. "Are you sitting down?"

"Lying down, actually," I said with a smile. "I'm in the hospital, remember?"

"Oh right," he said. "Sorry. Anyway, guess what...Ellison Shipwright's lawyers didn't take the out-of-court settlement."

"They didn't?" That got my attention because it was unusual. Corporations were almost always eager to get their ass out of the courtroom.

"Nope," Julian said. "They went after Ray Copeland *and* his doctor instead, sued the crap out of them for damages. I just got out of court a few hours ago."

"And...?"

I could hear Julian's high-voltage grin through the phone connection. "The judge nailed them both to the freaking wall, boss. Izzy found a string of other workman's comp cases Copeland's doctor had signed off on, and I ran them down - all bullshit. That doctor, he'll be owing money on the settlement he got slapped with until...well, forever."

"Good work, both of you," I said with a grin. "I bet

Mark Ellison was pleased."

"That isn't the word for it, boss. He wouldn't stop hugging me after we got out of court, and just now two of his kids stopped by with a bottle of whiskey. They said it was for us...it looks expensive."

I laughed; I'd been given things on occasion by exceptionally grateful clients but never a bottle of liquor.

"Old-school gratitude," I said. "What's the brand?"

"I can't pronounce it," he said.

"Means it's expensive," I said. "Spell it out for me."

"Okay." A pause. "L-A-P-H-R-O-A-I-G. The label says 'aged thirty one years'."

"Wow," I said. "I owe you a bonus check."

"Cool," he said. "What should I do with the whiskey?"

I grinned. "Put it in the safe we keep our case files in. We'll save it for when I get back."

"Really?"

"Yeah. Every detective agency needs an office bottle." I paused. "And Julian...good work. You're a badass detective now, for real."

"Thanks boss," he said.

"By the way, I never asked," I said. "How did the date with Nightingale go?"

"Uh...perilous," he said after an awkward pause. "Amanda's...um, really *intense*."

I restrained a laugh. "Met your match?"

Julian's voice grew soft. "Maybe, boss."

We exchanged goodbyes and I signed off. After that I dug into the backpack for my pistol. While rooting around I also discovered a pint of Mattie's moonshine. I smiled and shook my head. "I have a lot of paying forward to do," I said to myself, sliding a magazine into my pistol and working the slide. Both were difficult to do one-handed but I managed. The pistol went under my pillow, the rest of the hardware back into the backpack.

Touching the weapons brought a shiver to my spine. I thought of the hot rage I'd felt during the fight, and a few other things as well; how I'd damn near torn a man's balls off with my teeth. How close I'd come to killing another man with a piece of glass just because I'd wanted to. How good it had all felt, how natural, how *right*. I closed my eyes and lay back on my bed, the lump of my H & K a not-quite-comforting presence beneath my pillow.

There was the rustle of cloth against skin; I slid my hand under the pillow and opened my eyes. One of the nurses stood in the doorway.

"Oh," she said, "I'm sorry to wake you."

"I wasn't sleeping," I said, taking my hand off my piece and out from under the pillow. After giving her a second look I saw she had a gift basket in her hand, a cellophane-wrapped cornucopia the size of a large-breed dog. "What's that?"

"It showed up at our front desk, addressed to you," she said, setting it on the chair next to me. Curious, I plucked the card off the basket's handle and opened it. Under the fluffy Hallmark sentiment was a message scrawled in thick block letters.

Great job, and get well soon!

O.O.U.

-Crawley Boone

I blinked, confused; neither the message nor the name held any familiarity.

"Are you sure this is for me?"

"Like I said, it was addressed to you. Your room number and everything." She smiled brightly at me. "You're a popular person today."

"Sometimes that's a good thing," I said, fingering the card.

Chapter 38

The next nine weeks went by in a pain-wracked blur.

I thought I'd known busy times before but I was quite decisively proven wrong by the avalanche of two court cases, three branches of medicine and the voracious media machine, all vying for my time at once. The resulting collisions of interest and scheduling would have been hilarious, had I watched them happen to somebody else.

My shoulder turned out to have a torn rotator cuff requiring surgery and three painful weeks with my arm resembling half a bridge, so complete was the cast. My front tooth wasn't just chipped, but broken in half by its forcible encounter with the zipper on Sammy's jeans. My nose had to be re-broken and set again, as well as encased in a massive cast taking up half my face. Then there was slowly waiting for my cracked ribs to heal, along with the inevitable and incredible lingering body aches resulting from getting pummelled by people who knew how to do it. I swore and took pain pills and leaned on my friend group for help as much as my pride would allow.

The various legal entities wanting my attention

were totally unconcerned about my medical needs; court dates happen when they happen, and like the medical field courts don't give a damn about the havoc they wreak on the rest of your life. I gave opening testimony a day after the shoulder surgery, and thanks to a scheduling mishap I had a root canal at three pm and a deposition at five. Sounding cogent and reliable while looped out on Percocet is a trick and a half. So too is making yourself understood to a court stenographer with an upper lip half-paralyzed by Lidocaine.

I got through it all, however. Professionalism is being pounded into hamburger and going to court anyway. I took a certain perverse pleasure watching the opposing attorneys cringe when I took the stand half-covered in bruises and bandages. I was certain my appearance added a few sympathy points in the jury's eyes, in the drug trial and Andersen's civil case against Rick Strandell.

Thanks to Andersen's intern and her leak the media had a field day with both cases; when I wasn't in court or getting prodded by doctors I was inundated with phone calls; every courtroom I stepped out of had a pack of reporters waiting outside like starving dogs. In an absurd coincidence I was glad for the sorry state of my face. It meant that no pictures or video footage of me would be familiar to anyone who spotted me after my injuries healed. It was a small, backhanded silver lining in a thundercloud of suckitude. I ducked the cameras where I could and muttered "no comment" a lot at the ones I couldn't, declining any and all forms of interview that came over the phone. Every time it rang I thought of ovaries and eyeballs. Doing so helped a little, but not much.

As is the way of all things, eventually the situation settled down and I got a day to myself. I spent it visiting Lanie's grave.

I wasn't sure why I felt the need to go, but I found myself standing in a rain-soaked cemetery with a bouquet of roses and staring at a plain marble slab set into a wall of the same. Shelle had only been able to afford a crematory nook. Lanie's ashes were contained behind a placard which read:

ELAINE LAUREL HOOPER

BELOVED WIFE

BORN FEBRUARY 24 1994 - DIED MARCH 3 2014

"MAY YOUR SONG ALWAYS BE SUNG"

I set my bouquet against the cold marble. "Wherever you are, I hope you're comfortable."

"Me too," a voice said behind me.

Xander Harkness stood a few feet away, wrapped in a faded green overcoat and hunched over a medical cane; one foot was clad in the dirty white plaster of a cast. His face was gray and gaunt, long hair unbound and limp against his scalp. He gestured at my left arm's sling and smiled.

"Aren't we a pair," he said.

"Occupational hazards," I said.

"I know." He hobbled closer. "Been following the case since I left the hospital...ain't much else to do but watch television, laid up like I am."

"I envy you," I said.

"Don't," he said. "It gave me too much time for thinking."

Harkness pulled flower from under his coat and laid it on Lanie's marker; a stargazer lily, wrapped in green paper and clear plastic.

"I find myself coming up here when I can," he said. "Don't know why." He glanced at me. "I didn't expect to see you again."

"Didn't expect to be seen," I said.

"So what happens now, Miss Private Eye?"

"DA's talking about seeking the death penalty for Calloway," I said.

"Yeah, I heard that too." He grinned; it made his face resemble a skull with skin stretched over it. "Y'know, I heard once that Washington's the only state in the union with an active gallows."

"It's true," I said. "Death-row inmates can choose between that and lethal injection."

"The needle or the noose," Harkness said. "The law does occasionally have a taste for poetry."

"I doubt either will happen here," I said. "But we can be glad of one thing, Calloway's got nothing to trade for easy time...thanks to one of the others ratting him out on everything, the prosecution -"

"I don't give a damn," he snarled.

I stopped talking, brought up short by his sudden fury. Harkness placed a bony hand on Lanie's marker.

"We came up the same way, her and I," he said, voice quivering with tension. "Small town, parents who feared Christ more than cops, fucking at-risk teen boot camps where they starve you for being different and beat you when you say you're hungry." His mouth paled as he pressed it into a thin hard line. "It's why she trusted me and it's why she screwed me over." His nails scraped against the cold marble of Lanie's tomb. "I shouldn't have blamed her for doing that, you know. When you're from that place, you learn how to be hard."

"The people who killed her, they're going to pay," I said. "Justice won't bring Lanie back, but -"

"Justice." Harkness laughed, a sharp humorless caw that belonged in a raven's throat. "Such a strange word, justice. Calloway might've strangled Lanie, but he didn't kill her, oh no. She was dead before he got a rope around her neck, before that nice girl who married her ever even met her...hell, before I even laid eyes on her, she was a corpse. She'd been dead inside a long time. So, you tell me...you got any *justice* for her, really?"

Xander Harkness and I locked gazes just then. I resisted the urge to take a step back, so intense was his stare. The false fronts were gone and in their place burned something bright, raw and naked like tender skin long hidden from the sun. It half-frightened me, but once I saw it I couldn't look away.

"You go ahead, Miss Private Eye," he said. "You help put that bastard Billy Calloway in a concrete box along with all his friends - or send him to choose between the needle and the noose, whichever. It's the best you know how to do and hell, it's a good thing really. But all that he done...none of it is the real reason why Lanie's lying here." He thumped her grave marker with the handle of his cane.

"I have no idea what you're talking about," I said, meaning it in a way I wasn't used to.

"That's a good habit, admitting you don't know," he said. "Be sure you keep at it."

There were a good many things I could have said in response but none of them came out. *I have no daughter by that name* rang in my head and drowned out all my words. I was silent as the graves around me as Xander Harkness buttoned up his coat.

"I'll be on my way now," he said. "Thank you, Miss Private Eye, for doing what you did. I mean that. The world is full of decent folk who would've looked the other way."

He was nearly twenty feet away before I spoke again. "Amber," I called out.

He turned. "How's that?"

"My friends call me Amber," I heard myself say.

Rain struck my face and dripped off my chin; it did the same to the man who stood in front of me but neither of us reacted to it.

"Xander," he said.

"What are you going to do, Xander?"

"Grow up," he said.

Epilogue

It took several more weeks for the events surrounding Lanie Hooper's death to sort themselves out. I wasn't surprised.

Kevin Andersen's negligence suit against Deputy Sergeant Richard Strandell didn't even reach a courtroom; the Island County Sheriff's office dismissed him before the case went to trial. At the end Rachelle received a small settlement and Andersen broke even.

Andersen's bid for city council went well, flying high on the internet outrage that the Hooper case had introduced. It helped he also talked pretty, smiled big and looked good in a suit, but that much I'd already known. Before observing the proceedings I wondered why he'd felt the need to reach for hard-earned credibility in the first place. However, I did find myself changing my tune some after catching the highlights of his campaign on YouTube.

"Yes, I've done my time as a civil attorney," I watched him say to the camera, sporting his boyish grin. *"And yes, I'm aware that makes some of you watching wonder why I'm different. Well, here's the truth...I'm not."* A flash of applause, which he paused to

accept. *"I'm an attorney, like many others. This means I understand the law, and I understand why we have it. We have it because peace and order demand that we must. We live under the rule of law...which means its protections must be extended to every citizen, regardless of their creed or race, regardless of how much money they make or who they choose to marry."* This time the applause was much louder. *"As councilman I will work to extend the reality of this protection to all the citizens of Seattle, because I know full well the costs paid by those who live without it."*

People stood and clapped but I ignored them and watched Andersen; he blinked with nervousness and straightened his tie. Then an elegant Amazon with a pixie cut slid an arm around his waist and kissed him on the cheek. The relief in his face was palpable, as well as the glow of happiness.

"Behind every good man," I said to the screen, pausing the clip. I'd been wondering about the woman who'd been in bed with Andersen when I'd called, just like I'd wondered about the sudden change in his beliefs and behavior. Politics may have been politics, but I had to appreciate some legitimate change, at least in one man. I did plan on casting my ballot for Andersen in the November election. After all, he'd paid my bill promptly and without complaint.

Peter Weiss, Samuel Ellis and Steven Brinkley were convicted on a myriad of felony drug charges; Samuel Ellis' time was deferred, pending hospital time due to treatment for a ruptured testicle. Weiss' attorneys did their best to spin my actions in the worst light possible, but the bare fact that I'd been fighting against kidnapping, rape and murder threw a big monkey wrench into their impassioned rhetoric. Their clients' lack of anything interesting to trade for a softer sentence contributed to them receiving sixty-year sentences each. Even accounting for good time and various legal tricks I wouldn't be seeing them again until I was eligible to receive Social Security.

Calloway was tried separately from his compatriots, and the district attorney did indeed seek the death penalty; first-degree murder and contract killing were the charges, capital offenses according to Washington's little-used death penalty statute. Much social-political wrangling and media yammering surrounded the case, which became a social media darling as everyone with a pretense of caring sought to offer their opinion on rape culture, the death penalty, mental health and gun-owning America. I lost track of the number of causes which picked up the gage, but in the end it was all for naught.

Billy Calloway hung himself with a towel while awaiting trial.

Shelle Hooper had watched the news article detailing Calloway's death in my front room; she'd been staying at my apartment after agreeing to take a job with my firm. "I guess he figured it out," was all she'd said after the report ended. It was a mystery to me, how she felt about what she'd seen. I didn't ask and she didn't tell me.

Luke Brighton vanished into Witness Protection. His testimony ensured convictions on his former compatriots and had started a wide-ranging drug investigation run by the DEA. I never saw him again, and regretted that fact for strange reasons I could never quite put into words.

Acting on his information the DEA raided several chapters of the Freak Patrol Motorcycle Club, but despite a "thorough" - administrative speak for "desperate"- search of ten different MC chapter houses no connection between them and Weiss' heroin smuggling operation was discovered. I quietly dropped off a cardboard box loaded with gas cans and guns at the Freak Patrol's Tacoma branch...hoping to hell no law-abiding person saw me there all the while.

After that I healed up, went back to work and did my best to forget the details.

May showers pounded against my office window as I sorted through the paperwork for an insurance fraud case; a house had burned down under conditions that were improbable and the owner's insurance provider wanted to make certain it was an act of God before covering the damage. I'd already uncovered evidence that they were right to be suspicious, but needed something that would go well in a courtroom. I'd sent Julian and Shelle out to photograph the wreckage on the idea that he might be able to turn up evidence of wrongdoing. Ostensibly Shelle was assigned to Julian as an apprentice, but the understanding was she'd rein in his enthusiasm if he tried to play the cowboy again.

My shoulder twinged as I reached for a can of mixed nuts sitting on my desk. I swore and did the reaching again, slower. My doctor had informed me most of the pain would fade in a few months, but that some long-term discomfort was inevitable. Translation; I'd gotten hurt in a way that would never fully heal. I didn't like it, but things were what they were. I crunched down on the last of the cashews, the final remnant of the massive mystery gift basket I'd gotten at the Oak Harbor hospital.

My phone rang. As Izzy still didn't much care for phone work I lifted the receiver. "Eckart Investigations, this is Amber."

"It's Alvarez," a familiar voice said.

"Oh man," I said. "Sorry I haven't been at the gym. Shoulder surgery, I tore my rotator cuff."

"That plus a shitload of other things," he said. "I saw you on the news."

I sighed. "I'll be back in about three weeks," I said. "By the way, you're a good teacher."

"Yeah, you looked like you'd been in a scrap," he said. "I take it you applied my training."

"I did," I said.

"You do okay?"

"I'm here to talk, aren't I?"

He laughed.

"Hardy misses you," he said.

"His aim improving any?"

"Not really," he said. "You'll come back and be handing him his ass again." A pause. "I heard about the shit he pulled in the changing room. He ever does that again, you let me know."

I sighed. "I expected it, sooner or later. Don't worry about it."

"Like hell, Eckart. I run a clean gym. That means no

gangs, no hazing, no locker room prick-waving, no off-the-mat scrapping. Also means when any of that bullshit happens I need to know about it."

"Noted," I said with a sigh and a wince. I hadn't reported Hardy's little stunt because I'd assumed such things were normal in the fighting world and hadn't wanted to look like a wuss. I should've given Alvarez more credit than that.

"I'll remember," I said.

Izzy knocked on my door frame; when I looked over she mouthed *need to talk.* "Gotta go Alvarez, work beckons. See you in a few weeks."

"Look forward to it," he said and hung up. I set the phone back in its cradle.

"Boss," Izzy said, "you know how you got that big gift basket when you were in Oak Harbor?"

"The one we've been eating out of around here for the last few months?" I nodded. "Yeah. I guessed it was some old client wanting to say hi."

"That's what I thought," she said, "but I got curious because the message on the card was so weird. I went through our client records. We've never worked for a Crawley Boone."

Her eyes were wide with worry.

"Huh," I said. "What's got you spooked?"

"I Googled the name. You won't like what I found."

I sighed. "Izzy, just tell me."

"Crawley Boone," she said, "is the international president of the Freak Patrol MC."

I sat back in my chair. "You're kidding me."

"I wish," she said. "Oh and boss? I looked into that 'O.O.U' thing at the end of the message too. Apparently it stands for 'One Of Us'. It's a term the Freak Patrol uses to describe friends and allies."

"Well I'm flattered, but not interested," I said.

"From what I read, I got the impression it isn't something you can decline," she said. "You're supposed to get a tattoo."

"What?"

"Yeah. Otherwise, it's like a big-time insult."

"Oh, this is a *joke,*" I muttered.

"Like I said boss...I wish."

I took a deep breath and let it out slowly, drumming my fingers on my desk. Then I turned my chair around and put fingers to the keyboard.

"You ever find the design of the tat I'm supposed to

get?"

"Well yeah I - "she stopped talking. "Boss," she said slowly, "what are you doing?"

"What I always do," I said as I typed TATTOO PARLORS TACOMA WA FREAK PATROL MC into my search bar. "I'm rolling with the punches."

Made in the USA
Coppell, TX
12 May 2020